Scattered Showers

ALSO BY
RAINBOW ROWELL

Landline

Fangirl

Eleanor & Park

Attachments

THE SIMON SNOW TRILOGY

Any Way the Wind Blows

Wayward Son

Carry On

Rainbow Rowell

stories

Scattered Showers

with illustrations by Jim Tierney

WEDNESDAY BOOKS
NEW YORK

FOR CHRISTOPHER, MY FAVORITE TOUGH CROWD

First published in the United States by Wednesday Books, an imprint of St. Martin's Publishing Group

SCATTERED SHOWERS. Copyright © 2022 by Rainbow Rowell. All rights reserved. Printed in the United States of America. For information, address St. Martin's Publishing Group, 120 Broadway, New York, NY 10271.

www.wednesdaybooks.com

Designed by Devan Norman
Interior illustrations by Jim Tierney

"Midnights" originally published in *My True Love Gave to Me*, edited by Stephanie Perkins, Wednesday Books, 2014

"Kindred Spirits" originally published for World Book Day 2016 by Macmillan Children's Books

"The Prince and the Troll" originally published by Amazon Original Stories in *Faraway*, 2020

"If the Fates Allow" originally published by Amazon Original Stories, 2021

The Library of Congress Cataloging-in-Publication Data is available upon request.

ISBN 978-1-250-85541-1 (paper-over-board)
ISBN 978-1-250-85542-8 (ebook)

Our books may be purchased in bulk for promotional, educational, or business use. Please contact your local bookseller or the Macmillan Corporate and Premium Sales Department at 1-800-221-7945, extension 5442, or by email at MacmillanSpecialMarkets@macmillan.com.

First Edition: 2022

10 9 8 7 6 5 4 3 2 1

Contents

Midnights

December 31, 2014, almost midnight

IT WAS COLD OUT ON THE PATIO, UNDER THE DECK. Frigid. Dark.

Dark because Mags was outside at midnight, and dark because she was in the shadows.

This was the last place anyone would look for her—anyone, and especially Noel. She'd miss all the excitement.

Thank God. Mags should have thought of this years ago.

She leaned back against Alicia's house and started eating the Chex mix she'd brought out with her. (Alicia's mom made the best Chex mix.) Mags could hear the music playing inside, and then she couldn't—and that was a good sign. It meant that the countdown was starting.

"*Ten!*" she heard someone shout.

"*Nine!*" More people joined in.

"*Eight!*"

Mags was going to miss the whole thing. Perfect.

December 31, 2011, almost midnight

"Are there nuts in that?" the boy asked.

Mags paused, holding a cracker piled with pesto and cream cheese in front of her mouth. "I think there are pine nuts . . ." she said, crossing her eyes to look at it.

"Are pine nuts tree nuts?"

"I have no idea," Mags said. "I don't think pine nuts grow on pine trees, do they?"

The boy shrugged. He had shaggy brown hair and wide-open blue eyes. He was wearing a Pokémon T-shirt.

"I'm not much of a tree-nut expert," Mags said.

"Me neither," he said. "You'd think I would be—if I accidentally eat one, it could kill me. If there were something out there that could kill you, wouldn't you try to be an expert on it?"

"I don't know . . ." Mags shoved the cracker in her mouth and started chewing. "I don't know very much about cancer. Or car accidents."

"Yeah . . ." the boy said, looking sadly at the buffet table. He was skinny. And pale. "But tree nuts specifically have it out for me, for me *personally*. They're more like assassins than, like, possible dangers."

"Damn," Mags said, "what'd you ever do to tree nuts?"

The boy laughed. "Ate them, I guess."

The music, which had been really loud, stopped. "It's almost midnight!" somebody shouted.

They both looked around. Mags's friend Alicia, from homeroom, was standing on the couch. It was Alicia's party—the first New Year's Eve party that Mags, at fifteen, had ever been invited to.

"*Nine!*" Alicia yelled.

"*Eight!*" There were a few dozen people in the basement, and they were all shouting now.

"*Seven!*"

"I'm Noel," the boy said, holding out his hand.

Mags brushed all the pesto and traces of nuts off her hand and shook his. "Mags."

"*Four!*"

"*Three!*"

"It's nice to meet you, Mags."

"You, too, Noel. Congratulations on evading the tree nuts for another year."

"They almost had me with that pesto dip."

"Yeah." She nodded. "It was a close call."

December 31, 2012, almost midnight

Noel fell against the wall and slid down next to Mags, then bumped his shoulder against hers. He blew a paper party horn in her direction. "Hey."

"Hey." She smiled at him. He was wearing a plaid jacket, and his white shirt was open at the collar. Noel was pale and flushed easily. Right now he was pink from the top of his forehead to the second button of his shirt. "You're a dancing machine," she said.

"I like to dance, Mags."

"I know you do."

"And I only get so many opportunities."

She raised an eyebrow.

"I like to dance *in public*," Noel said. "With other people. It's a communal experience."

"I kept your tie safe," she said, and held out a red silk necktie. He'd been dancing on the coffee table when he threw it at her.

"Thank you," he said, taking it and slinging it around his neck.

"That was a good catch—but I was actually trying to lure you out onto the dance floor."

"That was a coffee table, Noel."

"There was room for two, Margaret."

Mags wrinkled her nose, considering. "I don't think there was."

"There's always room for you with me, on every coffee table," he said. "Because you are my best friend."

"Pony is your best friend."

Noel ran his fingers through his hair. It was sweaty and curly and fell past his ears. "Pony is also my best friend. And also Frankie. And Connor."

"And your mom," Mags said.

Noel turned his grin on her. "But especially you. It's our anniversary. I can't believe you wouldn't dance with me on our anniversary."

"I don't know what you're talking about," she said. (She knew exactly what he was talking about.)

"It happened right there." Noel pointed at the buffet table where Alicia's mom always laid out snacks. "I was having an allergic reaction, and you saved my life. You stuck an epinephrine pen into my heart."

"I ate some pesto," Mags said.

"Heroically," Noel agreed.

She sat up suddenly. "You didn't eat any of the chicken salad tonight, did you? There were almonds."

"Still saving my life," he said.

"*Did* you?"

"No. But I had some fruit cocktail. I think there were strawberries in it—my mouth is all tingly."

Mags squinted at him. "Are you okay?"

Noel looked okay. He looked flushed. And sweaty. He looked like his teeth were too wide for his mouth, and his mouth was too wide for his face.

"I'm fine," he said. "I'll tell you if my tongue gets puffy."

"Keep your lewd allergic reactions to yourself," she said.

Noel wiggled his eyebrows. "You should see what happens when I eat shellfish."

Mags rolled her eyes and tried not to laugh. After a second, she looked over at him again. "Wait, what happens when you eat shellfish?"

He waved his hand in front of his chest, halfheartedly. "I get a rash."

She frowned. "*How* are you still alive?"

"Through the efforts of everyday heroes like yourself."

"Don't eat the pink salad, either," she said. "It's shrimp."

Noel looped his red tie around her neck and smiled at her. Which was different than a grin. "Thanks."

"Thank *you*," she said, pulling the ends of the tie even and looking down at them. "It matches my sweater." Mags was wearing a giant sweater dress, some sort of Scandinavian design with a million colors.

"Everything matches your sweater," he said. "You look like a Christmas-themed Easter egg."

"I feel like a really colorful Muppet," she said. "One of the fuzzy ones."

"I like it," Noel said. "It's a feast for the senses."

She couldn't tell if he was making fun of her, so she changed the subject. "Where did Pony go?"

"Over there." Noel pointed across the room. "He wanted to get in position to be standing casually near Simini when midnight strikes."

"So he can kiss her?"

"Indeed," Noel said. "On the mouth, if all goes to plan."

"That's so gross," Mags said, fiddling with the ends of Noel's tie. "Kissing?"

"No . . . kissing is fine." She felt herself blushing. Fortunately she wasn't as pale as Noel; it wouldn't be painted all over her face and throat. "What's gross is using New Year's Eve as an excuse to kiss someone who might want not want to kiss you. Using it as a trick."

"Maybe Simini *does* want to kiss Pony."

"Or maybe it'll be really awkward," Mags said. "And she'll do it anyway because she feels like she has to."

"He's not going to maul her," Noel said. "He'll do the eye-contact thing."

"What eye-contact thing?"

Noel swung his head around and made eye contact with Mags. He raised his eyebrows hopefully; his eyes went all soft and possible. It was definitely a face that said, *Hey. Is it okay if I kiss you?*

"Oh," Mags said. "That's really good."

Noel snapped out of it—and made a face that said, *Well, duh.* "Of course it's good. I've kissed girls before."

"*Have* you?" Mags asked. She knew that Noel talked to girls. But she'd never heard of him having a girlfriend. And she *would* have heard of it—she was one of Noel's four to five best friends.

"Pfft," he said. "Three girls. Eight different occasions. I think I know how to make eye contact."

That was significantly more kissing than Mags had managed in her sixteen years.

She glanced over at Pony again. He was standing near the television, studying his phone. Simini was a few feet away, talking to her friends.

"Still," Mags said, "it feels like cheating."

"How is it cheating?" Noel asked, following her eyes. "Neither of them is in a relationship."

"Not that kind of cheating," Mags said. "More like . . . skipping ahead. If you like someone, you should have to make an effort. You should have to get to know the person—you should have to *work* for that first kiss."

"Pony and Simini already know each other."

"Right," she agreed, "but they've never gone out. Has Simini ever even *indicated* that she's interested?"

"Sometimes people need help," Noel said. "I mean—look at Pony."

Mags did. He was wearing black jeans and a black T-shirt. He had a half-grown-out mohawk now, but he'd had a ponytail back in middle school, so everyone still called him that. Pony was usually loud and funny, and sometimes loud and obnoxious. He was always drawing on his arm with ink pens.

"That guy has no idea how to tell a girl he likes her," Noel said. "None at all . . . Now, look at Simini."

Mags did. Simini was small and soft, and so shy that coming out of her shell wasn't even on the menu. If you wanted to talk to Simini, you had to climb inside her shell with her.

"Not everyone has our social graces," Noel said, sighing, and leaning into Mags's space to gesture toward Pony and Simini. "Not everyone knows how to reach out for the things they want. Maybe midnight is exactly what these two need to get rolling—would you begrudge them that?"

Mags turned to Noel. His face was just over her shoulder. He smelled warm. And like some sort of Walgreens body spray. "You're being melodramatic," she said.

"Life-or-death situations bring it out in me."

"Like coffee-table dancing?"

"No, the strawberries," he said, sticking out his tongue and trying to talk around it. "Duth it look puffy?"

Mags was trying to get a good look at Noel's tongue when the music dropped out.

"It's almost midnight!" Alicia shouted, standing near the television. The countdown was starting in Times Square. Mags saw Pony look up from his phone and inch toward Simini.

"*Nine!*" the room shouted.

"*Eight!*"

"Your tongue looks fine," Mags said, turning back to Noel.

He pulled his tongue back in his mouth and smiled.

Mags raised her eyebrows. She hardly realized she was doing it. "Happy anniversary, Noel."

Noel's eyes went soft. At least, she thought they did. "Happy anniversary, Mags."

"*Four!*"

And then Natalie ran over, slid down the wall next to Noel, and grabbed his shoulder.

Natalie was friends with both of them, but she wasn't a *best* friend. She had caramel-brown hair, and she always wore flannel shirts that gapped over her breasts. "Happy New Year!" she shouted at them.

"Not yet," Mags said.

"*One!*" everyone else yelled.

"Happy New Year," Noel said to Natalie.

Then Natalie leaned toward him, and he leaned toward her, and they kissed.

December 31, 2013, almost midnight

Noel was standing on the arm of the couch with his hands out to Mags.

Mags was walking past him, shaking her head.

"Come on!" he shouted over the music.

She shook her head *and* rolled her eyes.

"It's our last chance to dance together!" he said. "It's our senior year!"

"We have months left to dance," Mags said, stopping at the food table to get a mini quiche.

Noel walked down the couch, stepped onto the coffee table, then stretched one long leg out as far as he could to make it onto the love seat that was next to Mags.

"They're playing our song," he said.

"They're playing 'Baby Got Back,'" Mags said.

Noel grinned.

"Just for that," she said, "I'm never dancing with you."

"You never dance with me anyway," he said.

"I do everything else with you," Mags whined. It was true. She studied with Noel. She ate lunch with Noel. She picked Noel up on the way to school. "I even go with you to get a haircut."

He touched the back of his hair. It was brown and thick, and fell in loose curls down to his collar. "Mags, when you don't go, they cut it too short."

"I'm not complaining," she said. "I'm just sitting this round out."

"What're you eating?" he asked.

Mags looked down at the tray. "Some kind of quiche, I think."

"Can I eat it?"

She popped another one in her mouth and mushed it around. It didn't taste like tree nuts or strawberries or kiwi fruit or shellfish. "I think so," she said. She held up a quiche, and Noel leaned over and ate it out of her fingers. Standing on the love seat, he was seven and a half feet tall. He was wearing a ridiculous white suit. Three pieces. Where did somebody even find a three-piece white suit?

"S'good," he said. "Thanks." He reached for Mags's Coke, and she let him have it—then he jerked it away from his mouth and cocked his head. "Margaret. They're playing our song."

Mags listened. "Is this that Ke$ha song?"

"Dance with me. It's our anniversary."

"I don't like dancing with a bunch of people."

"But that's the best way to dance! Dancing is a communal experience!"

"For you," Mags said, pushing his thigh. He wavered, but didn't fall. "We're not the same person."

"I know," Noel said with a sigh. "*You* can eat tree nuts. Eat one of those brownies for me—let me watch."

Mags looked at the buffet and pointed to a plate of pecan brownies. "These?"

"Yeah," Noel said.

She picked up a brownie and took a bite. Crumbs fell on her flowered dress, and she brushed them off.

"Is it good?" he asked.

"Really good," she said. "Really dense. Moist." She took another bite.

"So unfair," Noel said, holding on to the back of the love seat and leaning farther over. "Let me see."

Mags opened her mouth and stuck out her tongue.

"Unfair," he said. "That looks delicious."

She closed her mouth and nodded.

"Finish your delicious brownie and dance with me," he said.

"The whole world is dancing with you," Mags said. "Leave me alone."

She grabbed another quiche and another brownie, then put Noel behind her.

There weren't that many places to sit in Alicia's basement; that's why Mags usually ended up on the floor. (And maybe why Noel usually ended up on the coffee table.) Pony had claimed the beanbag by the bar in the corner, and Simini was sitting on his lap. Simini smiled at Mags, and Mags smiled back and waved.

There wasn't any booze in the bar. Alicia's parents put it away whenever she had a party. All the barstools were taken, so Mags got a hand from somebody and sat up on the bar itself.

She watched Noel dance. (With Natalie. And then with Alicia and Connor. And then by himself, with his arms over his head.)

She watched everybody dance.

They had all their parties in this basement. After football games and school dances. Two years ago, Mags hadn't really known anybody in this room, except for Alicia. Now everybody here was either a best friend, or a friend, or someone she knew well enough to stay away from . . .

Or Noel.

Mags finished her brownie and watched Noel jump around.

Noel was her very best friend—even if she wasn't his. Noel was her *person*.

He was the first person she talked to in the morning, and the last person she texted at night. Not intentionally or methodically. That's just the way it was between them. If she didn't tell Noel about something, it was almost like it hadn't happened.

They'd been tight ever since they ended up in journalism class together, the second semester of sophomore year. (*That's* when they should celebrate their friendiversary—not on New Year's Eve.) And then they signed up for photography and tennis together.

They were so tight, Mags went with Noel to prom last year, even though he already had a date.

"Obviously, you're coming with us," Noel said.

"Is that okay with Amy?"

"Amy knows we're a package deal. She probably wouldn't even like me if I wasn't standing right next to you."

(Noel and Amy never went out again after prom. They weren't together long enough to break up.)

Mags was thinking about getting another brownie when someone suddenly turned off the music, and someone else flickered the lights. Alicia ran by the bar, shouting, "It's almost midnight!"

"Ten!" Pony called out a few seconds later.

Mags glanced around the room until she found Noel again—standing on the couch. He was already looking at her. He stepped onto the coffee table in Mags's direction and grinned, wolfishly. All of Noel's grins were a little bit wolfish; he had way too many teeth. Mags took a breath that shook on the way out. (Noel was her *person.*)

"*Eight!*" the room shouted.

Noel beckoned her with his hand.

Mags raised an eyebrow.

He waved at her again and made a face that said, *Come on, Mags.*

"*Four!*"

Then Frankie stepped onto the coffee table with Noel and slung an arm around his shoulders.

"*Three!*"

Noel turned to Frankie and grinned.

"*Two!*"

Frankie raised her eyebrows.

"*One!*"

Frankie leaned up into Noel. And Noel leaned down into Frankie. And they kissed.

December 31, 2014, about nine P.M.

Mags hadn't seen Noel yet this winter break. His family had gone to Walt Disney World for Christmas.

"*It's 80 degrees,*" he'd texted her, "*and I've been wearing mouse ears for 72 hours straight.*"

Mags hadn't seen Noel since August, when she went over to his house early one morning to say good-bye before his dad drove him to Notre Dame.

Noel didn't come home for Thanksgiving; plane tickets were too expensive.

She'd seen photos he'd posted online of *other* people. (People from his residence hall. People at parties. Girls.) And she and Noel had texted. They'd texted a lot. But Mags hadn't seen him since August—she hadn't heard his voice since then.

Honestly, she couldn't remember it. She couldn't remember ever thinking about Noel's voice before. Whether it was deep and rumbling. Or high and smooth. She couldn't remember what Noel sounded like—or what he looked like, not in motion. She could only see his face in the dozens of photos she still had saved on her phone.

"You're going to Alicia's, yeah?" he'd texted her yesterday. He was in an airport, on his way home.

"Where else would I go?" Mags texted back.

"Cool."

Mags got to Alicia's early and helped her clean out the basement, then helped Alicia's mom frost the brownies. Alicia was home from college in South Dakota; she had a tattoo on her back now of a meadowlark.

Mags didn't have any new tattoos. She hadn't changed at all. She hadn't even left Omaha—she'd gotten a scholarship to study industrial design at one of the schools in town. A full scholarship. It would have been stupid for Mags to leave.

Nobody showed up for the party on time, but everybody showed up. "Is Noel coming?" Alicia asked, when the doorbell had stopped ringing.

How would I know? Mags wanted to say. But she did know. "Yeah, he's coming," she said. "He'll be here." She'd gotten a little chocolate on the sleeve of her dress. She tried to scrape it off with her fingernail.

Mags had changed three times before she'd settled on this dress. At first she was going to wear a dress that Noel had always liked—gray poplin with deep red peonies—but she didn't want him to think that she hadn't had a single original thought since the last time she saw him.

So she'd changed. Then changed again. And ended up in this one, a cream-colored lace shift that she'd never worn before, with baroque-patterned pink-and-gold tights.

She stood in front of her bedroom mirror, staring at herself. At her dark brown hair. Her thick eyebrows and blunt chin. She tried to see herself the way Noel would see her, for the first time since August. Then she tried to pretend she didn't care.

Then she left.

She got halfway to her car, then ran back up to her room to put on the earrings Noel had given her last spring for her eighteenth birthday—angel wings.

Mags was talking to Pony when Noel finally arrived. Pony was in school in Iowa, studying engineering. He'd grown his hair back out into a ponytail, and Simini was tugging on it for no apparent reason, maybe just because it made her happy. She was studying art in Utah, but she was probably going to transfer to Iowa. Or Pony was going to move to Utah. Or they were going to meet in the middle. "What's in the middle?" Pony said. "Nebraska? Shit, honey, I guess we should move home."

Mags felt it when Noel walked in. (He came in through the back door, and a bunch of cold air came in with him.)

She looked up over Pony's shoulder and saw Noel, and Noel saw her—and he strode straight through the basement, over the love seat and up onto the coffee table and over the couch and through Pony and Simini, and wrapped his arms around Mags, swinging her in a circle.

"Mags!" Noel said.

"*Noel*," Mags whispered.

Noel hugged Pony and Simini, too. And Frankie and Alicia and Connor. And everybody. Noel was a hugger.

Then he came back to Mags and pinned her against the wall, crowding her as much as hugging her. "Oh, God, Mags," he said. "Never leave me."

"I never left you," she said to his chest. "I never go anywhere."

"Never let me leave you," he said to the top of her head.

"When do you go back to Notre Dame?" she asked.

"Sunday."

Noel was wearing wine-colored pants (softer than jeans, rougher than velvet), a blue-on-blue striped T-shirt, and a gray jacket with the collar turned up.

He was as pale as ever.

His eyes were as wide and as blue.

But his hair was cut short: buzzed over his ears and up the back, with long brown curls spilling out over his forehead. Mags brought her hand up to the back of his head. It felt like something was missing.

"You should have come with me, Margaret," he said. "The young woman who attacked me couldn't stop herself."

"No," she said, rubbing Noel's scalp. "It looks good. It suits you."

Everything was the same, and everything was different.

Same people. Same music. Same couches.

But they'd all grown apart for four months, and in wildly different directions.

Frankie brought beer and hid it under the couch, and Natalie was drunk when she got there. Connor brought his new college boyfriend, and everyone hated him—and Alicia kept trying to pull Connor aside to tell him so. The basement seemed more crowded than usual, and there wasn't as much dancing . . .

There was about as much dancing as there would be at a normal party—at somebody else's party. *Their* parties used to be *different*.

They used to be twenty-five people in a basement who knew each other so well, they never had to hold back.

Noel didn't dance tonight. He stuck with Pony and Simini and Frankie. He stuck by Mags's side, like he was glued there.

She was so glad that she and Noel hadn't stopped texting—that she still knew what he woke up worried about. Everybody else's inside jokes were seven months old, but Noel and Mags hadn't missed a beat.

Noel took a beer when Frankie offered him one. But when Mags rolled her eyes, he handed it to Pony.

"Is it weird being in Omaha?" Simini asked her. "Now that everybody's left?"

"It's like walking through the mall after it closes," Mags said. "I miss you guys so much."

Noel startled. "Hey," he said to Mags, pulling on her sleeve.

"What?"

"Come here, come here—come with me."

He was pulling her away from their friends, out of the basement, up the stairs. When they got to the first floor, he said, "Too far, can't hear the music."

"What?"

They went down the stairs again and stopped midway, and Noel switched places with her, so she was standing on the higher step. "Dance with me, Mags, they're playing our song."

Mags tipped her head. "'A Thousand Years'?"

"It's our actual song," he said. "Dance with me."

"How is this our song?" she asked.

"It was playing when we met," Noel said.

"When?"

"When we met," he said, rolling his hand, like he was hurrying her along.

"When we met *here*?"

"Yes. When we met. Downstairs. Sophomore year. And you saved my life."

"I never saved your life, Noel."

"Why do you always ruin this story?"

"You remember the song that was playing when we met?"

"I always remember the song that's playing," he said. "All the time."

That was true, he did. All Mags could think to say now was, "What?"

Noel groaned.

"I don't like to dance," she said.

"You don't like to dance *in front of people*," he said.

"That's true."

"Just a minute." Noel sighed and ran downstairs. "Don't go anywhere," he shouted up to her.

"I never go anywhere!" she shouted back.

She heard the song start over.

Then Noel was running back up the stairs. He stood on the step below her and held up his hands. "Please."

Mags sighed and lifted up her hands. She wasn't sure what to do with them . . .

Noel took one of her hands in his and put her other hand on his shoulder, curling his arm around her waist. "Jesus Christ," he said, "was that so hard?"

"I don't know why this is so important to you," she said. "Dancing."

"I don't know why it's so important to you," he said. "Not to dance with me."

She was a little bit taller than him like this. They were swaying.

Alicia's mom came down the stairs. "Hey, Mags. Hey, Noel—how's Notre Dame?"

Noel pulled Mags closer to let Mrs. Porter squeeze by. "Good," he said.

"You guys really fell asleep against Michigan."

"I'm not actually on the football team," Noel said.

"That's no excuse," Mrs. Porter said.

Noel didn't loosen his grip after Alicia's mom was past them. His arm was all the way around Mags's waist now, and their stomachs and chests were pressed together.

They'd touched a lot, over the years, as friends. Noel liked to touch. Noel hugged. And tickled and pulled hair. Noel pulled people into his lap. He apparently kissed anyone who raised their eyebrows at him on New Year's Eve . . .

But Noel had never held Mags like this.

Mags had never felt his belt buckle in her hip. She'd never tasted his breath.

Mrs. Porter came back up the stairs, and Noel held Mags even tighter.

"A Thousand Years" began again.

"Did you tell somebody to start it over?" Mags asked.

"I put it on repeat," he said. "They'll stop it when they notice."

"Was this on the *Twilight* soundtrack?"

"Dance with me, Mags."

"I am," she said.

"I know," he said. "Don't stop."

"Okay." Mags had been holding herself rigid, so that she'd still be standing upright, even if Noel let go. She stopped that now. She relaxed into his grip and let her arm slide over his shoulder. She touched the back of his hair again because she wanted to—because it was still missing.

"You don't like it," he said.

"I do like it," she said. "It's different."

"*You're* different."

Mags made a face that said, *You're crazy.*

"You are," Noel said.

"I'm exactly the same," she said. "I'm the only one who's the same."

"You're the most different."

"How?"

"I don't know," he said. "It's like we all left, and you let go—and *you're* the one who drifted away."

"That's bananas," Mags said. "I talk to you every day."

"It's not enough," he said. "I've never seen this dress before."

"You don't like my dress?"

"No." Noel shook his head. She wasn't used to seeing him like this. Agitated. "I like it. It's pretty. But it's different. You're different. I feel like I can't get close enough to you." He pushed his forehead into hers.

She pushed back. "We're pretty close, Noel."

He sighed, frustrated, and it filled her nose and mouth. "Why don't you have a boyfriend?"

Mags frowned. "Maybe I do."

He looked devastated and pulled his head back. "You wouldn't tell me something like that?"

"No," she said, "no—Noel, of course I would. I'd tell you. I just don't know what you want me to say. I don't know why I don't have a boyfriend."

"It's going to get worse," he said. "You're going to keep changing."

"Well, so are you," she said.

"I never change."

Mags laughed. "You're a kaleidoscope. You change every time I look away."

"Don't you hate that?" he asked.

Mags shook her head. Her nose rubbed against his. "I love it."

They'd stopped swaying.

"Are we still dancing?" she asked.

"We're still dancing. Don't get any big ideas, Margaret." He let go of her hand and wrapped that arm around her, too. "Don't go anywhere."

"I never go anywhere," Mags whispered.

He shook his head like she was a liar. "You're my *best* friend."

"You have lots of best friends," she said.

"No," he said. "Just you."

Mags held on to his neck with both arms. She pushed on his forehead. He smelled like skin.

"I can't get close enough," Noel said.

Somebody realized that the song was on repeat and skipped to the next one.

Somebody else realized that Mags and Noel were gone. Natalie came looking for Noel. "Noel! Come dance with me! They're playing our song!"

It was that Ke$ha song.

Noel pulled away from Mags. He grinned at her sheepishly. Like he'd been silly on the stairway, but she'd forgive him, wouldn't she? And there was a party downstairs, they should be at the party, right?

Noel went downstairs, and Mags followed.

The party had changed while they were gone: Everybody seemed a little bit younger again. They'd kicked off their shoes and were jumping on couches. They were singing all the words to the songs they always sang all the words to.

Noel took off his jacket and threw it to Mags. She caught it because she had good hands.

Noel looked good.

Long and pale. In dark red pants that no one else would wear. In a T-shirt that would have hung on him last year.

He looked so good.

And she loved him so much.

And Mags couldn't do it again.

She couldn't stand across the room and watch Noel kiss someone else. Not tonight. She couldn't watch somebody else get the kiss she'd been working so hard for since the moment they'd met.

So, a few minutes before midnight, Mags scooped up a handful of Chex mix and acted like she was going into the hall. Like maybe she was going to the bathroom. Or maybe she was going to check the filter on the furnace.

Then she slipped out the back door. No one would think to look for her outside in the snow.

It was cold, but Mags still had Noel's jacket, so she put it on. She leaned against the foundation of Alicia's house and ate Alicia's mom's Chex mix—Mrs. Porter made the best Chex mix—and listened to the music.

Then the music stopped, and the counting started.

And it was *good* that Mags was out here, because it would hurt too much to be in there. It always hurt too much, and this year, it might kill her.

"*Seven!*"

"*Six!*"

"Mags?" someone called.

It was Noel. She recognized his voice.

"Margaret?"

"*Four!*"

"Here," Mags said. Then, a little louder, "Here!" Because she was his best friend, and avoiding him was one thing, but hiding from him was another.

"*Two!*"

"Mags . . ."

She could see Noel then, in a shaft of moonlight breaking through the slats of the deck above them. His eyes had gone all soft, and he was raising his eyebrows.

"*One!*"

Mags nodded, and pushed with her shoulders away from the house.

Then Noel pushed her right back—pinning her as much as he was hugging her as much as he was crowding her against the wall.

He kissed her hard.

Mags hooked both arms around the back of his head, pressing their faces together, their chins and open mouths.

Noel held on to both of her shoulders.

After a few minutes—maybe more than a few minutes, after a while—they both seemed to trust the other not to go.

They eased up.

Mags petted Noel's curls, pushing them out of his face. Noel pinned her to the wall from his hips to his shoulders, kissing her to the rhythm of whatever song was playing inside now.

When he pulled away, she was going to tell him that she loved him; when he pulled away, she was going to tell him not to let go. "Don't," Mags said, when Noel finally lifted his head.

"Mags," he whispered. "My lips are going numb."

"Then don't kiss," she said. "But don't go."

"No . . ." Noel pushed away from her, and her whole front went cold. "My lips are going numb—were you eating strawberries?"

"Oh God," she said. "Chex mix."

"Chex mix?"

"Cashews," she said. "And probably other tree nuts."

"Ah," Noel said.

Mags was already dragging him away from the wall. "Do you have something with you?"

"Benadryl," he said. "In my car. But it makes me sleepy. I'm probably fine."

"Where are your keys?"

"In my pocket," he said, pointing at her, at his jacket.

Mags found the keys and kept pulling him. His car was parked on the street, and the Benadryl was in the glove compartment. Mags watched Noel swallow the pills, then stood with her arms folded, waiting for whatever came next.

"Can you breathe?" she asked.

"I can breathe."

"What usually happens?"

He grinned. "This has never happened before."

"You know what I mean."

"My mouth tingles. My tongue and lips swell up. I get hives. Do you want to check me for hives?" Wolfish.

"Then what?" she asked.

"Then nothing," he said. "Then I take Benadryl. I have an EpiPen, but I've never had to use it."

"I'm going to check you for hives," she said.

He grinned again and held out his arms. She looked at them. She lifted up his striped T-shirt . . . He was pale. And covered in goose bumps. And there were freckles she'd never known about on his chest.

"I don't think you have hives," she said.

"I can feel the Benadryl working already." He dropped his arms and put them around her.

"Don't kiss me again," Mags said.

"Immediately," Noel said. "I won't kiss you again immediately."

She leaned into him, her temple on his chin, and closed her eyes.

"I knew you'd save my life," he said.

"I wouldn't have had to save it if I didn't almost kill you."

"Don't give yourself too much credit. It's the tree nuts who are trying to kill me."

She nodded.

They were both quiet for a few minutes.

"Noel?"

"Yeah?"

She had to ask him this—she had to make herself ask it: "Are you just being melodramatic?"

"Mags, I promise. I wouldn't fake an allergic response."

"No," she said. "With the kiss."

"There was more than one kiss . . ."

"With all of them," she said. "Were you just—embellishing?"

Mags braced for him to say something silly.

"No," Noel said. Then, "Were you just humoring me?"

"God. No," she said. "Did it feel like I was humoring you?"

Noel shook his head, rubbing his chin into her temple.

"What are we doing?" Mags asked.

"I don't know . . ." he said eventually. "I know things have to change, but . . . I can't lose you. I don't think I get another one like you."

"I'm not going anywhere, Noel."

"You *are*," he said, squeezing her. "And it's okay. Just . . . I need you to take me with you."

Mags didn't know what to say to that.

It was cold. Noel was shivering. She should give him back his jacket.

"Mags?"

"Yeah?"

"What do *you* need?"

Mags swallowed.

In the three years she and Noel had been friends, she'd spent a lot of time pretending she didn't need anything more than what he was already giving her. She'd told herself there was a difference between wanting something and needing it . . .

"I need you to be my person," Mags said. "I need to see you.

And hear you. I need you to stay alive. And I need you to stop kissing other people just because they're standing next to you when the ball drops."

Noel laughed.

"I also need you not to laugh at me," she said.

He pulled his face back and looked at her. "No, you don't."

She kissed his chin without opening her mouth.

"You can have all those things," he said carefully. "You can have me, Mags, if you want me."

"I've always wanted you," she said, mortified by the extent to which it was true.

Noel leaned in to kiss her, and she dropped her forehead against his lips.

They were quiet.

And it was cold.

"Happy anniversary, Mags."

"Happy New Year, Noel."

Kindred Spirits

Monday, December 14, 2015

THERE WERE ALREADY TWO PEOPLE SITTING outside the theater when Elena got there, so she wouldn't be first in line. But that was okay. She was still here—she was still *doing this*.

She grabbed her sleeping bag, and the backpack she'd stocked with books and food and antibacterial wipes, and got out of the car as quickly as possible; it looked like her mom might make one last attempt to talk Elena out of this.

She rolled down her window to frown at Elena directly. "I don't see a porta potty."

Elena had said there would be a porta potty. "I'll figure it out," Elena said quietly. "These guys are figuring it out."

"They're men," her mom said. "They can pee anywhere."

"I'll hold it," Elena said.

"For four days?"

"Mom," Elena said. And what she meant was: *We've been through this. We've talked about it for weeks and weeks. I know you don't approve. But I'm still doing it.*

Elena dropped her gear on the sidewalk, behind a tall white boy who was second in line. "Okay," she said cheerfully to her mom. "I've got this. See you Thursday!"

Her mom was still frowning. "See you after lunch," she said, then rolled up her window and drove away.

Elena turned back to the line, smiling her best first-day-of-school smile. The guy next to her—he looked like he was probably about her age, seventeen or eighteen—didn't look up. First in line was a big white guy with a blond beard. He looked old enough to be one of Elena's teachers, and he was sitting in a foldout camping chair with his feet propped up on a giant cooler. "Hey!" he said happily. "Welcome to Star Wars, man! Welcome to the line!"

This, she quickly learned, was Troy. He'd been in line since Thursday morning. "I wanted to invest at least a week in this, you know? I really wanted to gather my focus."

The younger guy, Gabe, had gotten in line Thursday night.

"There was a couple who hung out with us Saturday for a few hours," Troy said, "but one of them forgot her sunglasses, so they went home. Weak!"

Elena hadn't brought any sunglasses. She squinted into the sun.

"I'm guessing this is your first line," Troy said.

"How can you tell?" she asked.

"I can tell," he said, chuckling. "I can always tell. It's Gabe's first line, too."

"We were eight when the last Star Wars movie came out," Gabe said, not looking up from his book.

"*Revenge of the Sith*!" Troy said. "That wasn't much of a line anyway. It was no *Empire*."

"Nothing is," Elena said.

Troy's face got somber. "Hear, hear, Elena. Hear, hear."

All right, so . . . she'd expected there to be more people here.

The Facebook group she'd found—Camp Star Wars: Omaha!!!—had eighty-five members, not including Elena, who was more of a lurker than a joiner. This was definitely the right theater; the Facebook posts had been very clear. (Maybe it was Troy who'd posted them.)

Elena had planned to continue her more-lurker-than-joiner strategy in the line. She thought she'd show up and then sort of disappear into the crowd until she got her sea legs. Her line legs. It was a pretty good strategy for most social situations: show up, fall back, let somebody else break the ice and take the spotlight. Somebody else always would. Extroverts were nothing if not dependable.

But even an expert mid-trovert like Elena couldn't lie low in a crowd of three. (Though this Gabe kid seemed to be trying.) Elena was going to be here for four days. She was going to have to talk to these people, at least until someone else showed up.

"Cold enough for you?" Troy asked.

"Actually I think I might be a little overdressed," Elena said.

She was wearing three layers on the bottom and four on top, and she had a big puffy coat if she needed it. If the temperature dropped dangerously low—which would be inevitable during a normal Omaha December—she'd have to go home. But the forecast was pretty mild. (Thanks, global warming?)

"What were they thinking when they scheduled this movie for December?" Troy said. "They weren't thinking of us, I can tell you that. *May*," he said, shaking his head. "May is when you release a Star Wars movie. If this were a May movie, the line would already be around the block."

"Lucky for us, I guess," Elena said. "We get to be first."

"Oh, I'd be first no matter what," Troy said. "I am here for it, you know?" He cupped his hands around his lips and shouted, "I'm here for it!"

Me, too, Elena thought.

Elena couldn't remember the first time she saw a Star Wars movie . . . in the same way she couldn't remember the first time she saw her parents. Star Wars had just always been there. There was a stuffed Chewbacca in her crib.

The original trilogy were her dad's favorite movies—he practically knew them by heart—so when Elena was little, like four or five, she'd say they were her favorite movies, too. Because she wanted to be just like him.

And then, as she got older, the movies started to actually sink in. Like, they went from something Elena could recite to something she could feel. She made them her own. And then she'd kept making them her own. However Elena changed or grew, Star Wars seemed to be there for her in a new way.

When she'd found out that there were going to be sequels—real sequels, Han and Leia and Luke sequels—she'd flipped out. That's when she'd decided to get in line.

She didn't want to miss this moment. Not just this moment in the world, but this moment in her life.

If you broke Elena's heart, Star Wars would spill out. This was a holy day for her—it was a cosmic event. This was her planets lining up. (Tatooine, Coruscant, Hoth.)

And Elena was going to be here for it.

∽

Her left foot was asleep.

She kept kicking the sidewalk, then stood up to bounce.

"Is your leg asleep again?" Troy said. "I'm worried about your circulation."

"It's fine," Elena said, stamping her foot.

She'd only been sitting for two hours, but she was so bored she could hardly stand it. She could literally hardly stand; even her blood vessels were bored.

She'd brought lots of books. (She'd planned to read Star Wars books whenever she had a quiet moment in line.) (Which was every moment so far.) But the wind kept blowing the pages, and the paper was so bright in the sun that reading made her eyes water.

None of that seemed to bother silent Gabe, who read his paperback without seeming to notice the sun, the traffic, Troy, Elena, or Elena's mom—who kept driving by slowly, like someone trying to buy drugs.

"The Imperial March" started playing, and Elena answered her phone.

"Why don't I pick you up now?" her mom said. "Then you can get back in line when there are more girls here."

"I'm fine," Elena said.

"You don't even know these men. They could be sexual predators."

"This doesn't seem like a very good place to prey," Elena whispered, glancing over at Gabe, who was still absorbed in his book. He was pale with curly, milk-chocolate-colored hair and rosy cheeks. He looked like Clark Kent's skinny cousin.

"You know you have to be extra careful," her mom said. "You look so young."

"We've been through this," Elena said.

They'd been through it a lot:

"You look twelve," her mom would say.

And Elena couldn't really argue. She was short and small. She could shop in the kids' section. And the fact that she was Vietnamese seemed to scramble non-Asians' perceptions of her. She was always being mistaken for a kid.

But what was she supposed to do about that? Act like a kid until she looked like an adult? Start smoking and spend too much time in the sun?

"Just because I look twelve doesn't mean you can treat me like I'm twelve," Elena would say. *"I'm going to college next year."*

"You told me there'd be other girls here," her mom said.

"There will be."

"Good. I'll bring you back after they get here."

"I've gotta go," Elena said. "I'm trying to conserve my phone battery."

"Elena—"

"I've got to go!" Elena hung up.

⟋⟍⟍⟍⟍

The first theater employees started showing up around two. One, who looked like the manager—a Latino guy in his thirties, wearing maroon pants and a matching tie—stopped in front of the line and crossed his arms. "So we've got a new addition, huh?"

Elena smiled.

He didn't smile back. "You know you can buy your ticket online, right?"

"I already bought my ticket," Elena said.

"Then you're guaranteed a seat. You don't have to wait in line."

"Um," Elena said. "That's okay."

"You can't talk her out of this," Troy said. "She's a true believer."

"I'm not trying to talk anybody out of anything," the manager said, looking harried. "I'm just explaining that this is an unnecessary gesture."

"All the best ones are," Troy said. "Now open the doors. My bladder is about to explode."

The manager sighed. "I don't have to let you use the restroom, you know."

"Give it up, Mark," Troy said. "They tried that during *Phantom Menace,* and it didn't work then either."

"I should make you hoof it to Starbucks," the manager said, walking toward the front doors and unlocking them.

Troy stood up and made a big show of stretching. "We take turns," he said to Elena, "in line order."

She nodded.

The manager, Mark, held the door for Troy, but was still looking at Elena. "Do your parents know you're here?"

"I'm eighteen," she said.

He looked surprised. "Well, all right. Then I guess you're old enough to waste your own time."

Elena was hoping Gabe would open up a little while Troy was gone. They'd been sitting next to each other for hours now, and he'd only said a few words. She thought maybe he was being so quiet because he didn't want to get Troy going on one of his stories. (Troy had *so* many stories—he'd camped out for every Star Wars opening since *The Empire Strikes Back*—and he was clearly pleased to have a captive audience.)

But Gabe, with his navy-blue peacoat and his gunmetal glasses, just sat there reading about the history of polio and ignoring her.

When Troy came out with an extra-large sack of popcorn, Gabe nodded at Elena. "Go ahead."

"I'm fine," Elena said. "I just got here." She wasn't fine; she had to pee so bad she was worried she was going to leak when she stood up.

Gabe didn't move. So Elena got up and walked into the theater. The manager kept an eye on her the whole time, like she might sneak in to see a movie. (She should. It was so *warm* inside the building.)

When she got back outside, Gabe took his turn.

"We have to save his spot," Troy said, "and look out for his things as if they were our own. Code of the Line." He held his bag of popcorn out over Gabe's sleeping bag.

Elena took some. "What invalidates the code?" she asked.

"What do you mean?"

"Like, are there any circumstances where someone loses their spot?"

"That is a fine question," he said. "I mean, some things are obvious. If someone takes off without telling anyone or leaving any collateral—they're out. I think there's a time limit, too. Like, you can't just go home and take a nap and expect to come back to your spot. Everybody else is here, earning it, you know? You don't get a free pass for that. Though there are always exceptions . . ."

"There are?"

"We're human. We had a guy in the *Phantom Menace* line who had to leave for therapy. We saved *his* place. But another guy tried to go to work, he said he was going to lose his job . . . We pushed his tent out of line."

"You did?" Popcorn fell out of Elena's mouth. She picked it up. "That's *brutal*."

"No"—Troy was grave—"that's life. We were all going to lose our jobs. I camped out for three weeks. You think I got three weeks' vacation? At the zoo?"

"You worked at the zoo?"

"You've got to sacrifice something for this experience," Troy said, refusing to be sidetracked. "That's why we're here. You've got to leave some blood on the altar. I mean, you heard Mark. If you just want to see the new Star Wars movie, you can buy your ticket online and then forget about it until showtime. But if you want to wait in line, you *wait in line,* you know?"

Elena was nodding. Gabe was standing on the sidewalk. "Did you just vote me out of the line?" he asked.

Troy laughed. "No, dude, you're good—you want some popcorn?"

Gabe took some and sat down.

⟨⟩

Elena had been imagining this day for months. She'd been planning it for weeks.

This wasn't what she'd been expecting from the line experience.

This was more like being in an elevator with two random people. Like being *stuck* in an elevator.

Elena had been expecting . . . well, more people, obviously. And more of a party. A celebration!

She'd thought it would be like all those photos she'd seen when she was a kid and the last Star Wars movies came out. All those fans out on the street, in communion with each other.

Elena had been too young to camp out then. Her dad wouldn't even let her *see* the prequels. He said she was too young. And then, when she grew up, he said they were too terrible. *"They'll just corrupt your love of Star Wars,"* he said. *"I wish I could unsee them."*

So even though Star Wars was Elena's whole life at ten, she didn't get to go to the party.

She was eighteen now. She could do whatever she wanted. *So where was the party?*

The afternoon was even more mind-numbing than the morning.

Her mom drove by three or four more times. Elena pretended not to notice. She read a few chapters of a Star Wars book. Troy pointed out that all the expanded-universe books weren't canon anymore—"Disney erased them from the timeline." Elena said she didn't care, that she liked them anyway.

At nightfall, people started showing up for the evening movies, and Troy got into a fight with Mark about refilling his popcorn. "It says, '*Endless refills same day only*,'" Troy said.

"You're perverting the intent," Mark said.

Elena kept hoping that some of the people walking toward the theater were there to join the line—there were two thirtysomething guys in Star Wars shirts who looked like good candidates, and a few college girls who looked nerdy enough—but they all walked right by.

Elena had stripped down to her Princess Leia T-shirt, but now that the sun was gone, she started reapplying her layers.

Maybe her mom was right. Maybe Elena should leave and come back when the line really got going . . .

What would Troy say? *"There was an Asian girl who hung out with us for a few hours; then her mom made her leave."*

No, this was it. If Elena bailed, she couldn't come back.

〜〜

She wrapped herself in her sleeping bag and pulled on a woolen hat with a big red pom-pom, taking a few more years off her appearance.

The fight with Mark seemed to have left Troy in a funk. He put in earbuds and watched Netflix on his phone. Elena watched him hungrily—she was dying to use her phone. Her whole world was in there. Sitting outside in the cold and dark would be so much more bearable if she could read fan fiction or text her friends. But she only had one backup battery pack to last four days . . . At least it was still bright enough to read. She was sitting just below a lit-up Star Wars poster.

Her mom pulled up in front of the theater again at ten. Elena got up and walked to the car.

"I don't like this," her mom said. "People are going to think you're homeless."

"No one will think that."

"Homeless people are going to bother you."

"Probably not."

"I talked to Dì Janet and she says you can buy your movie ticket online."

"That's not the point."

"It's just that—" Her mom rubbed her temple. "Elena, I think this is the dumbest thing you've ever done in your life."

"That's a good thing, Mom. Think about how much worse it could be."

Her mom frowned and handed her a warm covered dish. "You answer your texts tonight."

"I will."

Elena stepped away from the car.

"Don't worry about her!" Troy shouted from behind her. "She's in good hands!"

Elena's mom looked aghast. But she still drove away.

"I'm sorry," Troy said. "Did I make that worse? I meant the hands of the line."

"It's okay," Elena said, finding her spot against the wall.

Mark the theater manager came out one more time to give them a last call for the bathroom and concessions, which was pretty decent of him.

Troy was asleep by eleven, stretched out on his chair with an inflatable pillow wedged between him and the wall. He'd wrapped himself in fleece blankets, tipped his head back, and that was it.

Elena had planned to roll out her sleeping bag and sleep lying down. But that was back when she'd imagined a few dozen campers. It was different with just three people, and she felt too exposed at the end of the line. If she fell asleep lying down, someone could just drag her away in the night, and Troy and Gabe would never notice.

She didn't think she was afraid of Troy and Gabe themselves. Troy hadn't said anything pervy yet. Not even about Princess Leia. And Gabe seemed painstakingly uninterested in Elena.

Her mom didn't trust them, but her mom didn't trust any guys. She used to just have it in for white guys. (*"White guys are the worst. They rap 2 Live Crew lyrics at you and expect you to laugh."*) But ever since she and Elena's dad had separated four years ago, her mom had taken a stand against any and every man, especially where Elena was concerned. *"Learn from my mistakes,"* she said.

Learn what? Elena wondered. Avoid men? Avoid love? Avoid radiologists who buy movie-replica lightsabers?

Usually when her mom gave her warnings like this, Elena would just give her a thumbs-up. Like, *No prob, Bob.*

Because it really wasn't a problem. Avoid men? Done! This had literally never been an issue for her. When other girls complained about how to deal with unwanted male attention, Elena wouldn't feel jealous exactly, but she would feel curious—how does one go about attracting such attention? And is it impossible to attract just *some* of it? Just a small, manageable amount? Or was attention from boys all or nothing, like a tap that, once you'd found it, you could never turn off?

Elena's teeth were starting to chatter, and it wasn't even that cold out. But the cold of the ground had crept through her sleeping bag, through her jeans, through her long underwear and tights, and settled into her bones.

"You've gotta put something under your sleeping bag," Gabe said. "Or get off the ground."

She looked where his butt must be. He lifted up the side of his sleeping bag. He was sitting on cardboard, two or three pieces.

"Does that work?" she asked.

"It helps," he said.

"Well, I don't have a spare box on me . . ."

Gabe sighed. "Hold my spot."

He got up and shuffled out of his sleeping bag, walking down the street and disappearing behind the building. When he came back, he was carrying a few big cardboard boxes. *Raisinets. Sour Patch Kids.*

"You take mine," he said.

"What?"

"Move up, unless you don't want to sit between us. Troy's an excellent windbreak."

Elena shuffled over to Gabe's pile of boxes, pulling her things with her. Gabe quickly made himself a new nest and settled down again.

"It does help," Elena said. "Thanks."

She tested her instincts, to see if she felt any less safe sitting between these two strangers than she did on the end. No. She felt about the same. "You just want me to have to listen to Troy's stories," she whispered.

"We can switch back in the morning," Gabe said.

"Do you know him?" she asked. "Troy?"

"I didn't know him before," he said, "but I have been sitting next to him for four days."

Gabe picked up his book.

"Thanks," Elena said again.

Gabe didn't answer.

Tuesday, December 15, 2015

It didn't seem like Elena had slept, but she must have. She woke up slumped over her backpack with a patch of cold saliva on her chin.

"Star Wars!" someone was shouting from a car driving by.

"Star Wars!" Troy shouted back, raising his fist.

Yes, Elena thought, *Star Wars*. That's what this experience needed: more Star Wars.

Elena was going to rally.

So this wasn't the jubilant, communal, public display of affection she'd been expecting—it could still be *something*. It could still be memorable. She'd make it memorable.

"What does the Code of the Line say about going to Starbucks?" she asked.

Troy answered: "Totally acceptable as long as you bring back some for us."

Elena walked the six blocks to Starbucks and hung out in the bathroom for a while, painting little Yodas on her cheeks. She had the Starbucks barista write character names on their cups. Troy was Admiral Ackbar, Gabe was General Dodonna, and Elena was Mon Mothma.

When she got back to the line, she took out her phone and carefully took a selfie of herself with the guys behind her. Gabe wouldn't look at the camera, but Troy played along. *"Third in line!"* Elena posted on Instagram. Which sounded much better than *"Last in line!"*

"I dig your face paint," Troy said. "I've got a costume, but I'm saving it for opening night."

"Do you always wear a costume on opening night?" Elena asked.

"Oh yeah. Usually I camp in it."

"I want to hear about your costumes," Elena said.

"You mean opening-night costumes? Or all my Star Wars costumes, including Halloween and May the Fourth parties?"

"We want to hear about *all* of them," she said, glancing over at Gabe. "Right?"

Gabe was looking at her like she was out of her mind.

After they got through Troy's costumes, Elena quizzed him about highs and lows from past lines. Then she suggested they play Star Wars trivia, which she quickly realized wasn't a good idea, because she couldn't answer any questions about the prequels, and she didn't want Troy and Gabe to guess that she hadn't actually seen them.

Elena *could* have seen them by now. She could have watched all three prequels after her dad moved to Florida—but it still felt like she'd be betraying him. And even though her dad had betrayed her by leaving, she didn't feel like watching Star Wars movies just to spite him. That seemed like it really *would* corrupt her love for Star Wars. *"A Jedi uses the Force for knowledge and defense, never for attack."* (Yoda.)

Elena's mom drove by a few times that morning. Elena just waved and tried to look like she was having the time of her life.

Nobody new got in line.

The highlight of Tuesday afternoon was when a photographer from the newspaper came by to take their picture.

"I'm looking for the Star Wars line," he said. He had an oversized camera with a long black lens.

"That's us!" Troy said.

"Oh." He squinted at them. "I thought there was supposed to be a real line, like with people in costume."

"Come back on opening night," Troy said. "My Poe Dameron will knock your socks off."

The photographer looked at Elena's cheeks. "Is that Shrek?"

"It's Yoda," Gabe snapped. "For Christ's sake."

In the end, the photographer shot a close-up of Troy holding a photo of himself waiting in a much more interesting line fifteen years ago.

It was a humiliating setback for them as individuals and for the line as a whole.

(Ugh. They weren't a line. They were just three cold nerds.) (They were three suckers who showed up for a party that didn't exist.) (They were statistically insignificant!)

After the photographer left, Elena didn't start another cheerful conversation. Gabe excused himself to walk around the block. Troy watched TV on his phone.

Elena took out her phone just long enough to take a photo of her flowered sneakers. *"My legs are permanently asleep,"* she posted. *"#LineProblems."* Then she immediately put her phone away, before she could start wandering around online and enjoying herself.

When Gabe came back he was frowning more than Elena had ever seen a human being frown. Even her mother.

It was the longest afternoon of Elena's life.

By Tuesday evening, deep malaise had set in. Luke-staring-into-both-suns-of-Tatooine malaise.

Elena hid her face whenever moviegoers walked past. She only perked up when her mom came by around ten. *Gotta keep up appearances.*

When Elena stood up to go to the car, her whole body felt numb with cold and disuse. Her mom shoved a hot-water bottle out the window. "Here."

It was so hot that Elena dropped it. "Thanks," she said, picking it up.

"I don't think George Lucas would want you to do this," her mom said.

"I didn't know you knew who George Lucas was."

"Please. I was watching Star Wars movies before you were born. Your dad and I saw *Empire Strikes Back* five times in the theater."

"Lucky," Elena said.

"George Lucas is a father of daughters," her mother said. "He wouldn't want young girls freezing to death to prove their loyalty."

"This isn't about George Lucas," Elena said. "He isn't even that involved in the sequels."

"Come home," her mom said. "We'll watch *Empire Strikes Back* and I'll make hot cocoa."

"I can't," Elena said. "I'll lose my place in line."

"I think it will still be there for you in the morning."

"Good night, Mom."

Her mom sighed and held out a venti Starbucks cup. "Stay warm. I'll leave my ringer on tonight in case you change your mind."

Elena sat down with her coffee and tucked the hot-water bottle into her sleeping bag. It felt *amazing*.

"Call your mom," Gabe said flatly. "I want to watch *Empire Strikes Back* and drink hot cocoa."

She realized now that the coffee was a setup.

It was two in the morning, and Elena was going to wet her pants. She looked up the line. Troy was wrapped in sleeping bags and a polar fleece, like a mummy. Gabe had pulled his knees up and tucked his head down a few hours ago.

Elena had been sleeping. Badly. She felt groggy and out of sorts and her bladder actually *hurt*. She kept fidgeting. Gabe lifted his head. "What's wrong? Are you cold?"

"No," Elena said. "I mean, yes, of course. But no—I'm going to wet my pants."

"Don't do that," Gabe said.

"*I can't help it*. What am I supposed to do?"

"Go pee somewhere."

"Where?"

"I don't know. Behind a car or something."

"That's illegal!" Elena said. "And gross!"

"Not as gross as peeing your pants."

Elena closed her eyes. "Ughhhhhhhhhhh. Where have you guys been peeing?"

"Inside the theater," he said.

"Don't you ever have to go at night?"

He shrugged. "No."

Elena felt tears rolling down her cheeks.

"Don't cry," Gabe said. "That won't help."

She kept crying. It was going to happen soon.

"Okay," he said, standing up. "Come on."

"Where are we going?"

"To let you pee."

"We can't leave without telling Troy," she said. "Code of the Line."

"The Code of the Line also includes not soiling it. Come on."

Troy had an extra-large Coke cup, and Gabe grabbed it. Elena got up, carefully, and followed him around to the back of the theater.

"Okay," he said, holding out the cup. "You go behind the dumpster, pee in this cup, then put it in the dumpster."

"What if there are cameras?" Elena asked, taking the cup.

"I can't help you there. This isn't *Mission: Impossible,* you know?"

"But what if I need to pee more than this? I don't know how much I pee."

"If your bladder held more than forty-four ounces, you wouldn't have to go to the bathroom constantly."

She stood there, biting her lip.

"Elena."

"Yeah?"

"You don't have any other options here. Pee in the cup."

"Right," she said. She walked, carefully, to the other side of the dumpster. "I don't want you to listen!"

"Is this the first time you've peed around another human being?"

"Around a guy," she shouted, "yes!"

"I didn't ask for this!" Gabe shouted back. He started humming loudly—"The Imperial March." It made Elena feel like her mom was coming.

She carefully peeled down her layers and hovered over the cup, trying not to touch it, and trying not to splash, still sort of crying. Gabe kept up the loud humming. When Elena was done, she put the lid on the cup and walked out. "Okay," she said.

"Gross. You were supposed to throw it away."

"I'm going to pour it down a storm drain! So it doesn't spill on anyone."

"Whatever," Gabe said.

When she'd disposed of the pee, and the cup, she sat back down next to him and dug in her bag for a wet wipe.

"I should just go home," she said, scrubbing her hands.

"Do you have to pee again?"

"No."

"Then why do you want to go home?"

"Well, obviously I'm not prepared for this!" She waved her arm around, encompassing the cold, the line, the trash can, the storm drain . . . "And it isn't how I thought it was going to be."

"How'd you think it was going to be?" Gabe asked.

"I don't know—*fun*."

"You're camping on a sidewalk with strangers. Why would that be fun?"

"It always *looks* fun. In the pictures. Like, tent cities. And people meeting in line and making friends for life. Getting matching tattoos."

"You want to get a matching tattoo with Troy?"

"You know what I mean." She threw her wadded-up wet wipe onto the ground. "I thought it was going to be a celebration, like a way to be really excited about Star Wars with a bunch of other people who are really excited about Star Wars. Like in Troy's stories. Like the time they all camped out for two weeks to see *Return of the Jedi* and ended up with soul mates and nicknames. The practical jokes that went on for days! The lightsaber battles!"

"You could still end up with a nickname," Gabe said. "Right now I'm thinking something to do with pee. Or cups."

Elena wrapped her sleeping bag tighter.

"Maybe 'Refill' . . ." Gabe said. "And then I can call you 'Phil,' for short."

"Why are *you* here?" she asked, ignoring him. "If you knew it was going to be miserable."

"I'm here because I love Star Wars," he said. "Same as you." He folded his arms on his knees and tucked his head down.

"But you don't even talk to me," Elena said. "To either of us."

Gabe made a sarcastic noise, like *hrmph.*

"No, seriously," she said. "What's the point of getting in this line if you don't want to experience it with other people?"

"Maybe I just don't want to experience it with you," he said. "Have you thought of that?"

"Oh my God." She scrunched up her face. "*No.* I haven't thought of that. Is that true? Why are you so mean?"

"It's not true," he grumbled, lifting his head. "I'm just tired. And I'm not—a people person. Sorry I'm not meeting your Star Wars dream-line expectations."

"Me, too." She rubbed her hands together and blew in them.

"Why didn't your friends wait in line with you?" Gabe asked. "Then you could have had your party line."

"None of my friends like Star Wars."

"Everybody likes Star Wars," he said. "Everybody likes every-thing these days. The whole world is a nerd."

"Are you mad because other people like Star Wars? Are you mad because people *like me* like Star Wars?"

Gabe glowered at her. "Maybe."

"Well," she said, "my friends *do* like Star Wars. They're going to see it this weekend. But they don't like it like I do. They don't get a stomachache about it."

"Why does Star Wars give you a stomachache?"

"I don't know. I just care about it so much."

"I wasn't trying to call you a fake geek girl," Gabe said.

"I didn't say that you were."

"I mean, you obviously know the original trilogy inside out. And that's not even important, but you obviously do."

"I've yet to determine whether you're a fake geek boy," she said, pulling her sleeves down over her hands.

He laughed, and she was ninety percent sure it wasn't sarcastic.

"Here's what bothers me," he said, glowering slightly less, but still looking frustrated. "I'm a nerd, right? Like obviously. Classic nerd. I hate sports. I know every Weird Al song by heart. I don't know how to talk to most people. I'm probably going to get a job in computer science. Like, I know those are all stereotypes, but they're also true of me. That's who I am. And the thing about nerd culture being mainstream culture now means that there's no place to just be a nerd among other nerds—without being reminded that you're the nerd. Do you follow me?"

"Only sort of," Elena said.

"Okay. So. If I go to a football party at my brother's house, I don't know anything about football, and I'm the nerd. And if I go dancing with my friend who likes to dance, well, I don't dance, and I don't like loud music, so I'm the nerd. But *now,* even if I go see a comic-book movie, the whole world is there—so I'm still the nerd. I would have thought that a *Star Wars line* would be safe," he said, waving his arm around the way Elena had. "No way am I going to feel like a social outcast in a Star Wars line. No way am I going to have to sit next to one of the *cool girls* for four days."

"Whoa," Elena said. "I'm not a cool girl."

"Give me a break."

She held up her index finger. "I feel like I need to say that everyone should be welcome in a Star Wars line, socially successful or not, but also, *whoa.* I am a nerd," she said. "That's what this was supposed to be, a chance to talk to people who wouldn't care that I'm awkward in literally every other situation."

"That's not true," Gabe said, rolling his eyes.

"It is."

"You have friends. You have a clique. You walk down the hall like you own the place."

"You seem to have mistaken me for the movie *Mean Girls*," Elena said. "Also, are you saying you don't have friends at your school? Have you considered that maybe it's your silent pouting that drives people away?"

"I have friends," he said. "That's not the point."

"So you have *friends*, but you think I have a *clique*."

"I'm pretty sure of it."

"I feel like you're projecting your clearly problematic girl issues on me," she said.

Gabe rolled his eyes again. "I thought you said you couldn't talk to people," he said. "You don't seem to have any problems talking to me."

"I'm having *a lot* of problems talking to you."

"Okay, then, let's stop."

Was Gabe really mad? She couldn't tell.

Was Elena mad? She also couldn't tell . . .

Yes. *Yes*, Elena *was* mad. Who was Gabe to take her inventory like this? He didn't know her. And he was giving her zero benefit of the doubt; she'd been giving him nothing *but* benefit of the doubt for thirty-six hours.

"For what it's worth," she said, without looking at him, "I haven't thought, *Whoa, Gabe sure is a nerd* even once since I sat down."

He didn't say anything.

Elena squirmed. She wrapped her sleeping bag as tightly as she could and rearranged her legs. "Uggggggggch."

"I get it," he said. "You think I'm a jerk."

"No. *Yes*, but no—I have to pee again."

"You just went."

"I know, I can't help it. Sometimes it happens in waves."

"Can you wait?"

"*No.*"

Gabe sighed and stood up. "Come on. Let's go back to the dumpster."

"I threw away the cup!" Elena said.

"You still have your hot-water bottle—"

"*No.*"

Gabe clicked his tongue like he was thinking. Elena started rooting through her backpack. Everything she'd brought was in plastic bags.

"Aha!" Gabe said. He reached behind her sleeping bag and pulled out her Starbucks cup. "This is perfect—it's already got your name on it."

They left their sleeping bags and shuffled to the back of the theater. It was no less humiliating for Elena the second time around.

"You're definitely getting a nickname," Gabe said when they sat down again by the wall.

Elena crawled into her sleeping bag, feeling more unbelievably tired than unbelievably uncomfortable, like maybe she'd be able to get some sleep for real now.

"I was born at the wrong time," she said. "And in the wrong climate. It should be 1983, and I should be sitting outside Mann's Chinese Theatre in Hollywood, California."

"They're camping outside the Chinese Theatre tonight," Gabe said. "Troy says we're all one line."

"I'm probably last in that one, too," Elena said.

She rolled away from Gabe and fell asleep.

Wednesday, December 16, 2015

"The Force awakens!" Troy shouted.

Elena pulled her hat down over her eyes.

"Come on, Elena," Troy said. "We're hoping you'll go get coffee again."

"Because I'm a woman?"

"No. Because you probably have to pee," Gabe said.

Elena did. "Fine, tell me what you want."

Twenty minutes later she was staring at herself in the Starbucks mirror. She was starting to look like someone who slept on the street and washed up in Starbucks bathrooms.

There'd been an actual homeless person sitting outside the Starbucks when Elena walked in, and it made her feel like a big creep to think she was doing this for fun. (It wasn't even fun!)

She told the barista their names were Tarkin, Veers, and Ozzel.

"Feeling your dark side today, huh?" Troy said when she handed him his cup.

"Pretty much," Elena said, dropping to the ground. "Fear, anger, hate, suffering . . ."

"T minus one!" Troy said. "One more day. *One more day!* I can't believe we've waited ten years for this, though honestly I never thought it would come. *Real* sequels . . ."

"What's your favorite Star Wars movie?" Gabe asked. Uncharacteristically. Elena looked over at him.

"You might as well ask me who my favorite child is," Troy said.

"Do you have children?" Elena asked him.

"I meant hypothetically," Troy said. He exhaled hard. "This is tough, this is really tough. I'm gonna have to go with *The Empire Strikes Back*."

The next half hour was taken up by Troy justifying his choice.

At several points he considered changing his answer, but he kept landing back on Hoth.

"What about you, Elena?" Gabe finally asked.

She frowned at him. Suspicious. "*Empire*," she said. "For all the reasons Troy just said. Plus the kissing. What's yours?"

"*Episode Six*," Gabe said.

"*Jedi*?" she asked.

He nodded.

"Solid choice," Troy said. "Very solid."

Gabe didn't expound; instead he turned back to Elena. "So, what's your least favorite?"

"Why do I have to go first?"

"You don't have to," he said.

She held her coffee cup in both hands. "No, it's fine. *Jedi*. I still love it. But yeah."

Troy acted like he'd been shot. "*Jedi*?"

Gabe was shocked, too. "You think *Episode Six* is worse than *Episode Two*? Worse than Anakin and Padmé frolicking among the shaaks?"

"The shaaks!" Troy said. "Geonosis!"

Those sounded like nonsense words to Elena. She didn't want to be found out. She bit her lip. "I wasn't really considering the prequels. You said least *favorite*, not worst."

"Ahhhh," Troy said, "you did say that."

"True," Gabe said.

They moved on to Troy's least favorite (*III*—"the violence just struck me as mindless") and then to Gabe's (*II*—"love on the fields of Naboo").

And then Troy had to take a call from his girlfriend.

"So," Gabe said to Elena, "who's your favorite character?"

"What are you doing?" Elena said.

"Talking about Star Wars."

"Why?"

"I thought this was what you wanted."

"So now you're trying to give me what I want?"

Gabe sighed. "Not exactly. Just . . . maybe you were right."

"When?" she asked.

"When you said that the point of being in this line was to be excited about Star Wars with other people who love Star Wars."

"Of course I was right," Elena said. "That's obviously why people camp out like this. Nobody leaves their house to sit outside a theater for a week just so they can ignore other fans."

"So I was getting in my own way," Gabe admitted. "Okay?"

"Okay," Elena said carefully.

"So, who's your favorite character?" he asked again.

"You'll probably think it's basic."

"I'm not a jerk," he said.

"People who are jerks don't get to decide whether they're jerks. It's left up to a jury of their peers."

"I disagree. I do not identify as a jerk, so I'm not going to act like one."

"Fine," Elena said. "Princess Leia."

"Great choice," he said.

She was still suspicious. "What about you?"

⟜

The thing about Gabe being nice to Elena for unknown, suspicious reasons was . . . he was still being nice to her. And interesting. And funny. And good company.

She kept forgetting that it was all an act and possibly a ruse—and just enjoyed herself.

They were *all* enjoying themselves.

"Excuse me," someone said, interrupting a lively discussion about whom they'd each buy a drink for in the cantina.

The whole line looked up. There were two women standing on the sidewalk with bakery boxes. One of them cleared her throat. "We heard that people were camping out for Star Wars . . ."

"That's us!" Troy said, only slightly less enthusiastically than he'd said it yesterday.

"Where's everybody else?" she asked. "Are they around the back? Do you do this in shifts?"

"It's just us," Elena said.

"We're the Cupcake Gals," the other woman said. "We thought we'd bring Star Wars cupcakes? For the line?"

"Great!" Troy said.

The Cupcake Gals held on tight to their boxes.

"It's just . . ." the first woman said, "we were going to take a photo of the whole line, and post it on Instagram . . ."

"I can help you there!" Elena said. Those cupcakes were not going to just walk away. Not on Elena's watch.

Elena took a selfie of their line, the Cupcake Gals, and a theater employee all holding Star Wars cupcakes—it looked like a snapshot from a crowd—and promised to post it across all her channels. The lighting was perfect. Magic hour, no filter necessary. *#CupcakeGals #TheForceACAKEns #SalaciousCrumbs*

The Gals were completely satisfied and left both boxes of cupcakes.

"This is the first time I've been happy that there were only three of us," Elena said, helping herself to a second cupcake. It was frosted to look like Chewbacca.

"You *saved* these cupcakes," Gabe said. "Those women were going to walk away with them."

"I know," Elena said. "I could see it in their eyes. I would've stopped at nothing to change their minds."

"Thank God they were satisfied by a selfie then," Gabe said. His cupcake looked like Darth Vader, and his tongue was black.

"I'm really good at selfies," Elena said. "Especially for someone with short arms."

"Great job," Troy said. "You'll make someone a great provider someday."

"That day is today," she said, leaning back against the theater wall. "You're both welcome."

"Errrggh." Troy stretched, kicking out his feet. "Cupcake coma."

"How many did you eat?" Gabe asked.

"Four," Troy said. "I took down the Jedi Council. Time for a little midday siesta—the Force *asleepens*."

It was the warmest day yet. Elena wondered if she could take a nap, too. Maybe not. It seemed even weirder to be asleep on the street in the middle of the day than at night.

"You hate the prequels more than anyone I've met," Gabe said, licking his thumb. "These cupcakes are really good. You should tweet about them again."

"I don't hate the prequels," she said.

"We ranked our top thirty characters, and the only prequel character you listed was Queen Amidala."

That was the only prequel character Elena *knew* . . .

"I mean, you must really *hate* them," he said.

"All right," she said, "I feel like I owe you a debt, after you helped me last night . . . "

"You do. Not quite a life debt. But I did save you from peeing your pants *twice*."

" . . . so I'm going to tell you a secret—but you have to promise not to use it against me."

Gabe reached over Elena's legs to get another cupcake. "How could you possibly have a dark secret involving the Star Wars prequels? Are you responsible for Jar Jar Binks?"

"Do you promise?" she asked.

"Sure, I promise."

"I've never seen the prequels."

"*What?*" Gabe spat crumbs all over both of them. Elena shook them out of her ponytail. "How could that happen?"

"It *didn't* happen," she said. "I never saw them."

"Was it against your religion? Are you some sort of Star Wars purist?"

"Sort of," Elena said. "My dad was. He wouldn't let me see them."

"Did he lock you in a tower?"

"No. He just told me they were terrible. He said they'd . . . *corrupt* my love of Star Wars."

"And you never thought of watching them anyway?"

"Not really. It's my *dad*."

"How does he feel about the sequels? Are you here undercover?"

"I don't know," Elena said. "I haven't heard from him."

Gabe looked confused.

"He's sort of in Florida."

"'Sort of in Florida' is our band name," Gabe said.

"Don't tell Troy," she said.

"I won't. He'd probably make us watch all three movies on his phone."

Elena looked down. "Now you're probably thinking that I really am a fake geek girl."

"I try not to think that about anybody," Gabe said. "If anything, this makes you an uber Star Wars nerd. A Star Wars hipster. You're like one of those people who only listens to music on vinyl."

"Do you think I should watch the prequels?" she asked.

"How would I know? I mean, I'd watch them. I couldn't know there was more Star Wars out there that I hadn't tapped. You could have double the Star Wars in your life."

"Did the prequels corrupt your love of Star Wars?"

Gabe gave her a very Han Solo–like grin. "It was already corrupt, babe."

They both laughed. This was not the Gabe she'd been sitting next to for two days.

"I don't know," he said, more seriously. "I saw the prequels before the original trilogy."

"What?" It was Elena's turn to be shocked. "That's all wrong. That's a perversion."

"It is not! I think it's how George Lucas intended it—it's the higher order."

"George Lucas doesn't even know what he intended," Elena said. "He can't even decide who shot first."

"I saw the prequels in the theater," Gabe said. "When I was a kid. I thought they were awesome."

"And now?" she asked.

"They're my first love," he said. "I can't be objective."

Elena hugged herself. "I don't think I'll ever watch them. I feel like I'd be letting my dad down. Like he's going to show up some-day, and ask whether I've seen *Attack of the Clones,* and if I say yes, he'll take off again."

Gabe looked like he was thinking. "So . . ." he said, "you won't mind if I spoil them for you."

"I guess not," she said. "I mean, I already know what happens."

Gabe sat up straight and held both hands up between them. *"Turmoil has engulfed the Great Republic . . ."*

When Troy woke up from his nap, he didn't even ask what they were doing. He just joined in. His Yoda impression was *uncanny.*

"I knew you hadn't seen the prequels," Troy confided in Elena. "There were some pretty obvious gaps in your understanding of the Galactic Senate."

Troy's girlfriend, Sandra, brought them all pizza that night, and

when she got there she joined the dramatic reenactment. She said
they had to rewind so she could elaborate for Elena on how dashing
Obi-Wan was. "*Ewan McGregor*," she groaned. "I made Troy grow
a beard after the second movie."

"I also grew a Padawan braid," Troy said.

Troy and Sandra and Gabe acted out a lightsaber battle that
brought tears to Elena's eyes, probably because they were all three
singing the John Williams music. (Elena knew the prequel music;
she'd listened to all the scores.)

Some moviegoers stopped on their way out of the theater to
watch. Elena snapped a photo when Gabe fell to the ground. (*#Epic
#KnightFall #OnLine*) Everyone clapped.

When the crowd cleared, Elena noticed her mom parked at the
curb. Elena jumped up and ran over.

"Are you coming home?" her mom asked.

"Nope," Elena said. "Do you want to get in line?"

"No way. You get this craziness from your dad, not me."

The night was clear and cold. Sandra had talked Manager Mark
into refilling Elena's hot-water bottle at the coffee machine. Elena
hugged it under her sleeping bag.

"Hey," Gabe said, "I got you something."

"What?"

He handed her a movie-theater cup, one of the new Star Wars
ones. "Tonight you can pee in a collector's item."

"Ha ha," Elena said. "Did we eat all the cupcakes?"

Gabe handed her the box. There was one left. A very lonely
C-3PO. Elena picked up her phone and took a photo of it. Then
went to Instagram. *#LastDroidStanding*

Her phone battery was still seventy percent charged, and she only had twenty-four hours to get through, so Elena decided to indulge herself by thumbing through her Instagram feed, reading the comments on her posts from the last few days.

Her friends had all hearted them and left funny comments. God, Elena missed her friends. (Not that Troy and Gabe weren't great. She'd definitely miss them.) (Even Gabe.) (Especially Gabe.)

Her first post, from Monday, had the most comments. The photo of the line.

"Is that Gabe?" someone had posted.

"GABERS."

"It's Geekle!" Elena's friend Jocelyn had posted. *"ICKLE GEEKLE."*

Geekle? Elena thought.

She quickly texted Jocelyn: *"Who's Geekle?"*

"Geekle!" Jocelyn texted back. *"From Spanish class. He sits at the back. He's kind of geeky."*

"Is that why you call him Geekle?"

"IDK," Jocelyn sent. *"ICKLE GEEKLE. Tell him I said hi."*

Elena looked over at Gabe. He did look sort of familiar . . .

Jocelyn had nicknames for everyone, usually mean ones. "Ickle Geekle," whatever that meant, was mild. Jocelyn herself wasn't very mean, once you got to know her. She just thought she was funnier than she actually was. And she couldn't stand silence. She'd fill every second with stupid jokes.

Gabe. From Spanish class. Elena tried to picture him without his peacoat . . . While she was staring, Gabe took off his glasses and rubbed his eyes.

"You don't wear glasses!" she blurted out.

"What?" he said, putting his glasses back on.

"In school," she said. "You don't wear glasses."

Gabe's face fell. "No. I don't."

Gabe. Geekle. His Spanish name was *Gabriel*. Elena had never talked to him; she'd never really looked at him. (Which sounded worse than it was—Elena didn't go around *looking* at people. She minded her own business!)

This was bad. This was very bad.

"I'm sorry," she said.

"Why?"

"I didn't recognize you."

He shrugged. "Why would you?"

"Because we're in class together!"

"You apparently never noticed," he said. "There's no crime there."

"Did *you* recognize *me*?"

Gabe turned to look at her, rolling his eyes. "*Of course*. We've been in school together for four years."

"I—I don't know very many people."

"Yeah, why should you pay attention to anyone else . . . You've got your clique."

That was true, but not the way he was saying it. "We're not a clique," Elena said.

"Gang, then."

"*Gabe*."

"Army?"

"Why do you dislike us so much?"

"Because you're jerks," he said. "Because you call me Geekle—what does that even mean?"

"I don't know. I don't call you that!"

"Because you don't know I exist!"

"I know *now*," she said.

Gabe started to say something, then shook his head.

"Jocelyn just has a big mouth," Elena said. "She's harmless."

"To you," he said. "You guys think you're so far above everyone else."

"I don't think that."

"You walk around in a clump, looking all cute and matchy, and cast your clever little insults down on us plebes—"

"We never intentionally match!" Elena said.

"Whatever!"

They both sat back, arms crossed.

"It's not like that," she said. "We're not a clique. We're just friends."

Gabe huffed. "Do you know why I know you and your friends? But you don't know me and my friends?"

"Why?"

"Because we don't get in your way. We don't have nicknames for you, and if we did, we wouldn't shout them every day when you walked into Spanish."

"That's just Jocelyn," Elena said.

"That's your whole vibe," Gabe said.

"I don't even have a vibe!"

"Pfft!"

"So you hate me," she said. "You hated me before I even got in line."

"I didn't hate you," he said. "You're just . . . part of them."

"I'm also part of *this*."

"What's this? Star Wars? I don't have to like you because you like Star Wars. I don't have to like every bonehead with a stormtrooper tattoo."

"No," Elena said. "I'm part of *this*, part of the line."

"What does that count for?"

"I don't know," she said, "but it should count for something.

Look, I'm sorry Jocelyn calls you names. She's a loudmouth. She's been a loudmouth since fourth grade. We're all just *used* to her. And if you've noticed me at all at school, you've noticed that I don't exactly reach out. I have classes where I don't talk to *anybody*. Nobody in my math class even knows my name."

"I don't believe that . . ."

"I'm really sorry that I've never talked to you before. But you've never talked to me either. We're talking *now*, right?"

"I just . . ." Gabe gritted his teeth. "I *hate* it when she calls me Geekle."

"She calls me Eleh-nerd," Elena said. "And Short Stuff. Wednesday Addams. Virgin Daiquiri. Ukelena . . . Ukelele . . . Lele. My Little Pony. Thumbelina. Rumpelstiltskin . . ."

Gabe laughed a little. "Why do you let her call you all that?"

"I don't even hear it anymore," Elena said. "Plus it's different, I'm her friend. I can have her stop calling you names, if you want."

"It doesn't even matter," he said.

They were quiet for a minute. Elena was trying to figure out whether she was mad . . . She wasn't.

"Why didn't you tell me?" she asked. "That we already knew each other."

"I didn't want you to call me Geekle," Gabe said. "I didn't want it to catch on."

Elena nodded.

"We should sleep," he said. "This is our last night."

"Yeah," she said.

He pulled up his legs and folded his arms. *How did he sleep like that?*

Elena curled up as much as she could. She kept trying to get comfortable. It was so bright under the lights.

"Gabe?" she said after ten minutes or so.

"Yeah?"

"Are you asleep?"

"Sort of."

"Are you still mad?"

Gabe sighed. "In a larger sense, yes. At you, in this moment, no."

"Okay. Good."

Elena hunkered down again. She watched the cars driving by. She would be really, really glad to be home tomorrow night. After the movie. The movie . . .

"Gabe?" she said.

"What?"

"I can't sleep."

"Why not?"

"Star Wars!"

Thursday, December 17, 2015

Something strange happened at 6 A.M.

Darth Vader got in line.

It was one of Troy's friends. He kicked Troy's feet off the cooler and shouted, "The Force awakens!"

"Yeah, we've heard that one," Gabe grumbled, sitting up.

Elena was watching everything from a gap between her hat and her sleeping bag.

"I haven't slept in a week," Gabe said. "I think you can die of that. I think I'm dead."

Troy woke up and welcomed his friend, who eventually got in line behind them.

Elena and Gabe walked together to Starbucks. She gave him some of her baby wipes; they were both in dire need of a shower. Gabe looked like he was growing a beard. It was coming in redder than his hair. Elena painted new Yodas on her cheeks.

"You into Star Wars?" the barista asked.

"Nope," Gabe said.

"Yes," Elena said.

"I'm going to see it tonight," the barista said. "Midnight showing."

"Cool," Elena said.

"There are already people in line over there," he said. "Have you seen them? Just three miserable dorks sitting on the sidewalk."

Elena smiled brightly. "That's us!"

"What?"

"We're the three dorks—well, two of the three."

The barista was mortified; he gave them their coffee for free. "May the Force be with you!" Elena said.

When they got back, there were four new people in line.

By noon, there were twenty, at least half of them in costume.

By three, there were portable speakers on the sidewalk, and someone kept playing the victory parade music from *The Phantom Menace* over and over again. (It was only a minute and a half long.)

Elena consented to a ninety-second dance with Troy. Gabe turned him down.

Fifty more people showed up by dinnertime, and some of them brought pizza. Elena went up and down the line, posing for photos and posting them to Instagram. (Her hashtags were *inspired*.) Troy, who'd changed into his pilot costume, was a little wary of all the newcomers—"Jar-Jar-come-latelies."

"We have to keep our guard up," he said. "These people aren't part of the line covenant. They might try to surge at the end."

"We still have our tickets," Gabe said.

"I will be the first person to walk into that theater," Troy said. "You will be second. And Elena will be third. We are the line. These are just day guests."

"So are we sitting together?" Elena asked.

"Oh," Troy said. "Well, we can sit near each other. I've actually got a bunch of friends coming . . ."

"We can sit together," Gabe said, looking at Elena, but somehow *not* looking at Elena. "If you want."

"Sure," she said. "Let's see this through."

The newspaper photographer came back. The line wrapped around the block. Mark came out with a loudspeaker to give everybody directions.

"We've got two hours," Gabe said to Elena. "I think we've only got time for a tattoo *or* a nickname. Your pick."

"Let's not talk about nicknames," she said.

They'd packed up their stuff, and Mark said they could leave it in his office during the movie. "Thank you for not being drunk or disorderly," he said. "And for not littering. I hope you camp outside a different theater next time—I'd be happy to make a few recommendations."

"No chance," Troy said. "This is home."

Elena bounced up and down, pointing from side to side.

"What's that?" Gabe asked.

"It's my Star Wars dance," she said, bouncing and pointing.

After a few seconds, he joined her. Then Troy's friends picked it up. The dance traveled down the line. From the street, they must have looked like the Peanuts characters dancing.

There *was* a surge at the end—Troy was right! The line turned into a mob when Mark opened the doors. But Mark shouted at everyone and made sure the three original line members got in first. Gabe and Elena grabbed seats in the very middle of the theater.

"Oh my God," Elena said. "This is the most comfortable chair I've ever sat in. I feel like a princess."

"You look like a ruffian," Gabe said, but his eyes were closed. "It's so warm," he said. "I love inside."

"Inside is the best," she agreed. "Let's never go outside again."

The theater filled up, and everyone was loud and excited. Elena got a large popcorn and a small pop, and she went to the bathroom twice in the hour before the show started. "If I have to pee during the movie, I'm using this cup."

"It's what you do best," Gabe said.

"I can't believe I made it!" she said. "I can't believe we're here. I can't believe there's a new Star Wars movie."

"I can't believe how much I want a shower," Gabe said.

Elena started doing her Star Wars dance again. It worked just as well in a chair.

When the lights went down, she squealed.

She'd made it. She'd camped out. And she hadn't given up. And now it was here. Now it was starting.

The opening crawl began. *Episode VII: The Force Awakens.*

Elena felt all the stress and tension—all the adrenaline—of the last four days drain out of her body. She felt like she was sinking deep, deep into the warm, plush chair.

She'd made it. She was here. It was happening.

Friday, December 18, 2015

Elena woke up with her head on Gabe's shoulder. In a puddle of spit. Someone was trying to climb over her. "Excuse me," the person said. *Why would anyone be leaving during the opening credits . . .*

The opening credits. Star Wars movies didn't *have* opening credits.

Elena looked at Gabe. His head had fallen to the side, and his mouth was open. She shook his arm. *Violently.* "Gabe, Gabe, Gabe. Wake up! Gabe!"

He sat up like he'd been hit by lightning. "What?"

"We fell asleep," Elena said. "We fell asleep!"

"What?" He looked at the screen—"Oh my God!"—then back at Elena. "When did you fall asleep?"

"Immediately," she said. "As soon as the lights went off. Oh my gahhhhd."

"I saw the crawl," Gabe said. "And a ship, I think?"

"We missed the whole thing," Elena said. Her chin was trembling.

"We missed the whole thing," Gabe repeated. "We waited for a week, and then we missed the whole thing." He rested his elbows on his knees and buried his face in his hands. His shoulders started shaking.

Elena laid her hand on him—on the wet spot she'd left on his sleeve. She quickly pulled her hand away and wiped it on her jeans.

Gabe sat back in his seat with his fists still in his hair. He was laughing so hard he looked like he was in pain.

Elena stared at him, in shock.

And then she started giggling.

And then she started guffawing.

"Elena! Gabe!" Troy was moving with the crowd toward the door. "Was it everything?"

"I'm speechless!" Elena shouted.

Gabe just kept laughing. "We slept on the *street*," he sputtered out. "You peed in a *dumpster*!"

Elena laughed so hard, her stomach hurt.

There were moments in the laughing when she felt totally miserable and wanted to cry—*she missed the whole thing!*—but that just made her laugh harder.

"What do we do now?" Gabe asked. "Hit the street? Camp out until the next showing?"

"I'm going *home*," Elena said. "I'm going to sleep for twelve hours."

"Good idea," he said, sobering up a little. "Me, too."

Elena looked at him. At his curly brown hair and red stubble. She wondered what he'd look like when he hadn't been sleeping rough for a few days. (She'd know this if she ever picked up her head at school.) "We could come back tonight," she said. "We might be able to get tickets."

"I actually already have tickets," Gabe said, running his fingers through his hair. "I was going to come back at seven and see it again."

"Oh," Elena said. "Cool."

"You can have one . . ."

"I don't want to take someone else's ticket."

"It was for my cousin, and he can wait a day," Gabe said. "You've been waiting a week."

"I've been waiting my whole life," she said.

Gabe smiled at her.

Elena smiled back.

"Meet you tonight?" he said.

Elena nodded. "First person here gets in line."

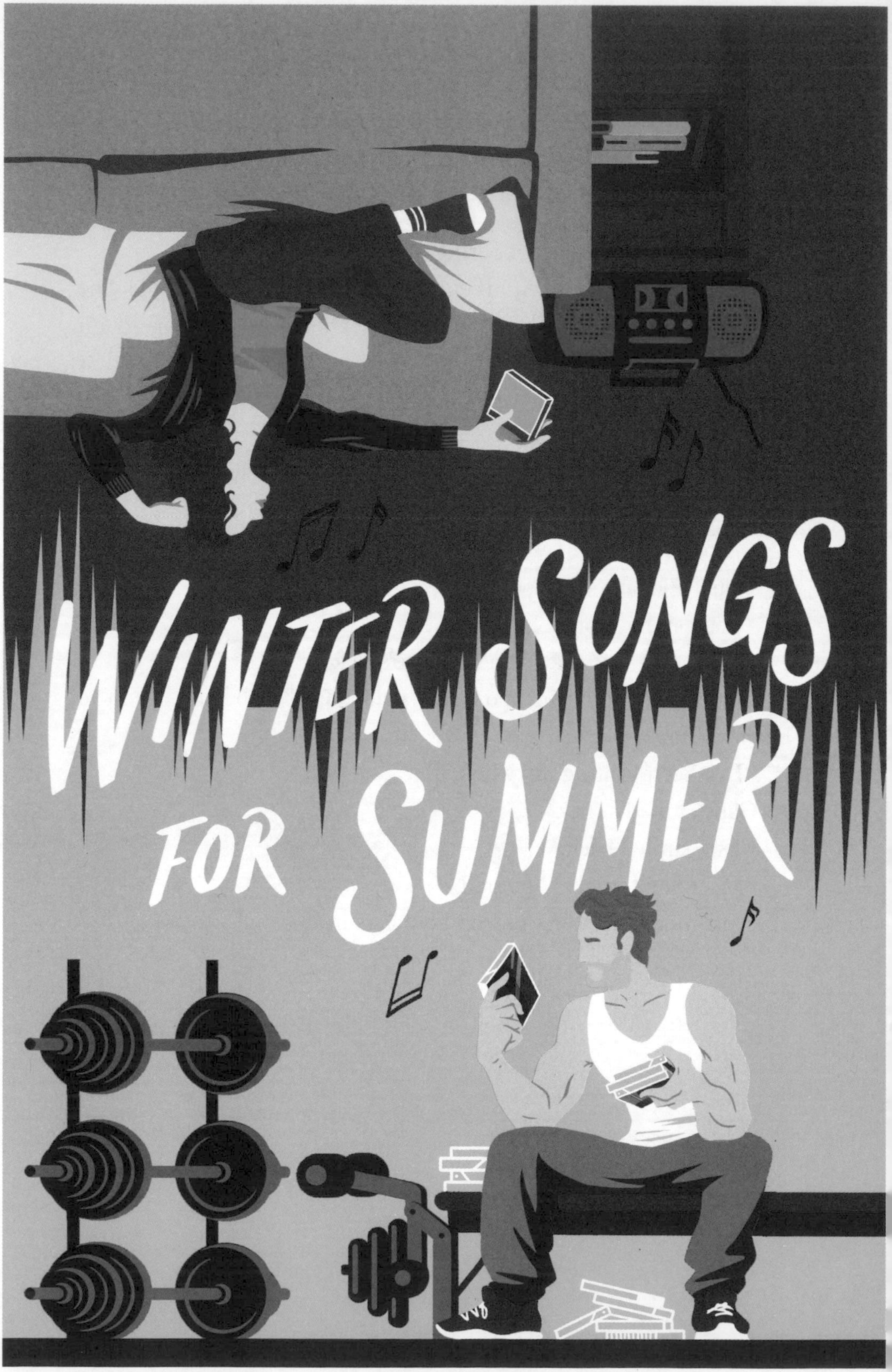

WINTER SONGS
FOR SUMMER

Winter Songs
for Summer

SUMMER WAS CURLED INTO A BALL ON HER DORM room floor.

Or as close as she could get to a ball.

She wasn't one of those girls who could collapse into nothing. She was curled into more of a boomerang shape. A miserable boomerang.

She should probably move onto the bed, but it felt more pathetic to lie on the floor, and the floor was closer to her speakers.

She had a small, all-in-one stereo with a dual cassette player and a radio and a three-CD carousel. It was her prize possession; she'd saved up for six months to buy it.

In the old days, when Summer wanted to listen to one song over and over, she'd have to hit *rewind* on the tape deck and then guess when to stop. Or sometimes she'd make a tape with the same song dubbed over and over—that was time-consuming.

Now she could put in a CD and press *repeat track*, and listen to the same song infinitely without ever getting up—without ever having to shift out of her misery.

It had really revolutionized this breakup.

Summer had been listening to "Silent All These Years" on repeat since she broke up with Charlie five days ago.

She'd been the one to break up with *him,* but there was no victory or solace in that fact. She'd only broken up with Charlie because she could tell that *he* wanted to break up with *her.* They'd been fighting all the time, over nothing, and she could tell by the way he looked at her that he didn't really like her much anymore. Summer wasn't sure that she liked him much, either—but that was cold comfort.

Charlie had been *in love* with her.

He absolutely had. For a while.

And now he wasn't.

And Summer didn't like the mathematical implications there. If the only person who'd ever been in love with her had gradually gotten bored with her, that didn't bode well for the next person to fall in love with Summer. If there *was* a next person.

What if there was only ever Charlie?

True love wasn't guaranteed. No one *owed* you love. And you couldn't earn it.

You just had to be in the right place for it.

Summer had been in the right place for it, with Charlie— Oldfather Hall. They were in the same modern languages class. Summer had been reading a book that Charlie had read, too, and he'd started talking to her about it.

Later he told her that he'd noticed her before that, that he'd liked her auburn hair and these earrings she wore sometimes, with little bells on them.

The henna eventually washed out of Summer's hair. And Charlie eventually told her that he felt like Summer had been misleading him from the very start—like the *first thing* he'd liked about her wasn't really a *thing* about her. Maybe everything he thought he liked about her was just a false flag . . .

It was so unfair. Summer didn't even wear makeup.

None of this boded well for Charlie, either. It meant he could be easily fooled and long delayed. They'd wasted more than a year on each other.

Summer had settled on "Silent All These Years" as her breakup song because it made her sad in ways she didn't even understand. The piano part at the beginning was so unsettling, and Tori Amos's voice crawled right under her skin . . .

"Years go by, will I still be waiting for somebody else to understand?"

Summer had sobbed the first time she listened to this song after the breakup—after Charlie left her room for the last time. It had felt so good to cry. Like her outsides matched her insides. (How often did that happen?) Like she was perfectly centered inside herself and her misery.

She wished she could *keep* crying like that.

The song lost its power the more that Summer listened to it. Now it was just keeping her suspended in a permanent state of dull grief.

Summer listened to the Tori Amos song while she got ready for class in the morning. Then she turned it on as soon as she got back. She'd even been listening to it when she worked on homework, in the hours when she couldn't afford to lie on the floor.

At some point, she would stop.

But stopping would be the start of getting over what had happened. And Summer had no interest in doing that. She wanted to stay right here, as long as she could, mourning the loss of Charlie. And more than that, mourning what she'd had with Charlie—being in love, belonging to someone, being part of something warm. And even more than that, mourning the loss of *herself.*

Summer had always been the sort of person who believed in true love. She wasn't a *hopeless* romantic, but she'd thought that when she said, *"I'll always love you,"* it was a promise she could keep.

It wasn't.

She'd know now that she couldn't be trusted.

Probably Summer would never make promises like that again—but if she did, she'd know they were written in disappearing ink.

And she'd know not to believe the next person who promised to always love *her*.

Summer was the sort of person that love didn't stick to. That was a terrible thing to know about yourself.

There was a knock at Summer's door.

Her friend Michelle usually stopped by her room after dinner, and they'd go work out at the rec center together. But Michelle knew that Summer was out of commission . . .

She might be checking on her. Summer didn't want to be checked on. She ignored the knocking.

But it didn't stop.

Summer got up and looked through the peephole in the door. She didn't know the person who was standing there. Or, like, she *did* know him—they lived in the same building—but she'd never talked to him.

It was that big, kind of gross guy who wore his gym clothes in the cafeteria and was always too loud in the elevators.

She thought about ignoring him, but he started knocking again while Summer was standing there—so she opened her door and frowned.

"Hey," the guy said, "I'm going to need you to turn that off."

"Turn what off?" ("Silent All These Years" had just started again.)

"The music."

"I'm listening to it."

"You're listening to it, I'm listening to it, floors ten through twelve are listening to it."

Normally Summer would apologize in a situation like this. She didn't want to impose on anyone. She didn't want to be a bad neighbor. But she *really* didn't like to be told what to do. And she felt, in her current state, *entitled* to some rude behavior.

Also, once, when Michelle was holding the elevator for Summer, this very guy had gotten impatient and smacked Michelle's hand away, and the elevator had closed while Summer was running for it.

"It's not that loud," she said.

"It's pretty fucking loud from where I'm trying to study for a quantum mechanics test. Your speakers are sitting on my ceiling."

She grimaced. She had no idea this guy lived directly below her. That was an unpleasant thought.

"I'm losing my mind," he said. "I can hear this song in my sleep. It follows me around campus like a ghost. That *Twilight Zone* piano . . . I can't take it. I know you're sad about your breakup—"

"How do you know that?" Had Charlie told him? Did Charlie talk to this Neanderthal? They did live on the same floor . . .

The guy rolled his eyes. "Well, I didn't think you were listening to 'Silent All These Years' on repeat because you were *happy*. Either you just got dumped, or you're having a stroke."

Summer was blinking. There were tears in her eyes. (It felt good.) "I didn't get *dumped*."

"Oh." The guy looked thoughtful. "You broke up with him? Good for you. It was about time."

Summer was crying a little harder. (It felt great.) "I don't want to talk to you about this."

"And I don't want to talk to you!" He waved his finger between them. "This is a win-win situation. Just put on headphones."

Her headphones were broken. "No."

"Okay, don't put on headphones, I don't care. But I will definitely tell my RA if I hear any more Tori Amos tonight."

Summer was really crying now. She knew it was mostly embarrassment and anger and the fact that she couldn't handle confrontation, but it felt *fantastic*. Like she'd tapped into herself again. Like something was moving inside her.

"Just leave me alone," she said.

She didn't slam the door in his face, but she closed it with vigor. Then she crawled onto her bed. She was still crying. It felt *so good*. It was such a *relief*. Like her emotions and body were in synch with her brain again. She cried into her pillow until she didn't have anything left. Maybe now she'd be able to sleep . . .

She was just drifting off when there was another knock at her door.

Summer got up and looked through the peephole. It was the big guy again. He had a dumb-looking tank top on. He *loved* tank tops. (Summer had seen more of this guy's armpit hair than her own.)

She opened the door. "I haven't been listening to anything." Her voice was hoarse.

"No, I know." He was looking at her with his eyebrows down, like he felt bad about something. "Look, I made you this."

He held out a CD in a clear case.

"What is it?"

"Music. That you can listen to."

"Are you critiquing the music I listen to when I'm grieving?"

"No!" He gestured when he talked—as if he wasn't big and loud enough. "I get it. You're upset. But if I have to grieve with you, I need a little variety."

Summer looked down at the CD. He'd written *Songs for Getting Over Dipshits* on the case.

"I can't believe you're trying to dictate what I listen to while I cry," she said, fully affronted. "You don't even know me. This is such a guy move."

"A *guy* move?"

"Yeah."

"Hey, I'm not the one who dumped you."

"He didn't *dump* me."

"If you dumped him"—he spread his arms—"why are you listening to suicide music?"

"It's not suicide music! And it's because I'm sad!"

The guy rubbed his face. He was also wearing weight-lifting gloves. Why couldn't he put those on when he got to the gym? Was he trying to draw attention to how big he was? That was unnecessary . . .

You know how, in high school, there were those guys who already looked like grown men? Like their necks were already thick, and their beards were already full?

This guy was the college version of that.

He looked like a *grown* grown man. He was a head taller than most people and proportionately wider, and he always seemed to have five-o'clock shadow. He was *too much*.

"I understand that you're sad," he said. "I'm just saying—there are lots of sad songs."

"I can hear your music, too, you know." (He listened to very aggressive rap music. Charlie said it was the *Judgment Night* soundtrack.) "I've never come down to harass you about it."

"If you ever need me to turn it down," he said, "I will."

Summer shook her head. She *hated* knowing that this guy lived below her. Now she'd be constantly thinking about what he could hear. "Just leave me alone," she said.

"Fine," he agreed.

"Fine."

He walked away before Summer could close the door in his face. She swung it shut and sat back on her bed looking down at the CD. Who was *he* calling a dipshit?

～ ⁀

Summer bought new headphones at the university bookstore for $7.99. She'd been saving up for a new pair of Vans, and now she'd have to wait another week. She blamed her downstairs neighbor for that. For the last day, she'd been more angry with him than she had been miserable about Charlie.

But then she saw Charlie at dinner—she'd just finished getting her food, and she'd walked out into the dining area, and there he was. In a Pavement T-shirt and a flannel shirt. Summer had panicked and whirled around. She walked the wrong way through the food line and out into the other side of the cafeteria, the north side.

Michelle hadn't been able to find her, so Summer ate alone.

After dinner, Summer skipped working out, and went and sat in front of her stereo, plugging in her new headphones.

She had to lie very close to the stereo, so they wouldn't come unplugged.

She started "Silent All These Years."

It was like sinking into a warm, unhappy bath. Like being gently raked from head to toe with familiar misery.

The song played over Summer and through her, and she settled into it, hollow and numb.

~~~

Summer had to move her stereo, so she could listen to music on her headphones while she worked at her desk. It meant she couldn't lie on the floor anymore. She hated wearing headphones. She hated feeling *tethered*. But it was worth it to never have to talk to her neighbor.

She'd eaten on the north side of the cafeteria again tonight. She'd tried to talk Michelle into eating on the north side from now on. But Michelle liked a guy who ate on the south side, and the rest of the girls on their floor all ate on the south side.

"Don't let Charlie change your life like this," Michelle said.

"It's not much of a change," Summer said. "It's literally just the other half of the cafeteria. They have all the same food."

"You know that the soft serve is better on the south side . . ."

Summer couldn't argue with that; it was true.

She ate dinner by herself for the rest of the week. Like a first-semester freshman.

Summer had listened to "Silent All These Years" so many times, she could hardly even feel it anymore. She could hardly even *hear* it. It was just the sound that her room made.

She wasn't sure she even remembered how to listen to other songs . . . She had a one-track mind now. Every other song sounded like a mistake someone made while they were trying to play "Silent All These Years."

She flipped through her CD crate, feeling tetchy and fickle.

She hated her new headphones. They'd taken her last eight dollars—but they were so cheap, they were already buzzing in one ear.

She'd shoved that CD from the guy downstairs in here with the rest of her CDs. She wondered what a guy like that considered breakup music . . . Metallica? Korn?

Summer ejected her Tori Amos CD and put the CD he'd given her into the carousel. She hit *play*.

She didn't recognize the first track . . .

Maybe she'd heard it on an oldies station?

Or in church? It kind of sounded like a church song. It didn't sound sad. How was this a breakup song? The lyrics weren't sad. The piano wasn't sad.

"Morning has broken, like the first morning . . ."

Summer's head dropped into her hands. There were tears streaming down her cheeks.

All she listened to for the rest of the night was "Morning Has Broken." On repeat. Trying to figure out why it was so devastating.

Why it reminded her of things she'd completely forgotten—like waking up with Charlie after the first time he'd slept in her dorm room and walking to class together in the rain.

How could a song she'd never heard before *remind* her of something?

Summer stopped crying after the first few times she listened to it. But she still felt . . . something new. Wretched in a new way. Like her misery was a sculpture, and she'd walked around to get a different view of it.

⟋⟋⟋

Track 2 was another song she only sort of recognized. Another song that you could sing in church. Another song that made Summer cry.

⟋⟋⟋

Track 3 was Metallica. She still cried. (It was acoustic.)

⟋⟋⟋

Track 4 was a Tori Amos song that she'd never heard before. Summer thought she'd heard *every* Tori Amos song before. (It was a cover of "Ain't No Sunshine," obviously a bootleg. The guy downstairs probably stole music from the Internet. He was probably really into Napster.)

The song reminded her of lying in bed with Charlie and watching cartoons. They'd always stayed in her room because Summer didn't want to get caught sneaking down to the boys' floor. Sneaking onto the boys' floor made her feel like a tramp. Letting Charlie into her room felt divine.

Summer cried.

⟋⟋⟋

Track 5 was a song Summer just couldn't get into.

She skipped to Track 6—Judy Collins. "Send in the Clowns." Judy Collins was sort of the 1973 version of Tori Amos. Summer cried a river.

It took three nights for Summer to get through the eighteen songs on the CD. Thirteen of them were exquisite. Two were just okay. And three were skippable.

The songs were mostly new to her, so they were slow to lose their power. She listened to the CD whenever she was in her room. Tethered to her stereo. Sometimes just leaning against her desk.

Her headphones gave out in the middle of writing a paper. Summer threw them across the room. She listened to the CD with the volume turned low.

She listened to the CD with the volume turned loud.

She lay on her floor, with her eyes closed, remembering how Charlie slept with his fingers coiled in her hair.

Summer went through the north side of the cafeteria line and out into the dining area, looking for a table.

The meathead from the tenth floor was sitting by himself, right next to the salad bar. He smiled when he saw Summer. It was a knowing smile. Like—*I know you're listening to that CD I gave you.*

Summer rolled her eyes and walked past him.

She knew he knew! She hadn't forgotten how space and sound worked. She couldn't afford new headphones right now. It was either listen to the CD and know he could hear it—or not listen to the CD, which was . . . untenable.

Summer stopped, just past his table, and came back around to the other side. He grinned up at her.

"Is anyone sitting here?" she asked.

He kicked the chair across from him, pushing it away from the table. He was wearing a neon tank top, and his weight-lifting gloves were sitting next to his tray. She sat down anyway.

"So," he said.

"So," Summer conceded.

"You usually sit on the south side."

"So do you."

He shrugged. "The line was shorter on this side tonight. I'm trying to get to the gym." He narrowed his eyes. "I know what you're doing over here—you're trying to avoid that dipshit."

She shrugged. "It seemed advisable."

"You should make *him* sit on this side, to avoid *you*. You can't let him get the good soft serve in the divorce."

"The soft serve is perfectly fine over here," she said.

The sides of his mouth pulled down. "Is it?"

"It must be." Summer spread her paper napkin in her lap. "All these people eat here every night. They seem happy."

The guy looked around. "The only people who eat on this side of the cafeteria are freshmen and the lactose-intolerant."

Summer shook her head. None of this mattered. She was too sad to eat ice cream. "I know you know," she said.

He was grinning at her. He had a very big head. And a very big smile. He looked like he hadn't shaved in a month. "What do I know?"

"That I'm listening to that CD you gave me. I like it, okay?"

He grinned down at his tray. He had two dinner plates wedged onto the tray, with two servings of roasted chicken. He'd covered it all with spinach and cottage cheese. He also had three bananas. "I *did* know that." He looked up at her. "It's pretty good shit, huh?"

"Yes," Summer said, sounding irritated, "it's very good. I listen to it all the time." She leaned over her own tray (where there was a very normal cheeseburger with a normal serving of French fries).

"How did you know? I mean—was that just a mix that you had left over from the last time you got dumped? Is that your go-to breakup mix?"

He looked offended. "No. I made it for you."

"But you don't even know me!" Summer practically shouted.

"You're right!" he practically shouted back. (He was so *loud*.) "But I know *a lot* about what kind of music you like."

Summer shuddered. Mostly for effect. "Are you *listening* to me listen to music?"

The guy looked at his food again and picked up a fork. "You're not making me feel bad about that. I'm not some creep. All I've done is bear with your obsessive-compulsive bullshit for the last two years and tried not to complain about it."

"You've lived under me for *two years*?" That seemed egregious.

"Why are you acting like that's a problem? I didn't *choose* it."

"So you just made me a breakup CD with songs you thought I'd like . . ."

"Because I've heard every song that you like a thousand times. Yeah." He took a bite of chicken and raw spinach and cottage cheese and . . . were those almonds? "And it worked," he said. "Now, at least you're listening to music that I like, too."

"You don't like music like that . . ."

He frowned at her. "What are you talking about? I made that CD."

"I've heard your music. It's all people screaming over heavy bass."

He looked confused for a second and chewed quietly. "Ohhhh," he finally said with his mouth full. "I listen to the *Judgment Night* soundtrack when I want to get pumped up for a test. That's not *all* I listen to."

"That's all I hear."

"Well, I normally wear headphones. Because I'm a good neighbor."

Summer looked at her food. She picked up her cheeseburger. "The thing I don't understand, about your CD . . ." She looked up. ". . . is why the happy songs make me feel worse than the sad ones."

"Happy songs are the saddest thing to listen to when you're unhappy," the guy said matter-of-factly. "That's just physics."

"That's not physics."

"They break your heart because they make you think about the last time you were happy." He took another bite. "Also, don't argue with me about physics. I'm a physics major. What's your major?"

"Secondary education."

"Okay, I won't argue with you about that."

Summer watched him eat his chicken and spinach and cottage cheese and almond slivers and . . . some little brown things that he sprinkled on his food from a Tupperware container; they looked like Grape-Nuts.

⟨⟩

When Summer woke up the next morning, someone had slid a CD under her door. She was half asleep, and for a minute she thought it was from Charlie, and her chest seized up a little bit. Charlie had never made her a mix CD.

Then she realized that it was from the guy downstairs, and she felt like he really should have just left it outside. Sliding something under someone's door was a little intimate.

He'd written *More Songs for Getting Over Dipshits* on the case.

Summer stared at it for a few seconds, tempted to sit down and listen right now, never mind her morning classes.

She opened up the case and put the CD in the player, so that all she'd have to do when she got home was push *play*.

⟨⟩

Track 1 was the Barenaked Ladies. Summer thought the Barenaked Ladies were corny. The song made her cry.

Track 2 was another corny song with some guy warbling over a harmonica. So corny: *"Once I was a hunter, and I brought home fresh meat for you."*

Summer lay on top of her comforter with her arms over her eyes, and felt like the song was pulling her heart out in pieces, through her toes and her fingertips.

The thing about Charlie was—he was the first person who Summer had ever noticed across a crowded room, who noticed her back.

She'd noticed lots of boys before. Crushed on them. Watched them.

But they didn't notice and crush and watch her back.

Charlie did. They'd looked at each other across the auditorium, and there were . . . maybe not fireworks. Maybe not bells. But there was *something.*

Summer was aware of him, and he was aware of her, and she was aware of him being aware of her.

Maybe that happened to other girls all the time. It had never happened to Summer before.

She wasn't ugly—not really. But she was the sort of girl who really pretty girls liked to hang around with because they wouldn't be a distraction. Summer wasn't a distraction.

She was a little short. She was a little fat. Her nose was a little big. Her best feature was probably her breasts, but she hated wearing anything that called attention to them—so they largely went unnoticed.

The guys who liked Summer in high school had gotten to know her first. She had plenty of personality.

But Summer didn't have to wear Charlie down or grow on him. He just saw her. And liked her. And wanted to be close to her.

How could something like that go wrong?

It was the closest Summer had ever come to feeling magic.

⟶

This new CD was one corny song after another. Paul McCartney! Paul McCartney and *Wings*!

Summer was laid low by every one.

None of them were skippable.

She kept seeing the guy downstairs in the cafeteria, and he kept smiling at her like he had her number—and she supposed he did.

He wore tank tops and T-shirts with the sleeves ripped off. Even though it was November. He carried that little container of brown stuff that he dumped on his food. He sat by himself.

Where had he found all these sad songs? Did he collect them? Summer needed to start listening to something other than the college radio station and bands that Charlie liked.

She was four days into the new CD when she stopped at the guy downstairs's table again. He kicked a chair out for her.

Summer sat down, letting her tray drop with a clatter that almost knocked over her chocolate milk.

He grinned at her. "How's it going?"

"You know how it's going," she said, picking up her spoon.

Summer had a bowl of chili and a side salad.

The guy had two plates again—pork chops, with raw broccoli, more cottage cheese, almonds, again, and his Tupperware granola.

He ate it all with a knife and a fork. His weight-lifting gloves were sitting next to his tray.

"He wasn't a dipshit," Summer said.

The guy glanced up at her. "Okay." He went back to eating.

"He really wasn't. He isn't."

The guy squinted one eye, like he disagreed with her.

"You don't even know him," she said.

"We live on the same floor."

"That's hardly intimate."

"I mean, I've seen him naked . . ."

Summer made a face. "Don't you guys have shower stalls?"

"We have stalls," the guy said, "but no curtains."

"That's a real maintenance problem," she said.

He gave her a frank look. "I've hung out with your ex-boyfriend. He doesn't rinse the sink after he brushes his teeth, and he never laughs at anyone else's jokes. He's kind of a dipshit, no offense."

"How can that be 'no offense'? I dated him for fourteen months."

"I get it. He's cute."

Charlie *was* cute. He had dark hair that brushed his collar and stayed perfectly tucked behind his ears. He had a pointy chin and prominent cheekbones. He looked like the cute, smart friend on a sitcom. He made Summer feel cuter and smarter. By association. "That's not why we dated," she said.

"You don't have to explain any of this to me."

"I know," she said. "I just—I don't like it when you call him that. Just because he didn't laugh at your jokes . . ."

"Did he ever laugh at yours?"

Summer bit the inside of her cheek—so that she wouldn't say something like *"Maybe I'm not funny"* just to win this argument.

"What are you even eating?" she asked.

"Protein," the guy said, chewing.

"What's that stuff you carry around in your little container? Is it steroids? Or Grape-Nuts? Is it steroid Grape-Nuts?"

He lowered his eyebrow, offended, but he still kind of laughed. "It's hemp hearts."

"Is that legal?"

"Yes, it's legal. They're good for you. Do you want to try some?"

"No, thank you. I might run for office someday."

He laughed again. "I thought you were going to be a secondary school teacher."

"I can do both."

He shrugged again, agreeably.

"Where are your friends?" she asked. When she used to see him at dinner, he'd be sitting with a big group of friends. All weird-looking. None as weird-looking as him.

"On the other side of the cafeteria," he said, "with the good soft serve. Where are yours?"

⌒

"Do you know that guy who lives in our dorm, who looks, like, thirty-five, and like he might be training for the WWF?"

"The World Wildlife Fund?" Michelle was on the stair machine next to Summer's.

Summer had started working out again most nights after dinner. But she still wasn't working out very hard. She never worked out as hard as Michelle. Summer left her machine on manual and set the difficulty to three. She couldn't get over thinking that, when it came to working out, it was the thought that counted.

"No," Summer said. "He's, like, really tall and really big, and he's always in gym clothes? And his hair is sweaty half the time?"

"Is he a football player?" Michelle was panting. Her bangs were sticking to her forehead.

"God no. Imagine a big nerd who's built like a football player. *You know*—the loud guy. With hair on his shoulders."

"The one who closed the elevator on you?"

"Yes!" Summer said, relieved.

"Yeah, I know him!"

"What's his name?"

"Oh," Michelle panted. "I don't know. He lives on Charlie's floor, doesn't he?"

"Yeah," Summer said.

"Why do you need to know?"

Because I missed my window to ask, Summer thought. "I just realized that I didn't know his name."

"Huh." Michelle was climbing the fake stairs very intensely. She didn't ask any more questions.

It would be very embarrassing to run into Charlie on his own floor.

But he did live on the other *end* of the floor. And he'd already be at dinner by now; he had a routine.

Summer walked quietly down the stairs (there was no reason to be quiet) and out onto the tenth floor. All the boys' names were written on construction paper and taped to their doors. No one had to share a room in their dorm; it was their privilege as upperclassmen.

She walked to room 1007. (Summer lived in 1107.) But there was no name on the door. Just a picture of a monster and some construction paper that said *CTHULHU*. She rolled her eyes.

The door opened—Summer jumped back.

"Summer," the guy said. (*How the hell did he know* her *name?*)

"Cthulhu," she said.

"What are you—" He glanced down the hall, toward Charlie's room. Then he looked at Summer again, his eyebrows up in the middle, like he felt sorry for her.

"There's an elevator problem on my floor," she lied.

"Let me show you to ours," he said, closing his door behind him.

Summer walked with him down the hall.

"Are you headed to dinner?" he asked.

"Yeah."

"Me, too."

That was obvious—he was wearing his weight-lifting gloves.

He didn't suggest that they go together. But they didn't really have any other polite options. They went through the north side of the cafeteria line together, and Summer watched him get two plates of sloppy joe mix, without any bread.

"Are you going to put cottage cheese on that?" she asked.

"I like cottage cheese."

"I like cottage cheese, too. But I don't use it as a condiment."

"It has more protein than dressing," he said, like that would clear things up for her.

Summer got chicken nuggets and French fries and a side salad with ranch dressing.

She followed him to a table and sat across from him. And watched him take off his gloves and sprinkle his hemp hearts.

"What does someone do with a physics major?" she asked.

"Physics."

She rolled her eyes.

He grinned up at her. "You can go to grad school. Teach physics. Do research. Work for the government. Work in a hundred different industries."

"That's a lot of options."

"There's a real demand for people who fundamentally understand how the world works."

"That seems like an overstatement," she said.

He shrugged. "Why do you want to teach high school?"

"I want to teach middle school."

"Why?"

"Because middle school is terrible."

"You're a sadist?"

"No. I think I could be a good field medic." She dragged a French fry through her ranch dressing. "Middle-school kids are such a mess—they're so emotional, they can't help it."

He stopped his chewing and crunching to smile at her.

"I know what you're thinking," she said.

He shrugged and kept chewing.

Summer tried to change the subject. "Charlie is a German major."

The guy chewed.

"He's also studying Russian."

He took another bite.

"Does he honestly not rinse the sink after he brushes his teeth?"

"Not once," the guy said.

"I was really in love with him," she said.

The guy didn't even nod.

"What's your name, anyway?"

He looked up at her, surprised. "You don't know my name?"

"How would I?"

He swallowed and took a drink of iced tea. "It's Benji."

"Benji? Like the dog?"

"That's a deep cut, but yeah."

"Benji," she said, examining him. He had dark brown hair—wavy and coarse-looking. The kind of coarse that's sort of shiny, like wire, and won't lie flat. It was big hair, even though it was short. He had a big head. His skin was ruddy. He must shave every morning . . . the scruff on his chin never turned into a beard. "How do you know so much about music?" she asked.

"I'm a good listener."

Summer started listening to the two CDs he'd given her back-to-back. There was a nice progression to them.

She didn't cry anymore, at any of the songs. But they still made her feel like she was paging through her relationship with Charlie from beginning to end.

She listened to the CDs, quietly, at night when she couldn't sleep.

Summer hated sleeping alone now that she knew what it was like to sleep next to someone else. Would there be years of this now? Forever of this?

Is this how everyone felt when they fell out of love? Was the world full of hollowed-out people? Was almost everyone in mourning, all of the time?

She ate dinner with Benji that week whenever they happened to be at the cafeteria at the same time.

He was very opinionated.

Charlie had also been very opinionated.

The difference was—Benji didn't seem to care whether Summer agreed with him. He didn't even seem to care whether Summer liked him. That was a real relief. Summer still felt too miserable and broken to be polite.

The only other person she'd been talking to lately was Michelle, when they worked out. It was generally okay. People expected you to be rude when you were out of breath.

Summer was headed down to dinner one night when the elevator stopped at Charlie's floor. Her heart stopped, too.

Then started.

It was Benji and his friends. She could hear him before the doors even opened. He smiled at her but didn't say anything. Was Benji embarrassed to talk to her in front of his friends? (That was a troubling thought!) They were all bullshitting about some movie or TV show or something. They were doing voices. Benji was the loudest. And the tallest. He was his own crowd.

Summer broke off from them when the elevator opened, but they still ended up at the cafeteria line at the same time. When the line split, north and south, Benji grabbed a tray and got in line behind her.

Summer shot him a wry look. He wry-ed her right back.

There was fried chicken for dinner. He got two plates. She already knew he was going to be disgusting and peel off the skin.

Summer got macaroni and cheese.

They sat down together, and Benji took off his weight-lifting gloves and dropped them by his tray.

He peeled the skin off his chicken and made a gross pile of it, then dumped a bowl of greens and cottage cheese on top of the chicken.

"Everything you eat must taste the same," she said.

"No."

"It must all taste like cottage cheese and spinach."

"Every sandwich doesn't taste like bread." He glanced up at her. "Is my dinner bothering you?"

"Yes."

"Is it imposing on your dinner somehow?"

"Visually, yes. Conceptually."

"Minimally, at best. How're you doing, Summer?"

"You know how I'm doing."

He still had ears. He knew she was still swimming in a sea of misery—he'd written the soundtrack.

Someone sat down next to Summer. She looked up. It was one of Benji's weird friends. Three more sat down.

"South side's closed," one of them said. "Somebody threw up in the salad bar."

More people were filing in from the south side, looking for tables. Summer saw Michelle and their friends from the eleventh floor.

She saw Charlie.

And Charlie saw her.

And everyone else in the room sort of faded away—it was just like it used to be, when she and Charlie first met. He nodded his head at her. Summer nodded back. And then he walked by. Summer could hear the piano part from "Silent All These Years" in the back of her head.

Charlie sat down at a table with Michelle and the rest of them.

He was sitting with Summer's friends, and Summer was sitting at a table full of the weirdest guys from the tenth floor, which was the weirdest floor in Schramm Hall. Weird people were drawn together.

Summer stood up. She wasn't hungry. She'd never played piano, but she thought that if she sat down at one right now, she'd be able to play the first fourteen notes of "Silent All These Years" on her very first try.

Benji caught up with her at the elevator.

Summer tried to close the doors on him, but he was already in.

"Are you okay?" he asked.

"I'm fine," she said. "It's literally nothing. He just *exists,* he's going to keep on existing—that's not traumatic, you know?"

Summer was crying; it didn't feel good.

Benji didn't say anything.

She glared up at him. "How much can you actually hear?" Her voice was broken.

Benji licked his bottom lip. Like he was thinking. And being careful. "I can only hear your stereo because you turn it up so loud. I can hear it when you drop something. And I can hear it when people shout."

Summer held on to his eyes. "Have you ever been dumped?"

"Yeah," he said. "But you haven't. You weren't."

"I only dumped Charlie because he was going to dump me. I could feel it coming. Like the shadow of it was already passing over me. I broke up with him first, just to protect myself. I didn't think I could live through hearing his reasons."

Benji didn't look away. "What were *your* reasons?"

"I told him that I thought we were growing apart—isn't that stupid? It doesn't even mean anything."

"I think people can grow apart . . ."

"Maybe in their forties, when they have separate interests and full-time jobs. We lived in the same *building*. We did *everything* together. We weren't growing apart! We just didn't like each other anymore!"

Benji was standing very still. He took up most of the elevator. "You can tell me all this," he said, "but you don't have to."

"I feel like you already know!" She was crying, for real. It felt terrible.

"No, I don't know."

"You heard us fighting!"

"I heard that you *were* fighting."

"But the songs . . ." Summer said.

"They're just songs."

"No." She was crying so hard. "They're not."

The elevator doors opened. They were still in the lobby. Summer ran out. She'd take the stairs.

～～

A half hour later, there was a knock at her door. Summer had Tori Amos on repeat.

Benji was standing outside her door.

She opened it, daring him with her whole face to mention the music. She wouldn't turn the volume down at gunpoint.

"Do you want to take a walk?" Benji asked.

He was wearing his weight-lifting gloves.

"Don't you have to work out?"

"I can go later."

Summer looked at him for a second. Then went and turned off her stereo. She grabbed a jacket.

She and Benji took the elevator without talking. They walked out onto Sixteenth Street, toward the heart of campus.

It made her think of Charlie.

"I'm sorry about the CDs," Benji said.

Summer didn't say anything.

"I meant them as a peace offering," he said. "I could hear you crying up there—I'd never heard you cry before, so I thought you must *really* be crying, and I felt like shit about it. I wanted to make up for it."

"I like the CDs," she said.

"I like that we're friends now," Benji said.

Summer looked up at him. *Were* they friends now? She was still getting used to his name.

"But I'm sorry," he said. "I didn't mean to fuck with your grieving. You were in the middle of something, and I shouldn't have introduced new variables."

"I like the CDs," Summer said again.

"I like being your friend," Benji said again.

They were probably friends . . . They ate dinner together almost every night.

Summer looked over at him. Up at him. He'd pulled a sweatshirt on over his tank top. It was a relief.

"Why do you wear weight-lifting gloves to dinner?"

He lowered an eyebrow, like that was a stupid question. "So that I don't lose them."

She stared at him, like that was a stupid answer.

"I don't have pockets," he said. (Benji wore baggy striped pants that only gym-rat meatheads wore.)

"So you're not just trying to tell everybody that you lift weights?"

He tucked his chin into his neck. "I don't need to *tell* people that I lift weights."

That made Summer laugh.

She supposed they were friends. What a revolting development.

"I don't think there was anything special about Charlie . . ." Summer said.

Benji let her talk.

"And I don't think there's anything special about me. There was nothing special about us falling in love and being wrong about it. It's the most ordinary thing in the world, and I think that's the worst part of all this—knowing how unremarkable our relationship was."

Benji was watching the sidewalk, listening.

"The most magical thing that's ever going to happen to me wasn't magical at all," she said. "It was cardboard, you know? I'm crying over *cardboard*."

Benji glanced over at her. He was licking his bottom lip. "That dipshit wasn't the most magical thing that's ever going to happen to you. How old are you, twenty?"

"I'm twenty-one," she said. "How old are you?"

"Twenty-one."

"You look forty."

Benji laughed. Too loud. People walking by looked at them. "That wasn't the most magical thing that's ever going to happen to you," he said.

There was a CD slid under her door when she woke up the next morning, and she knew that it was from Benji.

More Songs for Getting Further Over Dipshits.

Summer wished that she still had a Discman.

Track 1 was lovely. Joni Mitchell. "Blue." Summer was a sucker for women with high voices and pianos. That wasn't a secret.

Track 2 was a whispery rap song.

Track 3 was Wings again—Benji clearly had a thing for Wings. They weren't so bad.

Track 4 was more folk music. Guitars. Harmonies. It was a song that felt like morning.

Track 5 was cheesy. A song from the sixties—"Sunday Will Never Be the Same." Summer laughed and skipped it. (She'd listen to it all the way through, the next time around.)

None of these songs were sad, really.

None of them made Summer cry.

They made her feel a little tearful.

She thought of the time Charlie had surprised her on her birthday with red velvet cake. He really wasn't a dipshit. This would be so much easier if he was.

Benji wouldn't let her taste his hemp hearts. He said they were *slightly* illegal.

Hemp hearts tasted like pine nuts.

Summer had three slots in her CD carousel. She could listen to all three of Benji's CDs one after another. Three and a half hours of music. She liked the sliding noise the carousel made between discs.

"Have you ever been in love?" Summer asked.

Benji was eating a salad with grilled chicken strips and green peppers and all his usual garbage. "No. I mean—yes. Maybe." He glanced up at her. "I've had deep feelings."

"But you've been dumped . . ."

He nodded. "Yeah."

"What happened?"

"Um . . ."

"You don't have to tell me," she said.

"It's all right." Benji squared his broad (bare) shoulders. "Once was in high school. She wanted to date someone else."

"Oof, I'm sorry. Was it terrible?"

"Yeah."

"I'm sorry."

"I've dated a few people here," he said. "In college. Nothing serious . . . Well, one thing seemed serious. But it wasn't. I don't know. I've made out with a lot of girls at parties."

Summer was surprised. "You *have*?"

He looked a little offended, but he still laughed. "Yeah."

"This is like the opposite of finding out that someone has hidden depths. You have hidden shallows."

Benji just laughed.

"I'm not the make-out-at-parties type," she said.

"I can tell."

That seemed like an insult, but Summer brushed it off. "Are you worried that you'll never fall in love?"

He shook his head. "No."

"I am," she said.

"But you've already been in love."

"That only makes me *more* worried. I'm a romantic."

He nodded.

"I believe in true love," she said.

He nodded again.

"But I clearly don't know it when I see it. How can I ever say '*I love you*' again? I'll have to asterisk it—'*I think I love you, but the only other time I said this, I was wrong. I don't actually know what love looks or feels like. I think I love you, but what do I know?*'"

Benji just listened. He kept listening after she was done talking. He ate his salad, and Summer ate her pizza.

"I think you're getting this all wrong," he said after a while.

"How so?"

"I don't have the proof worked out yet," he said. "But you're wrong."

Summer frowned. What did Benji know.

He'd never even been *wrong* about being in love.

⟡

Summer ran into Benji in the elevator again on the way to dinner. He was alone this time. He had his whole stupid outfit on.

"That's it," she said. "Give me your hands."

He put out his hands. "Why?"

She started taking off one of his terrible gloves. It was probably *pickled* in dried sweat. "Because I can't take it anymore! You can't wear these to dinner!"

"But I don't have pockets!"

She was pulling the second one off. "I do."

She tucked the gloves into the front of her hoodie. "You can't just wear these all the time. It's unbearably weird."

"I told you—I wear them to dinner because I go straight to the gym, and I don't want to forget them."

"Put them in your bag!"

"I don't want to!"

"Benji, I am telling you this from the bottom of my heart, with the kindest intentions: It's gross, and you look like a meathead."

He seemed like he might grab the gloves out of her front pocket. "Who cares?"

"Me!" Summer said. "I have to look at you!"

That made him laugh for some reason. "Fine," he said, turning toward the elevator doors. "Because I look so much less like a meathead now."

"It's a matter of degrees," she said.

⟡

Benji found her on the StairMaster. He looked up at her with his big, brown eyes. They were green in the middle, and his eyelashes were so thick, they looked like all one piece.

She reached into her front pocket and pulled out his gloves. He took them from her.

Michelle was staring at him. He nodded at her and walked away.

"That's that guy," Michelle said when he was gone.

"His name's Benji," Summer said.

Summer found herself only listening to the third CD that Benji had given her—the first two made her too sad.

She listened to the radio sometimes, too.

She saw Charlie at the Student Union with another girl. They might just be friends. But it made Summer feel more ordinary than ever.

Just thinking about Charlie made Summer feel mundane and re-placeable.

Summer went down to dinner and, as usual, went looking for Benji's table. Her jaw dropped when she saw him.

"What happened to you—do you have a job interview?"

Benji was wearing normal jeans and a *Calvin and Hobbes* T-shirt. She sat down across from him.

"I'm going to change after dinner," he said. "Even though that means going all the way back to my room. And wasting ten min-utes. And getting to the rec center when all of the good mats are taken."

Benji looked almost like a normal person dressed like this. Still too big and loud and florid. But normal. Ish. His T-shirt strained over his arms.

"I know you don't want to hear this," Summer said, "but your arms look even bigger when you wear sleeves."

"I just feel," Benji said, tearing into the terrible mess on his dinner tray, "that I should be able to wear what I want in the comfort of my own home."

"Wear what you want," she said.

He huffed.

"But you look good."

He huffed again. "I'm doing this for you, you know."

"I'm glad," Summer said. "I appreciate it."

His eyes were narrow, and he was staring at her.

She smiled at him. "You look good."

She woke up to a new CD.

Winter Songs for Summer.

She took the other CDs out of her stereo, and put that one in.

Sometimes Benji's friends came to eat with them on the north side. They weren't so bad. (Though they were very loud.)

"It must be nice to have friends who sacrifice the premium ice cream for you," Summer said.

"You have that," Benji said.

Benji had a car. An old Crown Vic.

He drove Summer to the mall to buy her new Vans. Benji needed shoes, too, but his feet were so big, all he could do was tell the salesperson what size he wore, and they brought out everything that might fit from the back room. Four pairs.

Benji bought black Nike high-tops with white swooshes. They

got Orange Juliuses and listened to instrumental music on the way back to campus—you never knew what you were going to get with Benji.

Summer only saw Benji's armpit hair now when she saw him at the gym. They went at the same time since he'd started changing after dinner. He'd walk over there with her and Michelle.

Summer still liked to needle him . . .

"You can't lift weights while wearing sleeves? They sap your strength or something?"

"That's right, Delilah."

"You look so good in sleeves . . ."

"I'm not accommodating you at the gym, Summer. I'm allowed to look like a meathead there."

Michelle thought Benji was weird, and she didn't get any of his jokes. But she liked him okay. She agreed that he should stop wearing tank tops.

Benji tried to teach Summer how to lift weights. Her heart wasn't in it. But it was fun hanging out with him.

The tracks on *Winter Songs for Summer* all felt like clean, yellow light.

Like stepping out into the cold after you'd been working out. Or like—that feeling you get when you recognize a pattern.

There were lots of women singing in harmony. Lots of tinkly pianos. Cat Stevens made another appearance. And Judy Collins. And there was a song Summer had never heard by Pearl Jam. (She thought she'd heard every song by Pearl Jam.)

Every single song made Summer smile.

Well, almost every single song—the last track was "Silent All These Years." That one made her cry. She'd thought she didn't have any more tears left for that song, but it had something to do with the other songs on the CD . . . The journey of them. The momentum. Context mattered.

～つ

"Let me explain how you're wrong," Benji said.

They were walking home from the rec center. Michelle had left a while ago, but Summer had stayed to entertain Benji while he lifted.

It was February and frigid, so Benji was wearing a big down coat over his tank top. Summer wondered if he'd gone to the coat store, and they'd brought out the only three coats that might fit him.

"Go for it," Summer said. "Wrong about what?"

"Love," he said.

"Oh. Right." Summer hadn't thought about love lately. Though she still thought about Charlie. Everything still reminded her of him—they'd spent too much time together in all of Summer's usual places for her to shake him off completely. "Love," she said.

"You *weren't* wrong about being in love," Benji asserted.

"Yes, I was."

"No, listen—" He held up both hands. "Imagine, you move into Schramm Hall."

"I'm with you so far."

"And you go to the cafeteria for dinner."

"Right."

"And you sit on the north side, because why wouldn't you? The line is shorter."

"Okay."

"And you're eighteen, so you see the ice cream machine, and

you're like, '*Holy fuck, there's a soft-serve machine?! I'm gonna eat ice cream with every meal!*'"

"They only turn it on at dinner."

"You're new, you don't know that."

"Okay," she said.

"And so you have ice cream every night, and you're happy with it."

"Only because I don't know about the south side."

Benji whirled on her and grabbed the edge of her coat. "Only because you don't know about the south side!"

He kept hold of her coat.

"But you're not *wrong* about the north-side ice cream," he said. "It *is* good. It *is* special. It's still ice cream. You're still lucky to have it."

Summer nodded.

"It's not your fault," Benji said, "that you don't realize there's superior soft serve."

"This analogy has several weaknesses," Summer said. "Do you really think I was lucky to fall in love with Charlie?"

"I think he was lucky to fall in love with you."

She shook her head. She felt wobbly. "Wrap it up," she said. "What's your closing statement?"

He tugged on her coat. "You can trust yourself to fall in love, Summer. You'll know what it feels like to have something better."

Benji was towering over her. Summer's head was tipped all the way back, like a kid watching her balloon fly away. It was dark out, but she could see how intensely he was looking down at her. Even his eyes were too loud.

"I like being your friend," she said quietly.

"I like being your friend," he said, exhaling a step away from her.

Summer caught the front of his jacket. "No. Wait. It's just—It's hard for me to imagine you . . . wanting me. Like that."

"But I do," he said.

"But so did Charlie once, you know? And now he doesn't even *like* me!"

"I don't like anything that he likes!" Benji shouted. "That guy's a dipshit!"

Summer laughed. She fisted her hand in his coat. "I don't want to talk about Charlie," she said, shaking her head.

"Good."

Her voice dropped: "It just doesn't bode well for me. As a sustainable object of affection."

"Nothing that happened in the past applies to me," Benji said. "I'm an entirely new variable."

"An entirely new variable," Summer repeated, hanging on to his coat.

Benji touched her hand.

"I'm scared," she whispered. "I feel so much better. Now. Than I did. I *like* feeling better."

"Do you like *me*, Summer?"

Summer nodded. Once. Then again. She kept nodding. With her chin in the air.

Benji pulled her a little closer. "You can trust yourself to fall in love." He pulled her closer. "You can trust me to catch you."

Summer's eyes were swimming with tears. (It felt okay. It felt terrifying. It felt like morning.) She stood on tiptoe, but it wasn't enough. "I trust you," she swore.

Benji put his arms around Summer and swung her up onto a concrete ledge at the edge of the sidewalk. She barely had time to get her feet under her. They were eye to eye now, for the first time ever—Benji's eyes were swimming, too. Summer carefully put her arms around his neck. It was like hugging an oak tree. She laughed a little. She was still crying. She was scared.

He moved his face toward hers with more care than she thought he was capable of. Summer met him halfway. His lips were fuller than she was used to, his mouth was warmer. She hugged his big head. His hair was rough, it curled around her fingers. She liked him, she trusted him—even though she never knew what she was going to get with him. It was always pretty good. It was already better.

Benji pulled away a little. They were both laughing. Sort of. Softly. Summer blinked away a few tears. She stroked his head with her thumbs.

"Yeah?" Benji whispered.

"Yeah." Summer nodded.

He grabbed her waist again and spun her around. "Yeah!" he shouted.

～＿✎

There were problems.

Summer had already ruined her room with Charlie. Ruined her bed with good and terrible memories. She didn't want Benji in there.

So she stayed in Benji's room most nights after their ten o'clock curfew and had to sneak back to her own floor whenever she needed to use the girls' restroom, and then sneak back to Benji again.

She was bound to see Charlie someday, while she was sneaking around, and it was going to be awful. (Summer was over Charlie, but she didn't want to see him. She didn't want him imposing his gaze on her. On Benji.) (Benji didn't care if Charlie saw them. "Fuck that guy.")

Benji's room was a mess. He hardly owned any clothes, but every inch of space was filled with books and papers and computer components—and stacks and stacks of CDs. (He was only sort of big into Napster.)

His bed was always full of hemp seeds—he munched them like popcorn—and broken mechanical-pencil leads. The mattress wasn't big enough for the both of them together. It was just barely big enough for Benji alone.

And they couldn't *both* listen to music on his headphones, so they argued about how loud to turn the volume and whether the music would bother the girl who lived below him.

They lay on Benji's bed, Summer tucked between his chest and the wall, with his arm around her waist. Whatever terrible tank top he'd been wearing would get thrown onto the floor; Summer couldn't abide them.

They listened to music that reminded Summer of things that hadn't happened yet.

She was afraid to tell him that she loved him.

How could she say to him the same words she'd said to Charlie? Knowing how much different this was, between them. How far superior.

Summer hadn't been magic with Charlie. She'd only gotten glimpses of how good she could feel.

Benji was bigger than life. He was too loud. His face was too red.

Benji told Summer that he loved her. In words. And music. And fierce looks on the elevator.

"Benji . . ." Summer said. And what she meant was, *A thousand mix CDs won't be enough if you ever stop loving me.*

Summer met Benji in the cafeteria most nights. They both came straight from class. Sometimes Michelle sat with them. Not usually.

He was late tonight, and Summer wondered if she should eat her mashed potatoes before they got cold.

But then he was there, and he didn't have a tray. He was holding two bowls.

"What's this?" she asked.

He set a bowl of ice cream in front of her. "An appetizer."

Summer giggled. "Don't you need protein?"

"I'll have protein for dessert." He sat down with his own bowl. "And don't lecture me on nutrition. You eat like a seven-year-old."

"Benji . . ." Summer said. She hadn't touched her ice cream.

He took a bite, but he was listening.

"I'm still a romantic," she said.

"That's good to hear."

"I still believe in true love."

He nodded. "Your ice cream is already melting."

"*Benji,*" she whispered.

He looked up at Summer and grinned like he had her number.

He very definitely did.

The Snow Ball

IT WAS CHRISTMAS EVE EVE, AND OWEN AND Libby weren't going to watch *Meet Me in St. Louis* together.

Even though it was Christmas Eve *Eve,* and they *always* watched *Meet Me in St. Louis* together on Christmas Eve Eve.

Well . . . always for the last three years.

Libby and Owen met freshman year when they were both trying out for the fall play. Neither of them got a part. They ended up as stagehands, wearing black T-shirts and black work gloves, and realizing that they always had something to say to each other. Being with Owen was easy—Libby could be herself. (She couldn't even manage that when she was alone.)

They had everything important in common—and the ways that they were different were interesting, not irritating.

(Well. *Libby* never got irritated with *Owen.* He got irritated with her sometimes. But . . . everybody got irritated with Libby. Her mom said she was abrasive. The nice thing about Owen was that he didn't seem to *mind* being irritated with her. Like being irritated with her ultimately wasn't that irritating for him.)

They both loved acting. They loved theater. And old movies. They loved quoting their favorite things at each other. They loved having theme nights. Theme weeks. They loved rituals. They both *loved* Christmas.

It was Libby's idea to spend their first Christmas as best friends watching all their favorite Christmas movies together.

And then the next year, when they did it again, Owen had said, *"I guess this is our tradition now."*

Libby had *loved* that. That he'd said that. She loved having traditions with Owen. She loved that their whole friendship was a secret handshake.

This was their fourth Christmas as best friends. They'd watched *Elf* last night. And tomorrow they were going to watch *It's a Wonderful Life*.

And tonight was supposed to be *Meet Me in St. Louis*. They both loved Judy Garland. (Libby's mom said that probably meant that Owen was gay.) (Libby told her mom that was a very retro assumption.) (Libby kind of wished that Owen *was* gay. Then he'd probably stay home with her tonight.)

They were *supposed* to spend the night on the leather couch in Owen's family room. Owen was supposed to make popcorn, and Libby was supposed to eat it all.

And then, at the end of the movie, Owen would sing "Have Yourself a Merry Little Christmas." And Libby would tell him to stop being so maudlin, for Pete's sake.

It was tradition. *Their* tradition.

And what was Owen doing instead?

"So you're going to the Snow Ball . . ." Libby said. "The *Snow* Ball."

Owen ignored her. He was trying to tie his bow tie in the mirror.

Libby could see herself in the mirror, too—sitting behind Owen on his bed. She was making a face like one of those cats who looks disgusted with everything because they have really mean eyebrows.

"It's like a snowball," she said, "but also like a snow *ball*, get it?"

"God," Owen said, dropping his arms. "It's still crooked."

Libby looked at his pink bow tie. And his mermaid-green jacket. And his skinny black pants. He looked very . . . dapper.

Owen always looked nice, at least to Libby. He was careful with his clothes and his hair, and he projected confidence, even though he was smaller than most boys.

He always looked good. But tonight he looked shined up and special. Like a boy in a movie. (They were usually shorter than you expected, too.)

"You look fine," she said, falling back on his bed.

"You didn't even look."

"I looked."

He turned away from the mirror and bumped his knee against hers. "*Look.*"

Libby sat up and pushed her glasses up higher on her nose. Owen's wavy brown hair was slicked back. He'd shaved. (Owen shaved now.) His chin was sharp, and his brown eyes were bright. "Okay," she said. "I'm looking. What am I supposed to be looking at?"

"This tie," he said. "Is it ridiculous?"

"All ties are ridiculous."

"Libby."

She looked closely at his tie—then reached up and pulled it undone. "Yes."

His face fell. "Jesus Christ, Libby! That took me fifteen minutes to tie!"

"I'll bet it won't take that long next time."

He turned back to his reflection, gritting his teeth. "You're such a . . ."

"A what?" she asked the mirror.

He puffed his breath, avoiding her eyes while he reknotted his tie. "You don't *have* to be here, you know. If you don't want to be."

"You told me to come over! You told me to come help you get ready."

"Yeah, but you're *not* helping, Libby."

"Did you actually think I would?"

"*Yes.*" He glanced over his shoulder, then shook his head. "I *hoped* that you might rise to the occasion and psych me up. Be my corner man."

"What's a corner man?"

He ran his fingers along the tie, straightening it behind his collar. "That guy in a boxing match who, like, slaps you on the face, and throws water on you, and says 'You can do it!'"

"You should have told me that you wanted me to slap you," Libby said. "I would have done it, like, twelve times already."

Owen turned away from the mirror again and stood at the end of the bed, his bed, looming over her—as much as you *can* loom when you're only five foot six. (Libby was three inches taller than Owen. That never seemed to bother him.)

"You're supposed to be telling me I can do this," he said.

Libby frowned and scooted back on the bed, leaning against the headboard. She pulled one of his blue-striped pillows over her stomach. "Do what, tie a tie? You can; I just watched you. It was slow and pathetic and crooked in the end—but you got the job done. Go, you."

"Not the tie," Owen said, licking his bottom lip. Resting his tongue there. It was a tic—the gratuitous lip-licking. It called attention to how thin his lips were. His bottom lip was a smudge, and his top lip wasn't there at all. Really. It was just an edge, a rim, a thin pink bracket.

"Not the tie," he said again. "The whole thing. You *know* this is the first time I've ever gone to a dance. I'm a senior. I'm seventeen years old. And this is the first time I've gone to a dance—"

He was getting riled up now. Theatrical. Waving his arms around. (He'd done a Mark Twain monologue last year in forensics, and he'd never abandoned the gestures.)

"—because it's the first time that someone who I liked has actually said yes. You *know* I'm nervous, Libby, and you're my *best friend*. Can't you just *try* to be encouraging?"

Libby narrowed her eyes at him. There was hair in her eyes, so she pushed it behind her ear. "You. Can. Do. It," she said.

Owen closed his eyes and shook his head again. "Thanks a lot," he said bitterly.

"Whatever 'it' is," Libby went on. "What is 'it' anyway? Is it the dancing? Are you worried about the dancing?"

Owen huffed and went back to his bow tie, frowning down at the tails and squishing his chin into his neck so he could see what he was doing. "I'm not worried about the dancing."

"Because you're a good dancer," she said.

He glanced up at her. Suspiciously. "Thank you."

"You do that thing . . ." She wrinkled her nose and popped her neck back and forth.

He sighed and crossed one piece of the tie over the other, shaking his head.

"No, it's good," she said. "I like it. I like it when you snap your fingers, too." She snapped.

"I'm a perfectly good dancer, Libby."

"That's what I'm saying, Owen. You're a *perfectly good* dancer. So that must not be the '*it.*' The thing you're worried about."

He looked back at the mirror.

"Where are you taking her to dinner?" Libby asked.

"Mother India."

"Nice," she said. "Intimate. Did you make reservations?"

"They don't take reservations." He undid the knot he was working on and took another deep breath.

"Does Carmen like Indian food?"

"Kamrin," he said. "I *know* you know her name. She's in your creative writing class."

"Right," Libby said. "Karen."

"You're not funny, Libby."

Libby pushed the pillow off her lap. "That doesn't reflect poorly on me, you know. I can't help how unfunny I am. But *you* chose me as your best friend. It's your bad taste that's in question here."

"I didn't choose you," he muttered, watching his own neck in the mirror. His chin was lifted. His Adam's apple was suspended. "I picked you up like a weird rock or a feather, and forgot that I stuck you in my pocket until two years later."

"That's very poetic," Libby said. "You should be in my creative writing class. I'm pretty sure I'd remember your name, if you were."

"Kamrin likes Indian food," Owen said. "I asked her." His bow tie was tied again. And skewing badly to one side. Listing. Like a doomed cruise liner.

He grimaced and pulled it undone.

Owen's hands were very small. If he'd been born during the Industrial Revolution, he'd probably have a horrible job that called for a small stature and nimble fingers. He played marimba in the school band, and he was always tapping out some rhythm on his leg or his desk or the back of Libby's head.

"So you're not worried about the dancing," she said. "You've got dinner in order, you've got your pink tie . . . You finally got a girl you like to say yes . . . Is this the part where I slap you?"

Owen looked genuinely miserable for a second. He let go of the tie and slumped back onto his bed, his hands falling between his knees. "Never mind," he said.

Libby frowned. She wasn't used to Owen looking miserable. She wasn't used to him acting insecure.

She crawled forward on the bed and sat next to him. "Don't look like that."

"Like what," he said to the floor.

"I don't know. That."

"Leave me alone, Libby."

"Like, really alone? Or shut up for a minute?"

"Shut up for a minute."

She shut up. She watched herself in the mirror. She was wearing faded jeans and an Old Navy sweater with a penguin on it. Her hair was pulled into a ponytail, but half a dozen dark curls had worked their way free.

Owen looked dapper.

Libby looked . . . not. Libby looked like Libby. Tall and sloppy and careless. She looked like the kind of girl who'd never needed help zipping up a fancy dress.

She pushed a curl behind her ear and leaned toward him.

"You're a good dancer," she said again, more clearly.

"Thanks."

"And it's a dance. So you'll be fine."

"Right," he said, staring at the floor.

He had a sprig of something green attached to his lapel. "That's nice," she said. "What's that?"

"What?"

"On your jacket."

He glanced at his collar. "Mistletoe."

"Nice touch," she said.

"It's a Christmas dance."

"I know." Libby nodded. "*The Snow Ball.*"

He stared at the ground.

"Much Christmas," she said. "Very dance."

"You could come," he said, still looking at his knees, "if you want."

"What?" Libby sat back.

"You could come to the dance."

"With you and Camden?"

"Well, not to dinner—but you could meet us at the dance. A bunch of our friends will be there."

"No, thank you," she said.

"Why not?"

"Because I don't dance."

"I've seen you dance, Libby."

"*You* have," she said. "But no one else needs to."

"It might be fun."

"It's Christmas Eve *Eve,* Owen. There are traditions to uphold. Somebody has to watch *Meet Me in St. Louis*—it isn't going to watch itself. Somebody has to eat chocolate oranges and light a candle for Judy Garland."

He rolled his eyes. "I said I'd watch it with you tomorrow."

"Tomorrow is Christmas Eve. On Christmas Eve, we watch *It's a Wonderful Life*. Don't upset the natural order of things."

"You might like it," he said. "The dance."

"I won't like it."

"How do you know?"

"Because it's a *dance,* Owen. It's everyone I already don't like from school—but all dressed up and dancing. If I don't like them sitting in desks, why would I like them dancing?"

"It's not *about* them."

"It's about Kaitlin?"

"No. It's about you," he said. "Trying something new."

"Something new . . ."

"You only get so many high school dances in life." He waved his hand around. "You may as well go to *one*. So that you don't look back and feel like you missed out on something."

"Huh," Libby said. "Yeah. That's a compelling argument. Then, after the dance, maybe I should put my hand in the fireplace. Just so that I know how it feels. Just so I know I'm not *missing out* on something."

Owen fell back on the bed. "You're infuriating."

"Again," she said, turning to look down on him. "That's all on you. You *chose* me. You saw me on the shelf and thought, *That one— that one there. That's my best friend.*"

"I didn't choose you," Owen muttered, rubbing his eyes. "I picked you up because you looked interesting, and didn't realize I was still holding you until I'd already left the store."

"You're like E. E. Cummings or something," she said. "You should write these things down."

She fell back on the bed, too. Owen folded his arms. They were both staring at the ceiling now.

"I know that Jeremy Wheeler asked you to the Snow Ball . . ." Owen said.

"It's not a secret," she said.

"Jeremy's cute."

Jeremy was fine. "He looks like a guy in a Target ad."

"Everybody likes Jeremy Wheeler."

"Every time I see him," Libby said, "I think, *On sale this week at your neighborhood Target*."

"*You* like Jeremy Wheeler," Owen said.

"So what?" She raised up her hands. "Everybody likes him."

"Yeah, but *he* likes you."

"I'm likable," she said.

"No," Owen said, "you're not."

"*You* like me . . ."

"No." Owen sounded tired. "I just don't know what to do with you."

"You haven't found a place to set me down yet . . ."

"Exactly," Owen said.

Here will do, she thought.

Owen sat up and started over with his tie. He was being very brisk. And dapper. And on his way to a dance.

"You can do it," Libby said to the ceiling.

"Thanks."

"Whatever 'it' is."

"Thanks."

"Is '*it*' Carolyn?"

"Kamrin."

"Whatever. Is she '*it*'?"

Owen shrugged. "Maybe."

"Maybe," Libby repeated.

"I just don't want to mess this up," he said. "I think she really likes me—that never happens."

"That happens."

"Shut up, Libby."

"People like you." Libby lifted herself up on her elbows to look at him. "Who doesn't like you?"

"Shut up, you know what I mean."

"Who doesn't like you? Seriously, who is this person who doesn't like you? I want to dissect them and document it for science."

"Libby . . ."

"*Everyone* likes you, Owen."

Everyone *did* like Owen—even more than they liked Jeremy Wheeler. Libby had thought she and Owen were meant to be best friends because they were both misfits. They were both weirdos. But then Owen went and showed everyone that you could be weird *and* popular. Libby had thought those things were mutually exclusive. She'd wanted them to be. She'd wanted to keep Owen for herself.

"You know what I mean," he said, like he couldn't hear her internal monologue. He was staring at his neck in the mirror. "I mean girls. A girl like Kamrin has never liked me."

"What kind of girl is that?"

"Pretty," he said. "Decent. She's really cool, you know? She could go to this dance with anybody, but she said yes to me."

"Maybe you were just the first person to ask her."

Owen caught Libby's eyes in the mirror. "*Maybe I was.* Maybe it's a fluke—I don't care! I don't want to mess this up."

Libby rolled onto her side and let her cheek rest on the comforter.

Which smelled like Owen. Which was such a familiar smell, it practically didn't smell like anything at all. "How *could* you, even?" she asked. "Mess it up."

"Lots of ways," he said. "I'm afraid I'll mess it up without realizing I'm doing it. Like I'll break some rule I didn't even know existed."

"She writes poems that don't rhyme," Libby said.

"So?"

"In creative writing class."

"So?" he repeated. "Poems don't have to rhyme."

"But it's nice when they do," Libby said.

"I guess."

She twisted on the bed, so she could see him again in the mirror. *"The time has come, the Walrus said, to talk of many things. Of shoes and ships and sealing wax. Of cabbages and kings."* It was Libby's favorite poem. Lewis Carroll.

Owen ignored her. He pulled on one end of the bow tie, and it slid out from around his neck. "I'm just going to wear a regular necktie."

"Everyone else will be wearing regular neckties."

"Then I'll fit right in."

"You're living the dream, aren't you?"

"You don't have to be mean, Libby."

"I'm not."

Libby sat up. She was sitting right next to him. He smelled like mistletoe. Apparently.

"I'm being your corner man," she said. "Slap. Splash. *You can do it.*"

He closed his eyes.

"You can do it," she said again. She'd keep saying it, if he wanted her to. "Whatever it is. Dancing, dinner . . . Camry."

"Just say her name. You're running out of reasonable facsimiles."

Libby shrugged.

"We can watch the movie tomorrow, Libby."

"I'm watching something *else* tomorrow."

"It's just one night," he said.

"You better get to your dance," she said, "or you'll spend the rest of your life regretting it."

"Maybe I *like* school dances . . ."

"How would you know," she said quietly.

"Maybe I like Kamrin," he said even more quietly.

"Great," Libby whispered. "She said yes."

"Libby . . ." Owen turned to her. He looked pained. He sounded pained. "I just want to go to the dance and tell stupid jokes and listen to pop songs and maybe at the end of the night kiss somebody who isn't my grandmother—"

"Worthy goals."

He pointed at her. "—and you don't get to make me feel shitty about that."

She shrugged again. "How could I?"

He pointed harder. "You don't get to take that away."

"Where would I put it?"

"You're such a pain in the ass, Libby."

"And yet you chose me!"

"I didn't *choose* you!"

Libby was making an angry face. There were tears in her eyes. "Didn't you?"

"No." He shook his head and let it fall into his hands. He sounded resigned. "You were just there when I got here. I thought you were built in."

Libby drew her knees up and pulled her sweater down over them. They both stared at Owen's duvet cover. It was plaid.

"I don't have time to argue with you," Owen said.

"Do you want me to go home?"

"If you want."

"I'm sorry."

His head jerked up. "Really?"

She nodded.

"What are you sorry for? You're never sorry."

"I am so."

"Not with me," he said.

She clenched her jaw for a second. "Well, why should I be? Why would I want to hang out with someone who made me feel sorry all the time?"

"Why are you sorry *now*?"

She hugged her knees. "Because you told me to come over and help you get ready, and I don't think that I have."

"You haven't."

"Well. I'm sorry."

Owen licked his lips. "At some point . . ."

She waited.

"Libby, at some point, we won't spend every Friday night together."

"We aren't spending *this* Friday night together."

"Exactly!" he said. "At some point, this has to happen."

"At this point," she said. "Apparently."

"It's not fair!" Owen almost never lost his temper, but this was what it looked like when he did. "I asked *you* to the dance!"

"No, Jeremy Wheeler asked me to the dance," Libby said. "We were standing at the bus stop. He was all tall and nice and *Forty percent off outerwear, this week at Target.*"

"*No*," Owen said. "*I* asked you. Last year."

"You mean, to prom?"

"Yes! And you said no!"

"Because I didn't want to go to prom," Libby said. "I wanted to watch *Star Trek*."

"On your mom's VHS tapes."

"Right."

"You could have watched that anytime."

"Right," she agreed.

"I asked you to prom, and you said no."

What was his angle? "I remember," she said.

"Okay," he said. "So you have to give me tonight."

"I wanted to watch *Star Trek* last May, so I have to let you go to the Snow Ball tonight?"

Owen nodded. "*Yes.*"

"But you're going to go whether I let you or not."

"I am," he said. He licked his lips.

"So I'm not *letting* you," she said. "You're just *going.*"

"I want you to be happy for me."

"Why should I be happy for you? This dance sounds terrible."

"Not to me," he said.

"Because you're an idiot sometimes."

"Fair enough."

"I can't be happy for you, Owen."

He clenched his fists between his knees. "I asked *you* to prom, Libby . . ."

"I wanted to watch *Star Trek.*"

". . . and you said no."

"I asked *you* to watch *Star Trek* with me."

"*Star Trek* and prom aren't the same," Owen said.

"Agreed," Libby agreed. "One sucks."

"One means something!"

"Agreed!"

Owen licked his lips. He swallowed. He wound the tie around his fingers, licked his lips again, then let it unwind. "I don't know what you want from me."

"I want . . ." Libby didn't know either. She didn't have a bow tie to fiddle with, so she rubbed her face in her knees. "I want you to be my best friend."

"I am your best friend." He said it without even thinking about it.

"I don't want you to go to the dance, Owen."

"That's not *fair*."

"I don't care."

"I'm not trying to abandon you or leave you behind—*just come to the dance*."

"To the Snow Ball . . ." Libby said, considering it. (Well, *considering* considering it.)

"Come," he said. "Put on a dress. Or don't. Go to *one* high school dance. Mark it off your list."

"I don't have a list," she said.

"Well, I *do*." He reached over and put his hand on her forearm. That was unprecedented. When you've been someone's best friend for three years, almost nothing is unprecedented—but this was. "You have to let me have a list, Lib."

"I don't let you do anything," she whispered. "You do what you want."

"Ha." He didn't laugh. "I do what *you* want."

"But I thought doing what I wanted *was* what you wanted." Libby didn't understand why Owen was so upset. *She* was the one who should be upset! "You asked me if I wanted to go to prom," she said.

He nodded. "I did."

"And I *didn't* want to."

"I understand, Libby."

"No, you don't—I didn't want to go to prom; that didn't mean I was signing away all my mineral and property rights."

"Be less weird," he begged her. "Just for a few minutes."

"I mean, I didn't want to go to *prom*, Owen. I wanted to watch *Star Trek*."

"I remember."

"With *you*."

"I . . ." Owen stopped. He turned on the bed, so he was fully facing her. He still had her arm. "I actually *don't* know what you're talking about now, Libby."

"I didn't know that was '*it*,'" she said.

"What? That what was it?"

She looked at her knees. "Never mind."

"No—*not* never mind. *Libby.*"

"You should go," she said. "A girl that you like finally said yes."

"I asked you *first*," he said. "You said *no.*"

"To the prom," she said as quietly as she possibly could. "Not to you."

Owen started to say something. Then he licked his lips. He tilted his head. He didn't look at her. Then he did. "Libby . . ."

"You're holding on to my arm," she said.

"Do you want me to stop?"

"No."

"If I'd asked you to this Christmas dance," he said, "would you have said yes?"

"No."

"If I'd asked you . . . God, Libby, what would I have to ask? What do you want?"

She lifted up her head. She looked in his eyes. "I want you to stay home and watch Judy Garland with me."

"I got that part . . ."

"I don't want you to dance with pretty girls. Or worry about messing things up with them."

"Okay."

"I don't want you to kiss anyone. Except your grandmother."

"You're telling me what you *don't* want, not what you want . . ."

"Well, I'm better at that."

"I know."

His hand slipped down to hers. Completely unprecedented. And cold.

"Tell me what you want from me," he said.

"Can't we just be friends?" she asked. "We're really good at it."

"We're the best." He squeezed her hand. "Do you want me to let go?"

"No."

"What do I have to ask you," he asked, "to get a yes?"

"Would you rather take me to the Snow Ball than Kamrin?"

"*Yes,*" Owen said.

That was the best news Libby had heard all year. "I want to be on your list," she said quickly. "I don't want you to keep making it without me."

"Okay," he said.

"And I'll go to prom with you."

"We already missed prom."

"There's another one though, right? Eventually?"

"You'll go to prom with me five months from now?"

"Yes," she said.

"Do you want to?"

"No, but . . . I want *you,*" Libby said.

Owen squeezed her hand. He shoved his face forward. His chin jabbed into hers. He kissed her.

This was *with. Out. Precedent.*

Owen's lips were thin. The bottom one was just a smudge, and the top one was a line, an edge, an opening pressed against hers.

The kiss was short.

"Was that okay?" Owen whispered.

"Yes."

He tried it again. He pushed a little too hard with his mouth. Libby's hand came up to his chest.

"Still okay?" he asked.

"Yes," she whispered.

"I've never done that before."

"Me neither."

"Can we keep doing it for a minute?" he asked.

"Yes."

So they did.

When Owen pulled back, he ran his hand along Libby's hairline, untucking the curl from her ear and winding it around his finger. "I didn't think you wanted this," he said.

"You never asked."

"So I wasn't supposed to ask you to *prom;* I was supposed to ask if I could kiss you?"

"It's always better to be specific, Owen."

He huffed out a laugh. "I thought you said no to prom because you didn't want to ruin everything."

"What's everything?" She was still whispering.

"You and me. Friendship."

"I don't," she said. "But I'd rather we ruin it together than you ruin it with somebody else."

"But you *want* this, Libby?"

"I want you."

"I want you, too."

"That's nice to hear, Owen."

Owen laughed and shook his head at her. "You're really weird. And not in a normal way. You're genuinely odd, you know that?"

"I guess. Is that important?"

"You're weird. And you make everything difficult. And—could we have been kissing for the last year?"

"Probably even before that."

"Jesus. You're infuriating."

She pulled on his lapel. "But . . ."

"But, yeah . . ." He kissed her again. "I'm going to get really good at this, I promise."

"I believe you. *You can do it.*"

Owen kissed her. Every single kiss was softer and longer than the one before. Fibonacci sequence. They were never going to leave this room.

"Okay, Libby," he said the next time he pulled away. "*Jesus*. Okay."

"I'm glad we worked this out," she said, taking a breath.

He laughed. She smiled.

Then he pulled away from her. "You know I'm still going to the dance, right?"

Libby did *not* know that. "What? You can't!"

"I have to! Kamrin's waiting for me."

"But, *Owen*, what was the point of all this if you're still going to the Snow Ball?"

"I'm going to pretend that you didn't say that . . ."

"*Owen*."

"I'm not a monster, Libby. She's waiting for me."

"You're going to go with *her*?"

"I am."

"And you're going to *dance* with her?"

"I am. And I'll probably have a really great time because I am in a *fantastic* mood."

"*Owen!*"

"And then I'll come back to your house, or here if you want, and I'll watch *Meet Me in St. Louis* with you."

Owen stood up. He tied his bow tie. He watched Libby watching him in the mirror.

She wanted to argue with him, but she also wanted to run her fingertips over her lips.

When Owen turned back to face her, his tie was crooked. "Will you wait for me?"

She nodded. "Yes."

He unpinned the sprig of mistletoe from his jacket and attached it to Libby's sweater.

IF THE FATES ALLOW

If the Fates Allow

Christmas 2020

REAGAN WAS CARRYING TOO MUCH.

Her overnight bag and groceries, plus a glass pan of Jell-O salad—
too much Jell-O salad—because she didn't have a smaller glass dish,
and Grandma had always made it in a glass dish, so you could see all
the colors.

Reagan was carrying too much, and the driveway was slick as
fuck. There was snow on the ground, and her grandpa hadn't salted
the driveway or shoveled his walk. She couldn't really blame him—he
never went anywhere. Her parents dropped off his groceries once a
week.

She walked extra slow, taking small steps.

"Hey there!" a man called.

Reagan looked up, and her foot hit a patch of ice. She went down
quick, landing on one knee—and then on her hip, and then on the
groceries, twisting the whole time to keep the glass pan in the air.
"*Fuck.*"

"Holy shit!" the same voice swore. "Are you okay?"

"I'm fine!" Reagan shouted from the ground.

"Don't move!" Whoever it was was getting closer.

"*You* don't move—are you wearing a mask?"

"Oh . . . no."

"Then stay where you are!" Reagan set the Jell-O salad on the ground. "I'm fine!"

She pushed up onto her knees. She could see him now, the neighbors' son—the quiet one with no chin. Standing about ten feet away from her. He had his arms out like he was still about to help her up.

"Are you hurt?" he asked.

"No." She was a *little* hurt. Her knee felt scraped, and her hip was already throbbing. She lifted herself up onto her feet—

Then hit another patch of ice. The guy darted toward her. She caught her balance and pointed at him. "No!"

He stopped, his hands still up. She could see his breath.

"I swear to God, Mason"—Reagan didn't even remember that she remembered his name—"I have been quarantining for two weeks, and I am *not* giving my grandpa Covid because you can't listen."

"Okay," he said. Then he pulled his scarf up over his face—and Reagan thought at first that he was trying to hide his nonexistent chin. But then she realized he was trying not to blow germs at her. "Just be careful," he said.

"I was *being* careful before you tripped me!"

"Before I tripped you?"

"You yelled at me!"

"I was saying hello so that I didn't startle you."

"Well, good work!"

"Reagan?" someone new shouted. "Are you okay?"

She looked up. Her grandpa was standing at the front door.

"I'm fine, Grandpa!"

"Did you fall?"

"No, I'm fine!"

"Let me get my coat."

"No, Grandpa—stay!"

"Don't come out, Al—it's slick!"

"Is that you, Mason?"

"Yeah, don't come out—I'll help her."

"Don't you dare," Reagan hissed.

"Just go," Mason said. "Walk in the snow. It's safer."

He was right. She inched over to the snow, then stepped into it—even though she was wearing ankle boots, and the snow immediately fell over the tops. She got to the porch and up to the door—her grandpa was just coming back with his coat half on. Reagan hurried past him into the house and closed the door behind her.

And then there they were, she and her grandpa, standing not a foot apart. His coat was still hanging from one shoulder, and Reagan had tracked snow onto the carpet, and all she could think about in that moment was the air between them—the constant flow of droplets and microparticles. Her grandpa looked thinner than she remembered. Older than he'd looked just a few months ago. Like she could knock him over by breathing too hard.

This is okay. She'd taken every precaution. Reagan had been careful, anyway, for months—and then she'd practically sealed her little house off for two weeks so she could be here. She hadn't even opened her mail.

She was as clean as she could be; she wasn't going to hurt him.

"Hi, Grandpa," she said. And then she dropped her bags and stepped forward to give him a hug. It took him a second to catch up. Reagan didn't blame him; she hadn't hugged anyone in months, and neither of them had ever been huggers anyway. *Grandma* was the hugger. Grandma was the one who made you go find your grandpa and give him a hug. Reagan and her grandfather had probably never hugged before except under orders.

Reagan was the wrong choice for this.

If you could only spend Christmas with one person, no one in her family would pick her. (No one in the world would pick her.)

Reagan was the person you called when you wanted someone to talk you into leaving your husband. Or when you needed someone to call the bank to straighten out your overdraft fees.

Her niece called Reagan when she needed help getting birth control. And Reagan's mom called when she wanted someone to go to the Ford dealership with her dad, so they didn't end up paying too much for a truck.

No one called Reagan for comfort.

No one called Reagan to offer any.

No one ever said, *"I'm lonely, could you come by?"*—and no one ever came by.

Even before this bullshit.

Her grandpa felt more solid in her arms than he looked. He was a big guy once, and those bones were still there. "Thought maybe my hugging days were over," he said.

Reagan laughed and pulled away. "Me, too. It smells good in here."

"You thought I couldn't make a turkey?"

"No, I believed in you."

"I didn't bother with the potatoes."

"I brought potatoes," she said. "I told you I would."

"Well, all right . . ." He seemed awkward. Standing there in his own living room. Everything looked the same as it had when her grandma was alive. Either he kept the place pretty clean, or he'd cleaned up because Reagan was coming over.

"Well, all right," she said. "Let's get them started."

Grandpa turned toward the kitchen. Then the doorbell rang, and he turned back. Reagan caught his arm. "Don't answer that," she scolded. "You don't answer the door, do you?"

"Well, I look to see who it is. I get a lot of deliveries."

"I'll check. There's no reason for you to be answering the door right now. Nobody needs you."

She looked out the window. She didn't see anyone. Who was making deliveries on Christmas Day? Fucking Amazon Prime.

Reagan opened the door. The Jell-O salad was sitting on the welcome mat.

She picked it up, then went inside and wiped the glass down with a Clorox wipe.

~~~

Her mom texted while Reagan was peeling potatoes.

"I've been thinking and I just think it would be okay if you brought Grandpa over for dinner."

"You always think it would be okay," Reagan texted back.

"Well it has been so far!"

Her older sister, Caitlin, was on the thread, too.

"I mean," Caitlin texted, *"Mom's right. We haven't seen each other in nine months, and none of us have had Covid. So that's nine months we could have been seeing each other."*

Reagan wanted to say, *Maybe that's why we haven't had Covid.*

But she wasn't even *sure* that no one in her family had had Covid. They wouldn't tell her if they had. Half of them didn't wear masks—half of Nebraska wouldn't wear a mask. Her brother kept posting conspiracy theories on Facebook, and Reagan was the only one arguing with him.

Also, Reagan's family *had* seen each other. The rest of them had. They'd all gotten together for Thanksgiving. *"We're socially distanced over here,"* her mom had called to tell her.

"You put the leaf in the dining room table," Reagan replied. *"That's not social distancing."*

Only Reagan and her grandpa were taking this seriously. They each spent Thanksgiving alone—Grandpa here in Arnold, the little town where most of her family still lived, and Reagan a few hours away, in Lincoln.

"We're all so worried about you," her mom kept saying to her. *"You're becoming a recluse."*

"I'm simply following the recommendations of the CDC," Reagan would say.

"Oh, the CDC . . ."

Reagan didn't need to get Covid. She was fat and prone to bronchitis. She was exactly the sort of person who showed up in those "Who we've lost" retrospectives in the local newspaper.

If you asked Reagan, every single person in her family looked like someone in a Covid obituary. They were all fat. Her dad was diabetic. Her mom was a cancer survivor. Her sister still smoked. What were they playing at? They weren't lucky people. They were the sort of people who got laid off right before Christmas and got pregnant in the back seat of cars. Why were they willing to roll these dice?

Her grandpa had locked down right away.

"I'm worried about your grandpa," her mom said back in April. *"He won't let me come over."*

Good, Reagan had thought.

"He's still grieving," her mom said. *"He shouldn't be alone."*

Reagan couldn't really argue with that. There was no good argument. There was no answer. No good way to deal with any of this.

She'd called Grandpa on Thanksgiving Day and pitched him a plan for Christmas—she'd had to convince him it would be safe.

"I'll stay home for two weeks, Grandpa. I'll be totally quarantined."

"Well, I don't know that I want you to do that for me, Reagan . . ."

"I want *to do it."*

"That's a long time for a young person to stay home."

"I'd be home anyway, Grandpa." Reagan hadn't seen friends since March. She hadn't been on a single date.

"Well, I don't know . . ."

"I'm coming," she'd said. *"We're going to have Christmas together."*

Reagan didn't know how to make mashed potatoes. (Single people didn't make mashed potatoes.) But she'd looked up directions online, and it didn't seem hard.

Her grandpa made the gravy.

He'd already set the table with her grandma's red poinsettia tablecloth and gotten out two of the good plates, the not-quite-china with the purple flowers around the edges.

Reagan had never seen this table so empty.

Normally it was so crowded with food there was no room for your dinner plate. And no room for anyone under forty, anyway. Reagan had spent every Christmas of her life sitting at one of the card tables set up in the living room. The kids' tables.

This wasn't how she wanted to move up.

God, even if this were a normal Christmas, the only reason there'd be more room at the big table was because Grandma was gone. Would they even *have* Christmas here anymore? Or would Reagan's parents take over? Would their extended family split into smaller units, all the aunts and uncles doing their own thing? They were all grandparents now. All matriarchs and patriarchs. Who would get custody of Grandpa on Christmas—would it rotate? Maybe Reagan wouldn't see her cousins again until the next funeral. The next Zoom funeral.

Mother*fuck*, this was a bleak line of thinking. This was a bleak time to be alive. And this was definitely a bleak motherfucking table.

She set out the potatoes, the gravy boat, the lasagna pan full of green Jell-O salad, the dinner rolls Grandpa made from a can . . .

Grandpa brought out the turkey. Reagan laughed when she saw it.

"Why are you laughing at my turkey?"

"Because it's *massive*."

He set it down. "It's eighteen pounds."

"That's huge, Grandpa."

"I only know how to make an eighteen-pound turkey. I didn't feel like experimenting."

"I guess you'll have leftovers for sandwiches," she said.

"You can take some of it with you."

She nodded.

Grandpa sat at the head of the table, and Reagan sat next to him. He started carving the turkey with an electric knife that was probably older than she was. "It's your lucky day," he said. "You don't have to fight anybody for a drumstick."

She laughed. She was glad for his dumb jokes. They'd already run out of things to talk about in the kitchen. There wasn't much. He was a retired rancher who watched a lot of television. She was an accountant who worked from home. They talked about Covid news and theories. They'd read all the same newspaper stories. Her grandpa watched cable news but didn't trust it. Reagan had never really had a conversation with her grandfather before. They'd always been part of a larger group—always with her grandmother, usually with her parents. They didn't really have an existing dynamic. So they talked about the things that had brought them together today: Their worry. Their caution. Their firm belief that most people were idiots.

That was a nice discovery, that her grandpa seemed to dislike people as much as she did. Had he always been that way? Or was he just getting crotchety in old age and loneliness? Reagan had always been that way, and it was only getting worse.

"Your grandmother would want us to say grace," he said, after they'd piled up their plates.

"Hmm." Reagan was noncommittal. She'd already taken a bite of turkey.

"But if she wanted me to keep saying grace," he went on, "she should have outlived me."

The turkey caught in Reagan's throat. She looked up at him, to see if he was being bitter or morose—but he just looked matter-of-fact. He was buttering his roll.

Reagan finished swallowing. "She really should have."

He set the roll on his plate. "I kept telling her . . . that if she wanted me to get into heaven, she'd have to deliver me herself."

Reagan laughed. There were tears in her eyes. "That woman had no follow-through."

Her grandpa looked up at her. His eyes were shining, too. "Exactly."

"Do you think Grandma would have been as careful as you? Through all this?"

"Heck no, I would have had to nail our windows closed."

Reagan's grandmother had been a short, wide woman who dyed her hair red and always wore pink lipstick. She was active in her church, active in the community. The type of person who went to all of her grandkids' recitals and school plays, even after she had twenty of them.

She framed every school photo the grandkids ever gave her, always leaving the old ones inside so that the pictures stacked up and made the backs hard to close. Reagan's senior picture was sitting on a coffee table in the living room, and if you opened it up, her whole childhood would spring out.

"I can't even imagine your grandmother wearing a mask," Grandpa said.

"Maybe she'd get into it," Reagan said. "It would have given her something to do with her old quilting scraps."

"Those homemade masks aren't good for anything . . ."

"Better than nothing," she said.

"I've got some N95s for when I work with insulation. Remind me to give you a couple when you leave."

"All right." The potatoes were sticky, but the gravy was good. Reagan's whole plate was brown and white. The only green thing was her dish of Jell-O—she should have brought a vegetable. "My mom hates wearing a mask because she says they smear her lipstick. So then I say, 'Don't wear lipstick,' and she acts like I said, 'Don't wear pants.'"

Her grandpa laughed. But it turned sharp at the end. "I wish she'd be more careful."

"Me, too," Reagan said.

"To be honest, sometimes I'm glad your grandma didn't have to live through this. I think about it sometimes, that she never heard about it. She never worried about it. She never lost anyone to it. She left before she ever had to take on this burden. And I'm glad for that."

Reagan nodded.

She couldn't really think of anything to say after that. And her grandpa didn't seem to want to talk more, either. And there was no one to make them be sociable.

⌒

Reagan had quit smoking a long time ago. After college. Smoking used to make her feel like such a badass. But then she got out of school and started working—and smoking just made her feel hard. Even the way she held the cigarette in her hand and in her mouth . . . It was like she was always smirking. Always making a face like, *Well, isn't that fucking perfect.*

Reagan already felt hard enough. She didn't need any accessories. She didn't need to telegraph it out to the world.

Also she kept getting bronchitis. It was a fucking drag, so she quit.

But she still missed cigarettes. She missed having the excuse of them. The *"Be right back"*s. She missed the way decent people would leave you alone as soon as you pulled out the pack.

She still took cigarette breaks sometimes.

After dinner, she and her grandpa moved into the living room to watch television. Reagan didn't want to watch Fox News, so they settled on the Weather Channel. He sat in his easy chair, and Reagan sat on the couch, fiddling with a crochet hook she'd found tucked between the cushions.

After a half hour, she said, "I'm gonna get some air."

Her grandpa nodded.

She put on her coat and headed out onto the back deck. It was too cold for the snow to melt, but it wasn't freezing—or it was just barely freezing.

"Hey," someone said.

Reagan jumped.

It was Mason again, standing on his parents' deck. "I swear to God," he said. "I'm not trying to startle you."

"Jesus *Christ*, Mason."

"Sorry."

Reagan frowned at him. "What are you even doing out here?"

"Getting some air. Do you want me to put on a mask?"

She looked between them. They were at least twenty feet apart. And they were outdoors. "Yeah," she said. "If you're gonna keep talking to me."

Mason fished a mask out of his pocket.

Reagan did the same thing. She wasn't sure why she was bothering; she should just go back inside. "What are you out here avoiding?" she asked, sliding the elastic loops behind her ears.

"Who says I'm avoiding something?"

"Well, you're standing outside in the middle of winter. And you're not smoking a cigarette or waiting for a bus."

Mason laughed. "I'm just taking a moment for myself."

Reagan hummed. "Me, too."

"Hey, I'm, um . . . I'm sorry for your loss."

"Oh." She wasn't expecting him to say that. "Thanks. I guess that's what I'm out here avoiding."

"Your loss?"

"Pretty much. I thought I was doing my grandpa good by making sure he could still have a Christmas—but I think I'm just reminding him that it's Christmas and that she isn't here."

Mason didn't reply to that. Why should he? He was a complete stranger.

"Sorry," Reagan said. "I think I've forgotten how to talk to people."

He laughed again. "Don't worry about it. This is the first in-person conversation I've had with anyone other than my parents—and your grandpa and the UPS guy—in months."

"Yeah? You pretty locked down?"

"*Oh* yeah."

"I thought this was no-mask country," she said.

"Maybe it is, I wouldn't know. I don't leave the house."

Reagan smiled. He couldn't see it. "You live there with your parents?" she asked.

"No," he said. "I mean—I guess I don't know how to answer that question."

"O-kay . . ."

"Technically, I live in D.C. I have an apartment there. But I was going a little crazy after two months of isolation, and I was worried about my mom and dad . . ."

"So you came back to Arnold?"

"Yeah, I guess I did."

"You'd rather quarantine in Arnold, Nebraska, than in Washington, D.C.?"

"I mean . . . *yeah*." He was smiling. She could sort of hear it. She could imagine his chin disappearing. "Honestly," he said, "it's been nice. I took my brother's old room—it's huge. It's half the size of my apartment in D.C. And I can be outside here without wearing a mask. You know, usually. And my parents are much less irritating than I remembered from high school. I watch *M*A*S*H* every night with my mom. It's kinda *great*."

"So why are you out here getting some air?"

Mason was quiet for a second. Then he said, "I don't remember you being this chatty back in school."

"Well, I don't remember you at all."

He laughed.

"Seriously," she said, "were we in school together?" She wasn't trying to be mean. (She didn't have to try. It came naturally.) She only recognized him as her grandparents' neighbor.

"There's just the one high school, Reagan."

"Yeah, but you're a lot younger than me, right?"

"I'm two years younger than you."

"*Really?* I thought you won the state wrestling thing when I was in college."

"That was my brother, Brook."

"Oh yeah?"

"Yeah. We were in band together—you and me."

"I think I blocked that out. I hated band."

"I could tell," he said. "You were terrible."

"I didn't even play half the time. I just moved the clarinet around." She reached in her pocket for cigarettes. She didn't have any. She hadn't had any for years. "Sorry I don't really remember you."

"That's all right. We were all trying to stay in your blind spot anyhow."

"What does that mean?"

"It means you were mean as shit."

"I was not."

"Yes, you were—you called my friend 'Mr. Toad.'"

Reagan cackled. "You were friends with Mr. Toad?"

"I was."

"How's he doing?"

"All right. He manages the nursing home."

"Oof. What a time to work at a nursing home."

"Yeah . . ."

They were quiet again.

"Your grandpa is careful," Mason said, like he could hear her worrying. "Your parents come by, and they talk through the storm door."

"That's good," Reagan said.

"I should have salted his driveway."

"What?"

"I didn't realize it had iced up, or that he was having company."

"Oh God, don't worry about that—that's not your job."

Mason shrugged. His hands were in his coat pockets. "Well . . ."

"He says you shovel the walk, so the mailman can get up to the porch."

"Only if your dad hasn't come by."

"Well, that's still nice of you. Thanks."

"It's nothing. I didn't do it to impress you."

Reagan made a face. "Why *would* you do it to impress me?"

"I . . ." Mason was probably making a face that she couldn't see. "That's what I'm saying."

"Anyway," she grumbled, "I'm not that impressed." Reagan should go inside. She should sit on her grandparents' couch and scroll Instagram and silently judge everyone she knew for having big-ass family dinners. "So you work from home?" she asked. "I mean, remotely?"

"Yeah," Mason said.

"What do you do?"

"I fact-check audio content for news websites."

"That does not seem like a job a real person would have."

He laughed into his mask. "My eight-year-old self would be mortified, but it's interesting work."

"What did your eight-year-old self want to be?"

"Professional rodeo cowboy. What about you?"

"Oh, my eight-year-old self would be thrilled with my life. She just wanted to get the hell out of Arnold."

Mason laughed some more. He leaned against his deck railing. Reagan took half a step back from hers.

"You live in Lincoln," he said, "right? What do you do?"

"Accounting. For the Department of Agriculture."

"You like it?"

"It's fine. I can do it from home. I'm lucky," she said—because you had to say that, that you were lucky you *could* be careful. Even though most people around Reagan who *could* be careful *weren't*.

"Yeah, me, too," Mason said, nodding.

The conversation died again. He was looking down at the ground between their decks.

"I don't feel lucky," Reagan said out loud.

He looked up. "Yeah? Me, neither."

She couldn't really see him. It was dark, and he was wearing a fabric mask that sat high on his face, under his glasses. She hadn't taken a good look at him before he put it on. He had longish hair, with a little bit of wave to it, but she couldn't tell what color. He was taller than her, probably. Nondescript in his baggy jeans and heavy canvas coat. She wouldn't be able to pick him out of a lineup, even if it happened right this moment. He could be anybody.

"I am hiding," he said.

"What?"

"I'm hiding out here. My brother and his family came over after dinner. To exchange gifts. And we were all supposed to stay outside. But it was cold. And . . ." He shook his head. "It felt ridiculous. To be out on the porch, standing six feet apart. So my mom said, 'This is stupid, just come in,' and they did."

"And you came out here?"

"I did."

"What did you tell your family?"

"I didn't say anything. I just walked right through the house, out the back door."

"Are they going to be mad at you?"

"Maybe. They won't mention it, though."

"Why not?"

"Because we don't do that. We're stoic, Germanic types—inscrutable plainsmen. Aren't you?"

"No," Reagan said. "My family is very scrutable. Our closest neighbors growing up were five miles away, and they could still hear my sister and me fighting."

"Well . . . nobody will say anything. If I go back in."

"If?"

"Well, my brother's family just broke down our wall, you know? They crossed our perimeter."

"I do know."

"Any one of them could have Covid. They have three kids—kids don't even get symptoms half the time. They could be giving my parents Covid right now."

"Probably not."

"How do *you* know what's probable?" He raised his voice and his shoulders. "How does anyone? It's like—the air in there is different now. And if I go back in, I'm part of it. I keep thinking about all the terrible things that could happen from this moment on. Taking care of my parents. Taking care of myself. You can't even visit someone in the hospital, you know?"

"I know."

"And my brother will feel like shit if that happens. He's not a bad person."

"Is this the wrestler?"

"Yeah. I mean, not anymore. But yeah."

"So you're going to . . . what?"

"I don't know," he said. "You must think I'm crazy. Paranoid."

"I would have," she said, "before. But now . . . I don't even know what it means to be crazy. If you're as careful as you're supposed to be, you seem neurotic. I feel neurotic. Now. And I never used to be. I'm the sort of person who'd share an ice cream cone with a dog."

"That's disgusting."

"I know. But I've never cared about that sort of thing. I go swimming in lakes. I wear shoes in the house. If I drop my hot dog in the grass, I'll just brush it off and eat it."

Mason laughed.

"But now I wipe down my mail."

"They say you don't have to wipe down your mail," he said.

"I know, but I'm in the habit now."

"You get a lot of mail? I don't get any mail."

"I'm a homeowner with a retirement plan," she said.

"Now you're just bragging."

Reagan laughed. She leaned on the railing of the deck. She was tired of standing.

"They're in there eating pie," Mason said.

"How long has it been since you've all gotten together?"

"Indoors? Months. Probably June or July."

She nodded.

"Is *your* family all being careful?" he asked.

"God no, they're all at my mom's house. They've been acting normal this whole time. I haven't seen my mom since March."

"I'm sorry."

"It's all right. She still calls me every other day. And texts me weird YouTube videos."

Mason laughed. "I don't think my mom knows how to get on YouTube."

"Count your fucking blessings."

"I do." He looked down again, still kind of chuckling. "It's not fair," he said, more seriously. "I made that pie."

"I'm impressed," Reagan said. "I struggled with the Jell-O salad."

He looked up. "I thought that might be Jell-O salad . . . What kind did you make?"

"Green."

"Green is the *best*," he said.

"Green *is* the best," she agreed.

"*I'm* impressed."

Reagan smiled at him. Only because he couldn't see it. "Wait right there."

She turned around and walked into the house. Into the kitchen. The Jell-O was in the fridge.

"You talking to somebody?" her grandpa called from the living room.

"Just Mason," she said.

"I like that Mason. He's got a job in Washington."

"Mm-hmm." Reagan got two everyday bowls out of the cupboard. Blue-and-white Pfaltzgraff. "Do you want anything while I'm in here?"

"No, thanks. I'm still stuffed."

"All right." Reagan took the bowls out onto the deck. Mason was still standing there, with his hands in his pockets. He laughed when he saw her.

"I'm not sure how to do this," she said.

"You could set it on the deck, then back away from it."

"Yeah, all right." She set one of the bowls down and then stepped back.

Mason sat on the edge of his deck and slid under the wood railing, hopping to the ground. It wasn't much of a drop. He took the bowl and climbed back onto the deck, using the stairs. Then he leaned against the railing across from Reagan again. "It looks perfect," he said. "Are there layers?"

"It's just Cool Whip and cherries," Reagan said. "Also—there are pecans in there."

"Yeah there are."

"In case you're allergic."

"I'm not."

"Well, good."

He was looking at it.

"You can eat it," she said.

"Now?"

"Yeah, we'll just keep our distance."

"All right." He sat down at one end of his deck.

Reagan sat on her grandpa's deck, at the other end. Mason took off his mask and smiled over at her. She'd been a little hard on his chin before—it was present. He had a square face. Narrow eyes. Lips that didn't quite close over his smile. He looked like a chipmunk. She definitely would have pointed that out in high school; he was right to steer clear of her.

He was already taking a bite. "That's the stuff," he said.

Reagan took off her mask. She always had room for Jell-O salad.

"Is that pineapple?" he asked.

"Yeah. Pineapple, pecans, and cream cheese."

"And marshmallows."

"You've got quite a palate over there," she said.

"My grandma used to make this."

"Mine, too."

"God." He was grinning at the bowl. "This stuff is like a time machine."

Reagan was smiling at him. "I'm glad you like it."

"She used to make the other one, too. With the, um . . ." He squinted and snapped his fingers. "Pretzels."

"With raspberry Jell-O."

He pointed at her. "Yes!"

Reagan shook her head like he was being stupid, but she was laughing.

"I love that one," Mason said, taking another bite. "My mom never makes anything like this. She says my grandma cooked everything with packets of Jell-O and cans of soup."

"We used to give my grandma such a hard time," Reagan said. "It cracked us up that she called this a salad. '*You kids want some more salad?*'"

Mason laughed.

"I couldn't imagine Christmas without it," she said.

He looked up at her, still smiling. He tipped his head a little.

Reagan looked away. "So do you still have friends around here?"

"Oh . . ." he said, "you know."

"Not really."

"Some of the people from high school are still here. But I see them more on Facebook than anywhere else. I'm not exactly hanging out at the Co-op."

"I guess not," Reagan said.

"What about you? You still have friends in Arnold?"

"I'm not sure I ever had friends in Arnold."

He waved his hand, dismissing her. "You can't lie to me about that—I remember you and your friends. I always thought you were going to marry Levi Stewart."

Reagan curled her top lip. "Why'd you think that?"

"Everyone thought that."

"Not me."

He pulled his head back. "That's harsh."

"Pfft. Levi's fine. He's got a wife and three kids and fifty bison." She still talked to Levi once a week, even though they broke up in college. (Reagan didn't let many people into her life—but once she'd gone to the effort, she didn't like to let go of them.)

"Bison, huh? That sounds interesting."

"You should friend him on Facebook, he'll tell you all about it."

Mason was finished with his Jell-O already. He was putting his mask back on. Reagan was sorry to see his smile go.

It was colder now that she was sitting on the deck. She shivered.

"Here," Mason said. Then he tossed something onto her deck. Two somethings.

"What are those?" Reagan was squinting over at them.

"Handwarmers—I guess I should have asked if you wanted them. Are you worried about surface contact?"

"Um . . ." Reagan had hand sanitizer in her coat pocket. Mason watched her spray the handwarmers. He didn't make fun of her. She slipped the paper pouches into her pockets. They really were warm—how did that even work? "Oh," she said. "That's *nice*. You sure you don't need them?"

"Nah, I'm fine. I've been warming my hands this whole time."

She sat down again, hanging her feet off the deck. "Just watching me suffer."

"Exactly."

Mason was sitting at the very end of his deck, leaning against the beam. Both decks looked like they'd been built by the same person.

Unfinished cedar, with one railing. If you were a kid, you could fall right under the rail. Reagan and her cousins used to push each other off.

Reagan looked down at her feet. "Sorry I don't remember who you were going to marry in high school," she said.

"It's okay," Mason said. "I didn't marry her."

Reagan nodded, at another loss for words. What had this pandemic done to her? She'd never been much of a talker, but she'd always been able to find words when she wanted them. Now her head and mouth felt empty. She felt like she carried emptiness around with her, a six-foot radius of it.

"*Reagan*," Mason hissed. "Look!" He was pointing away from the deck. Three mule deer were running through her grandpa's yard. Nearly silent in the snow.

There were only two houses on this road, and they backed up to a field, with an old fence that stretched behind both yards. (This must have been one property once.) The first two deer got to the fence and sailed over it, out into the field. The third one stumbled. It stumbled and didn't get up.

"Shit," Mason said, sliding off his deck.

Reagan watched him run across the yard. "Careful," she said, too quietly for him to hear. He was already closer to that deer than he should be. "Careful!"

She hopped off the deck and landed in the snow. Her hip twinged, and her knee hurt more sharply. "Fuck," she muttered, still watching Mason. He was walking up to the deer with his hands out in front of him. Reagan followed—but hung back, staying well away from both of them. "What are you doing?" she shout-whispered.

"It's caught in the fence," Mason said.

The deer was staring at him. Completely still. It hadn't made a sound.

Reagan crept to the side to get a closer look. It looked like the deer had managed to snag its foot between two crossbars and a small tree that was growing right next to the fence.

Mason was still inching toward it, with his hands out.

"What are you *doing*?" Reagan asked again.

"I'm going to help it get free."

"It'll get itself free."

"I don't think it will. It's wedged pretty good."

The deer broke into frantic movement, struggling against the fence.

"It's going to injure itself," Mason said.

"It's going to injure *you*."

This wasn't a fawn or a hungry little doe; the deer was as long as Reagan was tall—it must have weighed two hundred pounds.

"Shhhh," Mason was saying. Maybe to the deer, maybe to Reagan. He was crouching behind it, which seemed like the dumbest decision in the world.

"*Mason,*" Reagan whispered.

"It's all right," he said, reaching for the trapped hoof. "Her other legs are on the other side of the fence."

"I think that's a buck."

"She's not a buck, look at her head."

The deer struggled again. Mason froze. Reagan took another anxious step toward them.

When the deer stilled, Mason shot forward. He bent the tree back and grabbed the trapped hoof, lifting it free.

The deer pulled the leg forward—and in the same motion, kicked its other hind leg through the fence, catching Mason in the chest.

"Oof," he said, falling backward.

The deer ran away, and Reagan ran to Mason. "Jesus Christ!" she shouted. "I told you!"

Mason was lying on his back in the snow. Reagan went down on her knees beside him. Her right knee hurt like a motherfucker. "Are you okay?" she asked, touching his arm.

His eyes were wide. "I'm fine," he said. "Just surprised. Is she okay?"

"The *deer*?"

He nodded.

"She's fine," Reagan said. "She'll live to spread ticks and disease, and destroy crops. Where'd she get you?"

He pointed to his shoulder.

"Can you move it?"

He rotated his shoulder. He was broader than he looked from a distance. Broad even under his coat. His neck was thick, and one of his ears was partly inverted, probably from an old injury. He had snow in his ears and his hair. His hair was much darker than Reagan's, almost black.

"Did you hit your head?" she asked.

"No. I think I'm okay."

"That was so stupid, Mason—that could have been your *face*."

"I think I'm okay," he repeated. He lifted his head up out of the snow and pushed up onto his elbows.

Reagan moved away from him.

He stood up, so she stood up, too. The pain in her knee flared. She hissed, shifting her weight off it.

Mason caught her arm. "Are you okay?"

"I'm fine." Reagan looked up at him. He was an inch or two taller than her. Not very tall. "That could have been your *neck*," she said. "That was *so stupid*."

"Okay," he said, nodding. "You're right. I'm sorry."

"God damn it," Reagan said. Her heart was still pounding.

Mason looked worried. There was snow on his glasses, and his mask had fallen below his nose. He was holding her arm. "I'm sorry, okay? Are you hurt?"

"*No*," Reagan said. "I'm just . . ."

Mason was holding her arm. He was standing right next to her.

She'd put herself this close to him, and she wasn't even wearing a mask—*where was her mask?* He was so close, she could see his chest moving.

He reached up, slowly, with his free hand, and tugged his mask back into place over his nose.

Reagan watched him through the fog of her own breath.

Then she reached up, with her own free hand, to touch his cloth-covered cheek.

He didn't move away.

She pulled his mask down. Slowly. Deliberately. Under his soft chin.

Mason watched her face. He wasn't smiling, but she could still see his two front teeth.

Reagan made a fist in the suede collar of his coat and pulled herself closer to him.

His head dipped forward, more fiercely than she was expecting, to kiss her.

She closed her eyes and just let it happen for a few seconds—he was kissing her. He was in her space. Past her perimeter. This was the second person to touch her today. The second person in ten months. (If Reagan had known in February what was coming, she would have thrown her body into more arms.) (She didn't need people the way other people needed people, but she still needed . . . *something*.) Mason squeezed her arm. She felt herself waking up. She pulled hard on his collar and kissed him hungrily—he tasted green. *God. God damn it.* He wrapped his arm around her waist and held her even closer. They were both wearing thick coats. Reagan was still wearing her ankle boots. Her feet were drenched. That deer was probably long gone. *God damn it. Damn it. Damn it.*

Mason pulled his mouth away. "Hey," he whispered. "Are you okay?"

Reagan was fine.

"Reagan . . ."

She was fine. She was alive. She was lucky.

"You're crying," he said, loosening his arm, letting go of her elbow. "I'm sorry . . ."

"No." She shook her head. "It's not . . ." She didn't have the rest of that sentence. She was at a loss for everything. Mason was just standing there, with Reagan's hand holding his collar. She pushed her face into his shoulder.

"All right," he said, touching her back again gently. "It's okay."

It wasn't. It maybe never would be. Reagan was crying like . . . like she was someone else. Someone she'd judge too harshly to pity.

"All right," Mason was whispering.

Reagan let go of his collar. She lifted her head. She looked up at his face. She didn't remember him from high school. She shook her head but couldn't find anything useful in it.

She took a step away from him and thought about apologizing, but she wasn't sure how. She ran back toward the house, past the deck and around the front.

When she rang the doorbell, her grandpa answered it.

Christmas 2021

The house was full of Reagan's relatives.

It still felt surreal to Reagan, to be this close to people. It still felt unsafe.

But her grandfather had decided it was probably as safe as it was going to get. Half the family was vaccinated, he argued, and the other half had already had Covid—a few of them had had both. *"I'm tired of waiting for it to get better, honey. It feels like we should all get together before it gets worse."*

Grandpa had just gotten his booster shot, and he was feeling invincible.

Reagan couldn't imagine that feeling.

She'd spent too much of the last two years feeling paranoid and vulnerable. She'd gotten through Thanksgiving at her mom's house by sitting next to an open window. And she got through most other social situations by avoiding them. She was still working remotely, by choice. And she still used the drive-up lane for groceries.

She'd tried going out with her friends a few times, this summer, when the future had felt brighter—but even then, it was hard not to look around a crowded bar and wonder how everyone there had spent the last year. *Had they been the ones making it all worse?*

Her friends said she was bitter. Levi said she had PTSD.

"I'm not so sure about that P," Reagan told him. (Easy for Levi to shrug it all off. He was surrounded by fresh air and bison.)

Her family wouldn't even talk to her about Covid anymore. Reagan's sister Caitlin had been down for about two months this spring, and she was still having trouble climbing stairs—but she'd told Reagan to stop checking in with her. *"I can feel you judging me."*

Reagan didn't know how to tell her sister that she only sort of judged her. That she wished Caitlin had been more careful, but that she also didn't believe that being careful was enough. And more than all that, she was just *worried* about her. She was constantly worried about all of them.

Reagan's mother had called the week before Christmas to make sure Reagan was coming home. *"You worry too much,"* her mom said. *"The CDC says the risk for vaccinated people—"*

Reagan had cut her off. *"Oh, the CDC . . ."*

"Sometimes I think you don't want *to get back to normal, Reagan. Sometimes I think you like it* better *this way."*

Sometimes Reagan agreed with her.

But Reagan had made the drive out to Arnold, anyway. She'd even come a day early to carry the folding chairs up from Grandpa's basement and to wash all the not-quite-china. And here she was, sitting at a table crowded with family—and even more crowded with food. (She'd claimed a chair at the grown-ups' table without consulting anyone. Her thirty-eight-year-old brother was at one of the kids' tables, and Reagan didn't feel a tiny bit bad about it.)

She was sitting between her mom and her aunt, facing the window that looked out on the house next door. Reagan had spent the last twenty-four hours not looking in that direction, but now she was stuck.

The neighbors had a full house today, too; the street outside was bumper-to-bumper trucks and SUVs. The two houses were set so close that Reagan could see right into the neighbors' dining room. She could see people sitting at the table . . .

She could see Mason staring right at her.

Reagan froze.

He was smiling at her. His gentle little chipmunk smile. He slowly raised a hand and moved his fingers to wave. Reagan nodded, but she wasn't sure he'd see it, so she raised her hand, too, then quickly put it back under the table.

"Who are you waving at?" her mom asked.

"One of the kids next door."

"We should close those curtains." Her mom flagged down one of the great-grandkids who was walking by the window. "Grace, close those curtains."

"Leave them open," Reagan's grandpa said. "This isn't a funeral."

"Dad, the McCrackens are watching us eat."

"They aren't watching us eat. They've got satellite TV over there. They've got better things to do."

Reagan avoided the window for the rest of the meal. The few times she glanced up, Mason was sitting there, probably talking to someone; it was hard to tell. Then she glanced up again, and someone else was sitting there. She relaxed a little after that.

After dinner, she helped her mom and her aunts clear the table. Reagan picked up the glass lasagna pan of Jell-O salad that she'd brought. It was still half-full. She grabbed two wet spoons out of the dish drainer and headed out the back door. "Be right back."

He was standing on his deck, leaning on the railing, looking out into the field. She'd known she'd find him out here . . .

No, that wasn't quite true. She'd just hoped that she would.

Mason turned when he heard her door open. He smiled a little. "Hey."

"Hey," Reagan said. "Who're you hiding from this time?"

"I'm not hiding," he said.

It was still full daylight. Winter daylight—bright yellow shot with gray. Mason was wearing a red sweater with Rudolph on the front. His face was flushed. It wasn't cold enough for a heavy coat—there wasn't any snow on the ground—but he had on a faded denim jacket with a flannel collar. His hair was cut short over his neck and ears. That must have been Covid hair, last year. This was what he really looked like.

Reagan held out the pan of Jell-O salad.

He lowered an eyebrow.

"I've got spoons," she said.

Mason laughed and sat down on the edge of his deck, hopping off.

He came around the side of her grandpa's deck, taking the steps. Reagan prepared herself for it. She still wasn't good in these moments, when someone was approaching her.

She saw the top of Mason's head on the stairs. And then the rest of him. She could see his body more clearly than she had last year. He had broad shoulders and a barrel chest. Thick arms. A belly. He looked young. The way country boys look young. Even this side of thirty.

When he got to the deck, Reagan took a step back. He stepped back, too, to the edge of the stairs.

She kind of shrugged the pan at him. Like she wasn't sure what to do next. There weren't any chairs out here, and she was already losing her nerve.

"I have a mask," Mason said, reaching into his pocket.

"It's okay," Reagan said. "We're outdoors. And . . . it's okay."

"Here . . ." Mason backed down a few steps and sat, leaving room for Reagan at the top. "Yeah?"

"Yeah," she said, sitting. She stuck a spoon in the pan and passed it down to him.

He took it. "Is that what I think it is?"

It absolutely was. Raspberry pretzel Jell-O salad. Reagan didn't say anything. Just watched him take a bite.

"Oh my God," he said. "Why don't people still make this?"

Reagan laughed. He held the pan out to her, and she took a bite, too.

Mason was clean-shaven. His eyes were blue. He was square-faced and handsome.

He motioned at the front of his sweater with his spoon. "We do this ugly-Christmas-sweater thing now."

Reagan nodded. "My family does that, too."

He looked down at her chest, confused. She was wearing a snug black V-neck.

"Not me," she said. "Fuck that."

Mason laughed and offered her the pan again.

Reagan took another bite of Jell-O salad. There were three layers—raspberry Jell-O, whipped cream cheese with sugar, and crushed pretzels. "So are you back in D.C. now?"

"I was," he said, "for a month or two. Then I bought a house in Omaha."

Her head jerked up. "You moved back to *Nebraska*?"

Mason nodded. He was more earnest-looking this close. In the daylight. (And he'd already seemed pretty earnest in the dark.) "Yeah, D.C. just felt too far, after everything. And my apartment seemed so small . . . So I bought a house in Omaha. My brother says I got ripped off, but it's *palatial* compared to what I could afford back east. I feel like a Major League Baseball player."

Reagan laughed. This was a lot of laughing. "Did you quit your job?"

"No. I'm still remote."

"Me, too."

"That's good." He frowned. "I mean, is that good?"

"It's what I wanted," she said.

"Well then, good." He took another bite of Jell-O salad. He had the pan in his lap. "I'm eating a lot of this, is that okay?"

"God, yeah," she said, "my nieces and nephews won't touch it. They say dessert shouldn't be salty."

"Okay," he said with his mouth full, "well, *one*, this isn't a dessert; it's a salad. And, *two*, the saltiness is the best part."

"You can have as much as you want," she said.

"I will."

Reagan smiled—then bit both her lips for a second. "Was, um . . . was everything okay last year?"

Mason looked up into her eyes. "Last year? You mean . . ."

"With your family," she said. "Your brother coming into the house."

"Oh, yeah." He shook his head. "It was fine. I mean, of course it was, right? What were the chances?"

She nodded. "Did you get vaccinated?"

"Fuck yeah," he said. "I don't care if it makes me grow another leg. I was first in line."

Reagan nodded some more. "Yeah, same."

"Give me some of that hot, fresh gene therapy," Mason went on, chewing. "I mean . . . hopefully we *don't* all grow extra legs . . ."

"Yeah," Reagan agreed. "Hopefully. If we all die, the only people left will be these shitheads." She waved her spoon around. Indicating half the county and both her brothers.

"That's a little harsh," he said.

I'm a little harsh, she thought.

Mason was smiling up at her. "I always thought you had red hair. In high school."

"I did," she said. "I stopped dyeing it last year. I didn't want to do it myself, and then I just got used to this color."

"That's your natural hair color?"

She nodded.

"It's great," he said, still smiling that chipmunky smile. "It's exactly the color of wildflower honey."

"Dirty blond?"

He shook his head, but he looked more amused than anything. "Harsh . . ."

"Mason," Reagan said, more serious. Her eyebrows were low, and she'd squared her shoulders. "Last year. I'm sorry that I—"

"Hey. It's okay. You don't have to—"

"No, I want to—"

"Reagan." His voice was gentle. His whole posture was gentle. "It was just a moment in the woods, right?"

"What?"

"You know, the Sondheim musical?"

"What the fuck are you talking about?"

Mason huffed out a laugh. "I don't know. Just—you don't have to—"

"I'm sorry I ran away," she said. "I'm sorry I cried." She licked her lips. "I'm sorry I reacted like kissing you was a bad thing. *It wasn't.*"

Mason had stopped arguing with her. He'd stopped smiling.

"It was not a bad thing," Reagan said as clearly as she could. "Kissing you."

"It wasn't," he said.

She shook her head no.

"No," he said, "I'm agreeing. It very much wasn't. Also. From my perspective."

"Okay," she said. "Well, good."

"All right," Mason said, nodding.

Reagan nodded.

He scratched his head with the hand that wasn't holding a spoon and grinned at her. "This Jell-O salad has served its purpose, don't you think?" He held up the pan.

Reagan looked down at it. She took it from him and set it behind her.

As soon as the Jell-O was out of the way, Mason was pushing up, over her lap, to kiss her. He'd turned so that he was kneeling on one stair, with his other leg stretched behind him.

She hadn't kissed anyone else in the last year.

It was an extraordinary dry spell, for Reagan—she was a curmudgeon, but she'd never been a monk.

The pandemic had changed her.

She'd gotten a lot pickier about who she let get this close. She'd gotten kind of fixated on repercussions.

But Reagan had kissed Mason before, and nothing bad had happened. It was a purely good moment in the middle of a very bad time. She hadn't forgotten it. She hadn't stopped wondering what might have happened if she could have kept her shit together.

Mason was leaning over her. He had one hand on the railing and one under her chin. She liked the way he kissed—gentle, but with purpose. She put her arms around him, to hold him steady.

They kissed for a long time. Until Mason pulled away to look at her.

"What," Reagan whispered.

"I was making sure you weren't crying."

She poked his ribs. "Shut up."

"You're shaking," he said.

"I'm just cold."

"It is December." He was standing up, taking off his jacket.

"I'm not going to wear your jacket," she said. "I'm not a fifteen-year-old cheerleader."

"You *were* a fifteen-year-old cheerleader," he said, holding out the jacket.

She took it. "How do you remember that? I got kicked out after one semester."

He shrugged. "Put on the jacket, so I can kiss you again without feeling guilty."

Reagan did. It was quilted inside, and still warm from him.

Mason sat down beside her on the top step. She had to scoot over to make room. He leaned behind her to take another bite of Jell-O salad.

She craned her head to look over her shoulder. "You can take that with you," she said. "You don't have to finish it right now."

Mason smiled with all of his teeth. He slid his arm around her waist. "I'll get the dish back to you."

Reagan looked down the steps, out into the yard, past the fence. "Yeah," she said. "All right."

You can read more about Reagan
in the novel *Fangirl*.

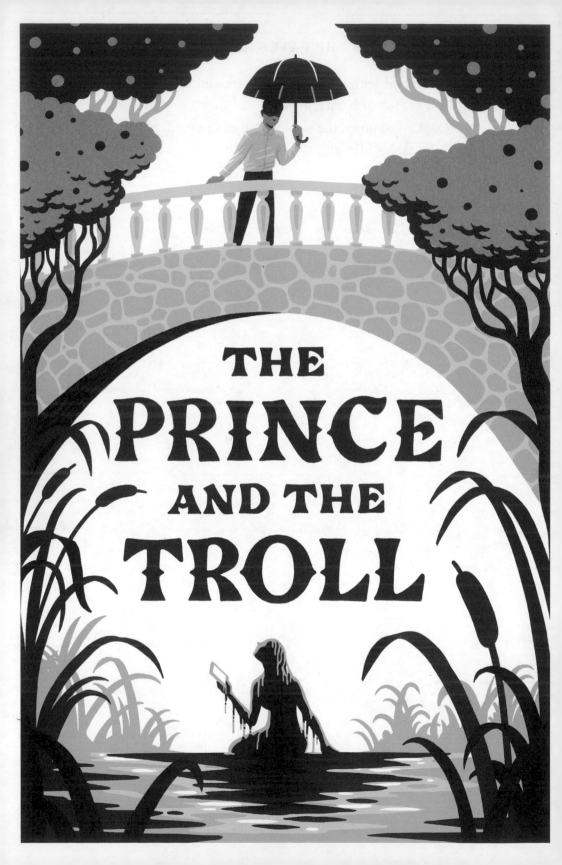

THE
PRINCE
AND THE
TROLL

The Prince
and the Troll

ONCE UPON A TIME, IN A LAND, THERE LIVED A BOY.

Well, he *was* a boy, but now he's a man. Tall and strong and full of purpose. With middling blue eyes and middling brown hair, and a smile for almost everyone he meets.

He has work that makes him feel useful.

He has a house that makes him feel safe.

And he's lucky to live right along the road—the long, wide road. He can see the smoothest part of it from his window.

He may as well be a prince.

One warm January day, the man was walking along the wide road from his safe house to his useful work when he dropped his phone over a bridge. *"Damn it all to darkness!"* He hadn't even noticed the bridge.

The man leaned over the railing to see if he could spot his phone. He brought his hand up to shield his eyes from the sun.

He didn't see the phone. But he saw two eyes looking up at him from the mud.

"Oh," he said. "Hey."

"Hi," the two eyes said. Well. The mouth below the two eyes said it. Whatever it was down there pushed some muddy hair out of its face to see him better.

"I sort of dropped my phone," he said.

"Oh." It sounded like maybe a feminine-type thing. "That sucks."

"Yeah . . ."

"Let me see if I can find it." The muddy thing sloshed around a bit, turning up some pieces of concrete and an empty Dasani bottle. "Oh no . . ." It held something up. "Is this your phone?"

"I can't tell," the young man said. "What kind is it?"

The mudthing shook the phone in its handthing. "It's the new kind with the three cameras."

The man sighed. "Yeah. That's mine."

"Sorry."

"No, that's okay. It's my fault. I was distracted."

"You have to be careful on bridges . . ."

"Yeah, that's what my mother always tells me."

The mudthing rose up a bit out of the muck. "Do you want me to throw it up to you?"

"Yeah, that'd be cool. Maybe I could put it in some rice overnight . . ."

"I've heard they sell magic beans . . ."

"I've heard that, too." He held both hands out.

The mudthing tossed his phone up—but not nearly far enough. It fell back into the gunk. "Sorry, let me try again. Webbed fingers, you know."

The phone flew up into the air again. The man leaned farther out over the railing, his feet lifting off the smooth paving stones. The phone fell through his grasping fingers.

"Sorry!" she called up.

"No, that was me," he said. "Try again?"

He caught it the third time, and they both laughed out loud. "Got it!" he said. "Thank you!"

"Yeah, sure, happy to help."

He tried to wipe some of the mud from his phone, deciding he'd better not turn it on just yet.

"You're lucky the river dried up," the mudthing said. "You would have lost it for sure in the current."

"Yeah, no kidding . . ." He looked down at her again. She was still mostly covered in mud. Her face disappeared when she blinked. (Though he supposed her face disappeared when *he* blinked, too . . . This was more thinking than the man was used to doing on his way to work.) "I guess I'll get going," he said. "Thanks again."

"Anytime," she said.

"Well, I hope not."

"Ha ha," she said. "Seriously."

He was walking again. He couldn't see her anymore. "Have a great day!" he shouted over his shoulder.

"Watch where you're walking!" she shouted back.

The walk to work felt longer without his phone to distract him. *This is good for me,* he thought. *I always mean to stop and smell the flowers. Or at least to notice them.*

All the best flowers grew by the road.

They grew all year long, now.

⌒

The next day, the young man woke in his soft bed, in his safe house. He hurried out onto the road. (He liked the road, everyone did. He was lucky to live so close.)

This time when he got to the bridge, he tucked his phone—it still worked, thank goodness—into his back pocket. He still felt like it might fly out over the railing, isn't that crazy? He kept touching his pocket to make sure it was there.

Thinking of it made him think of the mudthing. He wondered if she was down there today. *It's not like she just hangs out, waiting for people to drop their phones,* he thought. But he stopped anyway in the middle of the bridge. He leaned out over the railing. "Hello?"

There was a slopping sound beneath him.

"Oh," she said. "It's you. Hello." She lifted herself up out of the riverbed, pushing some of the mud away from her face. "Did you drop something?"

"No . . ." he said.

"Do you want to? Maybe a volleyball this time? We could play a little catch."

He laughed. "I just thought I'd say hello."

"Oh . . . That's nice. Hello."

"So, um . . ." He cleared his throat. He hadn't really thought this through. "Do you live here? Under the bridge?"

"I guess I do," she said. "Do you live up there?"

"Along the road," he said.

"That's lucky."

"It is." He brought his hand up to shield his eyes again. "Are you—I mean, I hope this isn't impolite—"

"Go ahead."

"Are you a troll?"

She laughed. "Because I live under a bridge?"

"Well, yeah," he said. "I don't mean to—"

"No, it's okay. I guess I am a troll. I live under bridges and call out to innocent boys."

"I'm not—I mean, you didn't call out to me."

"I will next time," she said. "Just to say hello."

"That would be nice," he said. Which was the wrong thing. He should have said something jokey.

She cleared her throat. He guessed she had a throat.

"Well," he said, "I suppose I should go to work."

"To your job?"

"Yeah."

"Do you like it?"

"I really do," he said. "It makes me feel useful."

"What is it?"

"Oh. It's kind of hard to explain. It's like—I monitor a section of the road. It's maintenance. Resource management. There's a little bit of graphic design."

"That does sound useful," she said. "For people who use the road."

"It is!" he said. "Well, anyway . . . it was nice talking to you."

"You, too."

He walked away from the bridge, smiling, and took his phone out of his pocket.

～～

"Hello!" The man leaned over the railing.

He waited.

"Hello?" he called again.

The womanish thing rose up out of the mud. "Oh, hello. I wasn't expecting to see you."

"Yeah, I wasn't sure you'd be around this time of day."

"I'm here pretty much all the time."

"Oh. That's nice. I mean . . ." He faltered. "*Is* it nice? It's nice for me. To find you here."

She smiled at that. He could see her teeth. She had teeth.

"I brought you something," he said, "to thank you."

"You already said thank you."

"Well, I know, but I was stopping for coffee anyway. There's a Starbucks just down the road."

"You brought me Starbucks?"

"Do you not like Starbucks?"

"No, of course I do. Just, um . . ." She was looking up at him from her patch of mud.

He looked down at his hands, at the two paper cups. "Oh," he said. "I see what you're getting at . . . I could drop it, I guess?"

"You could," she said. "That seems like something you would do."

He laughed. She laughed, too.

"I wish I could just bring it down to you . . ." he said.

"Too bad this isn't a wishing well," she said, another joke. Then she said, "Actually this *might* have been a wishing well, once upon a time."

"I can't believe I was so stupid," the man said. (He's not a prince, but he may as well be.) "I'd bring it down to you if I could, if there was a path."

"I believe you," she said.

He believed her.

～～

"What are you doing?" she shouted.

It was the next day, at the same time, and the man was climbing over the ornamental hedge that separated the road from everything else.

"I'm just trying to get over these shrubs."

"Be careful, they just sprayed!"

"I'm being careful," he said, snagging his pants on some thorns.

"You're going to spill your Starbucks," she said.

"It's your Starbucks," he said.

"Well, then you *really* shouldn't spill it."

He laughed. His foot was stuck in some branches. It didn't hurt. The thorns didn't hurt either. But it was embarrassing. The whole thing was embarrassing. He felt silly. "This is why no one leaves the road," he said to himself. "Maybe I'll just leave the coffee here for you?" he called. He couldn't quite see her from here, from the middle of the hedge. He'd never really seen her.

"I won't be able to reach it," she said. "You may as well take it to work—maybe someone else will drink it."

"Yeah, okay," he said. "I guess it's the thought that counts?"

"Did your mother tell you that?"

⟋⟍

"Did you come back to visit that hedge?"

It was the next day. He was midway through the bushes. She was already laughing at him.

"I'm bringing you Starbucks!" he shouted.

"I've heard that before," she said.

"Ha ha!" He kept working his way through, letting the thorns catch in his sleeve. He'd intentionally worn his cheapest sweater.

"Even when you get past the hedge, you're going to have to slosh down through mud."

"It's okay. I wore my worst clothes."

"I'm flattered."

"Ugh, sorry. I'm just—" He felt his foot land in the mud on the other side of the hedge. "Ha!" He pulled his other foot through the shrub. "Aha!"

"Are you okay?"

"Yeah! I'm good. I'm—" He was off the road. He couldn't see it anymore. It was just on the other side of the hedge. He could go back. Maybe he should go back?

"You didn't spill the coffee."

He turned toward her voice. He could see her better now. Could see her person-like shape, leaning on a rock at the edge of the old riverbed.

He walked toward her. "Hi."

"Hi," she said.

He was standing above her now. "I, um—"

She reached her hand-like thing toward him.

"Plain or vanilla?" he asked.

"Give me the one you'd want yourself," she said.

He laughed and gave her the vanilla. "That's very selfish of you."

"Oh, please, you get Starbucks every day."

I could bring you coffee every day, he almost said. (And the thing is, he really could. It wouldn't take much. This hadn't taken much.) (He didn't say it.)

"You could sit down," she said.

He looked down at the mud.

"Go on, you're already wearing your worst pants."

"That's true."

He sat down carefully, a few feet away from her, away from the center of the riverbed, where the mud was dark and thick. She wiped some sludge away from her lips to sip her coffee. She had lips.

He'd hoped the mud was just good, clean mud. But the smell was terrible now that he was sitting in it.

"The river smelled better," she said. He must have been making a face.

"No," he said, "it's fine." He sort of remembered the river. They'd needed it for the road. Whatever the road needed, they took.

She took another sip of the coffee. There was whipped cream on her lip. And mud on the lid. "That's really lovely," she said.

"I'm glad you like it," he said.

She took another drink. "It's seriously good."

"I know."

"It's amazing that you can have it every day."

"Some people say it's a waste of money," he said. "But I always feel like it's worth it. Small, good things are worth it."

"Totally," she said. "Treat yourself." She looked up at him. The mud was sliding down her shoulders, clinging to her long hair. (Hair, too.) "Thank you," she said, looking down at her coffee, "Adam."

His stomach pitched. His face fell. "How . . . How do you know my name?"

She smiled. "It was written on the cup."

"I . . . That's not . . . I wasn't supposed to tell you my name."

"No," she said, "it's fine. You're thinking of fairies."

"And dwarves," he said.

"Right, dwarves."

"And elves."

"But not bridge trolls," she said. "Really, Adam, I'm, like, the only creature you're safe giving your name to."

He laughed. He was embarrassed. And relieved. (Though not completely.) "What about you?"

"I told you, I can't hurt you."

"What's your name, I mean."

"I can't tell you that," she said between sips. "*Everyone* knows you can't trust princes."

"I'm not a prince."

He may as well be.

～～

"Those aren't your worst pants," she said, tilting her head to the side to examine him.

"My worst pants are in the dryer," he replied. "Vanilla or Cinnamon Dolce?"

"Which one do you like best?"

He handed her the Cinnamon Dolce. "I can't stay too long, I'm running late."

"What do you do up there?" she asked.

"I already told you," he said.

"Not really . . ."

"What do *you* do down here?"

She shrugged, settling back into the mud with her latte. "Nothing useful."

"That's not true," he said. "Sometimes you throw phones into the air."

She tilted her head again. "You think I'm at my most useful when I'm being useful to you?"

"No," he said. "I don't know what to think."

He didn't.

"Tell me about the road," she said one day. It was a beautiful February day. Sunny. Every day was sunny. Though some people said it would have to rain again, eventually.

"I love the road," he said. "Everyone does."

"Is it very smooth?"

"*So* smooth."

"And wide?"

"*So* wide," he said, smiling. "And it smells wonderful."

"That's very rude, Adam."

"Oh, I'm sorry."

"No, it's okay. I know what it smells like down here. I have a nose." She did, in fact.

"And there are flowers by the road," he said, "fewer than before—but still the best flowers. There are no flowers anywhere that you can't see from the road." He wished that she could see it.

"What's the best part?" she asked.

"The best part?"

"The best part, besides the Starbucks."

"I almost hate to tell you this, but there are *so many* Starbucks."

She sighed and laid her head down on her rock. Sometimes, she'd sit up on the rock. He liked that. She looked more like a something then—and less like part of the mud.

Today she was lying in the mud, with her head and arms on the rock, like it took too much effort to sit up any farther. "What's the *very best* part of the road?" she asked.

The man—we may as well call him Adam, he already gave up his name—stopped to really think. Finally, he said, "The road goes everywhere you'd want to go. Everywhere you'd think of going. It never ends. And you're never alone there. And everything you'd ever want is right there on the road."

"That's not the *one* best part," she said. "That's too many things."

"Fine," he said, "okay—the best part of being on the road is that when you're on it, it's all that you can see."

Her eyes were closed.

"That probably doesn't make sense to you," he said.

"No, it does." She wrinkled her nose, and the mud on her face cracked.

~

"What is *that*?"

"Strawberry Açaí Refresher."

"It's pink!"

"It's seasonal."

"Well, hand it over, Adam. Don't be shy."

Adam still felt shy here. He handed her the drink and settled down on the riverbank. It still hadn't rained—it never really rained, something to do with the road. He could sit much closer to her now without ruining his khakis.

"This is delicious," she said. "Why didn't you get one for yourself?"

"I'm cutting back," he said.

"On Strawberry Açaí Refreshers?"

"On carbs, mostly."

"*Ah*. Bridge trolls don't really have to worry about carbs."

"Lucky," he said.

"Yes," she said, "I'm so lucky."

He laughed, uncomfortably. He didn't really know what bridge trolls worried about; he was a little afraid to ask. (No, that's not right—he wasn't *afraid*, really. He just didn't want to know.) "I wish I knew your name," he said.

"What do you call me in your head?"

He blushed. "That's presumptuous."

She sipped loudly at her drink. It was already empty. "So much ice," she murmured.

"*She*," he said. "I call you *she. Her.*"

"*Now* who's being presumptuous," she said, her tongue hugging every round consonant. (Her tongue.)

"I'm sorry," he said. "Am I wrong?"

"No," she said. "You're right. Lucky guess." She tipped the ice down onto the mud, over what was surely her bottom half. "Do they sell water at Starbucks?"

"No," he said.

She seemed disappointed. "Oh."

"I mean, I guess they do sell *bottled* water, but they'll just give you a cup of water if you ask. Filtered."

"*Oh.*"

"I could bring you water tomorrow."

"Instead of a pink drink?"

"I could bring you both. They have drink carriers."

⌣⌢

"Is it true, what they say about the road?" She (she, she, *she*) had drunk half her venti water, then poured the rest between her chest and the rock. She was thick under all the thick mud. He could almost see her.

She slid up a bit on the rock.

"What do they say?" he asked.

"That the wizard's crows watch you at every moment."

"Oh, yeah, that's true."

"Even in your houses?"

"Yeah, I guess so. I don't really think about it."

"How could you not think about that?"

"They're just crows," he said. "You get used to it."

She shuddered. "They're not *just* crows. They're like . . . flying *eyeballs.*"

"Yeah, but it's not like the wizard can watch all of us at once."

"I suppose."

"And what's he going to see if he's looking at me? Me, sleeping? Me, making a sandwich?"

"So you like being watched by a dark wizard?"

"We don't know that he's dark."

"I mean, his armies of crows seem like a clue . . ."

"Look, I don't *like* the crows. They're just . . . It's such a small price to pay to live on the road."

"I'll take your word for it, Adam."

"Oh, listen to you!" He was flustered. "I wish I knew your name—I'd win more of these arguments if I knew your name!"

That made her laugh. (He did make her laugh. At least once every day.) "Fine," she said, "the crows are good. The crows are grand. If they see you choking, they can caw for help."

"That's true, you know."

"So the crows aren't the worst part of living on the road. What is?"

"What do you mean?"

"What's the very worst part of living on the road?"

"We weren't talking about that."

"We are now." She'd finished her pink drink, too, and was chewing on the ice.

"I guess, the worst part . . ." It wasn't good to talk about the bad parts. (And not because the crows were listening as well as watching.) (Not *just* because of that.) "You shouldn't focus on the bad things," he said. "Because you draw them toward you. Happiness is about focusing on good things and drawing *those* things toward you."

She closed her eyes tight. She wrinkled her nose. Bits of dust fell on her cheeks.

"What—" he started.

"Shhhh!" she shushed.

His voice dropped to a whisper: *"What are you doing?"*

So did hers: *"I'm focusing on good things."*

"Like what?"

"Rain."

"Rain?"

"Good things," she whispered. *"Rain. Mud. You."*

His heart jumped. (He had a heart.) *"Me?"*

She closed her eyes even tighter. *"You . . . coming back tomorrow, with Starbucks."*

"Behold the power of positive thinking!" she shouted before he was even over the hedge. He'd worn a gap in the shrub there and beaten a path down to the riverbed.

"Hello, you," he said, sitting down with a drink carrier.

"Hello, Adam."

"I brought two Frappuccinos, and before you ask which one I'd pick for myself, they're both caramel. Because I would pick caramel."

"Hmm." She stuck out her lower lip. (It wasn't a surprise; he knew she had lips.) (It was still good, though.) "I like having a choice."

He handed her a caramel Frappuccino. "But you always pick the one I like best."

"That's part of what makes it delicious! The microaggression."

"Oh yeah?"

"Yeah!"

"Well, I brought you something else." He took a venti cup of water from the drink carrier and dumped it on her.

She gasped.

It ran nearly-not-dirty streaks in her possibly black (possibly dark green?) (or a kind of brown?) hair.

And then she laughed more than he'd ever seen her laugh before. "You made me spill my Frappuccino!" she said, still laughing, tears burning tracks through the dried mud on her cheeks.

"You can have mine," he said.

She took it. She drank it all. She licked the whipped cream out of the domed lid. Then she dropped the cup into the riverbed.

"Hey, give me that," he said. "I'll recycle it."

"Oh, Adam." She laughed until her cheeks were sticky.

⟡

He was lying on his back with his head in the dirt. He couldn't even see her like this. There were crows circling overhead. It didn't matter, there were always crows.

"Adam?"

He felt something tugging at his foot.

When he sat up, he saw that his shoelace was undone. She'd never touched him before. Or his shoelaces.

He raised himself up on his elbows to look at her. She'd pulled herself to the edge of the riverbed. He'd never seen her so far out of the mud. It cracked and puckered around her.

"Hey," he said, "don't do that."

"What's wrong?" Her face looked strained. All this effort seemed painful.

"Don't do that," he said. "Get back."

She huddled back into the most fetid part of the riverbed. Away from him, away from her rock. "Tell me what's wrong."

"I'm sorry I didn't bring coffee," he said.

"It's okay, I don't need coffee. Tell me."

Maybe he should just tell her. Maybe he could . . . "There was a Tragedy on the road today."

"I'm sorry," she said.

"It's okay," he said. And it *was* okay. It *would be* okay. *He* was okay. "Tragedies just happen sometimes," he said. (It was what people said after a Tragedy.)

"Yes," she agreed. "Some things are unavoidable."

"Yes," he said. But that wasn't true. "I mean, *no*. It's not like that. Tragedies on the road happen even when they don't have to."

She was still looking at him. She was still confused.

"They *could* be avoided," he explained. "But we *don't* avoid them."

"Why not?"

"I can't explain it!" he shouted at her. (He'd never really shouted at her.) "It's part of living on the road! It's a small price to pay!"

"Okay, Adam."

"You live under a bridge!"

"I know."

"You wouldn't understand!"

"Fine, I *don't* understand!"

He stood up; he scrambled up the side of the dry riverbed. "I'm going to get coffee."

"Is Starbucks even open? The Tragedy—"

"Starbucks is always open!"

∼◞

"I'm sorry I shouted at you," Adam said.

She was lying in the darkest part of the mud. If she thought he couldn't see her, she was wrong. He'd gotten really good at seeing her.

"I brought Frappuccinos . . ."

He walked to the edge of the riverbed and set down a drink carrier and an armful of snacks. There were chocolate-dipped graham crackers. And bagel balls with cream cheese in the middle. And special coffee-fighting breath mints.

Then he sat back from the pile. In case she didn't want to come anywhere near him. "I got Java Chip and Midnight Mint Mocha. I'd pick the mint."

She was lying on her back. He could see the mud rising and cracking with her breath.

"The worst part of living on the road," he said, as evenly as he could, "isn't the crows. Or the Collapses—you've probably heard about the Collapses. It isn't even the Tragedies . . ."

Her eyes were closed.

"The worst part of living on the road," he said, not very evenly, "is that you can't fall down. If you fall down, you fall off." No, that wasn't true. He'd never lied to her. "If you fall down, they push you off. If someone falls, *we push*—"

Adam leaned forward. His elbows were on his knees, his head was hanging. He was—he couldn't stop—

He heard her dragging herself through what was left of the sludge. A heavy slither.

He didn't look up. He didn't want her to see him like this.

She pulled herself between his ankles.

She rested her head on the ground beneath his tears.

He heard her dragging herself through what was left of the sludge. A heavy slither.

"There's something I want to talk to you about."

"Coffee first," she said, "then talk."

He was hurrying down the path, skidding on the gravel. He was late. He'd been getting something ready.

She was in the middle of the riverbed, where there was still a little mud. Her arms were reaching out to him. "Remember yesterday when I said I don't need coffee? That was wrong—I do need coffee. You can never stop bringing me coffee, Adam. I've just cursed you, sorry."

He held out two iced drinks. "I didn't think bridge trolls could *curse* people."

She took the macchiato. "Hmm. I guess you're right—that's fairies, isn't it? Why do fairies get all the fun?"

"I'm sorry I'm late."

"It's okay," she said. "You don't have to keep coming. That wasn't a real curse."

"I know. I come because I want to come."

"Good." She started to burrow back into her patch of muck.

"Wait—" He caught her by the wrist. (It was undoubtedly a wrist.)

Her eyes whipped up. Her lips pulled back. She hissed.

Adam let go—but he didn't look away. He sat down in the mud with her. "Please wait. I want to talk to you . . . *This* is where I would say your name if I knew it. For emphasis."

"So noted," she said. She was still sort of hissing.

"I would say your name, and then I would say—I come here every day, because I *want* to come here. Because I want to see *you*."

"I know that. Adam."

"You do?"

"Well, I didn't figure you enjoyed the smell. Or the view."

(The view from the riverbed was dismal. The fact that it hasn't been mentioned yet only proves that point; it was exactly the sort of thing you couldn't see from the road.)

"I have a house," he said, getting back on track. She was always pulling him off track.

"You told me about it once. You said it was safe."

"*Yes*. I have a safe house with a soft bed. I have a warm hearth. Fresh bread, every day. Running water."

She'd pulled her arm away, but she was still there, peeking out at him from behind long, dirt-caked ropes of hair.

"It's right on the road," he said. "The smoothest part of it."

"You're very lucky," she said.

"*You* could be lucky!" He hadn't meant to shout it. "*Darling . . .*" he whispered. "I could make you lucky."

She was hidden behind the ropes. "You shouldn't call me that."

"I wouldn't have to if you'd tell me your name."

She was being very still. Adam understood that he should be still, too. That they were both trying not to crack.

She wrapped her finger-like things around his ankle. They really were webbed. "Adam," she said, "I can't live on the road. I'm a bridge troll."

"I could build a bridge," he said. He wasn't sure where.

"Don't be stupid," she said.

"Don't be mean."

"I'm a *bridge troll*!"

"What do bridge trolls even do?" Adam demanded.

She wrapped her other hand around his other ankle.

He reached out to touch her cheek. (It felt like silt. But it was certainly a cheek.)

"We eat stones!" she hissed. "And children's bones! But mostly we trick men into our clutches."

"Fine," Adam said, "I'm tricked!"

Her fingers were so tight around his ankles. "I can't live on the road with you!"

"Because of the crows?"

"The crows?! *No*."

"You made me feel weak because of the crows."

"Oh, Adam, you *are* weak. Sometimes it's the thing I like best about you. You're so fucking soft."

He rubbed his fingers along her cheek, pushing through the dirt, wanting to see what was underneath.

"It isn't the crows," she said.

"Is it the Bouts of Delirium?"

"You've never mentioned the Bouts of Delirium."

"I was going to mention them, when you agreed to live with me. I was going to warn you about everything. I wanted to show you the road first. So you'd understand."

She was letting him scrape the muck away from her cheek. She was reaching her fingers up the cuffs of his jeans.

"Adam, you know what the road is doing, don't you?"

"I know more about the road than you do. I grew up there!"

"Then you know," she said, "that the road is killing *every-thing*."

He hadn't expected her to say that. Maybe you didn't expect her to say that. Magical creatures are usually more cryptic.

"Not *everything*," Adam said.

She laughed. (He did make her laugh. At least once a day.)

"Everything," she said, "*eventually*."

"But not today," he said. This felt like an important thing to say. This felt like the *right* thing to say, and it must have been at least a little right, because she was clutching at the back of his calves now and pulling herself up between his legs.

"This is why you should come live with me on the road," he said. (He was begging, really.) "Because the road will be the last thing to die. And until it dies, it will be so safe. And so warm. And so easy."

"Adam." She fell forward on his chest. He shifted his arms to catch her—to pull her up, his hands on either side of her rib cage. She was heavy in his arms, not as slick as she'd once been, colder than he expected.

"My love," he said. (If only she'd tell him her name, he wouldn't be this embarrassing.)

"I can't live with you," she said.

"Yes, you can," he whispered. He tried to hiss it, but his tongue wasn't built for sibilance. *"I want you."*

"My love," she said, and she didn't even have an excuse to sound embarrassing. "Go home. Come back tomorrow. Bring me coffee."

"The coffee seems silly now," he said. "I would have brought you gold. I could have brought you frankincense and myrrh—I know where to find them. You can get them lots of places up there."

"Come back tomorrow," she said, "and bring me something sweet. Bring me something dear that you didn't have to fight for."

Adam left.

But first he cried.

He didn't go back to work—what was the point? He went back home and climbed into his clean, soft bed without changing out of his muddy clothes.

He closed his eyes. He focused hard. On good things: rain, *her.*

Eventually, he slept.

It was raining when Adam woke up. It had been so long since it rained.

My mother was right, he thought. *Good things come to good people.*

He squeezed through the hedge and nearly lost his balance on the other side. The ground was wet. He'd brought lattes today. She might like something hot.

It was raining hard; Adam may have focused too much. Everything that had been dry and dusty was wet and running. Even the river had come back to life, a muddy stream rushing under the bridge.

"Hello!" Adam shouted. "I'm here!"

He looked out to the center of the channel, where she liked to wait for him. The last place to dry out, the first place to get wet.

"I'm here," he called out again. "I've got a Peppermint Mocha and a Chestnut Praline. Not only would I choose the mint, but I actually hate the chestnut. That's a full-on aggression!"

She didn't answer. He couldn't see her. It was raining too hard. And the wind was blowing.

Adam sat down at the edge of the riverbed and waited. The coffee got cold.

"Hello!" he shouted.

He was standing on the bridge, leaning over the railing. The rain was still coming down. The river was so high it had devoured his path along the bank.

The Starbucks closest to Adam's house was closed. But the one down the road was open. He'd brought her hot coffee with cream and sugar.

"Hello!" he shouted.

Had she been swept away? Or drowned? Had she left to find a different bridge?

Someone tapped him on the shoulder. For a second he thought it might be her.

It wasn't. It was an older woman, wearing a fashionable raincoat. "What are you doing?" she asked him, her eyes wide and fearful. "It's slippery—you'll fall!"

Adam smiled at her. "Thank you. I'll be careful."

He turned back to the river and stopped smiling. He leaned farther over the rail. "Are you there?"

He didn't bring coffee today.

The river was lapping at the edge of the bridge. Adam was alone there. Everyone else had taken shelter or was looking for higher ground; his mother said she'd found some. He held on to the railing.

"I'm here!" he shouted.

And then he held his phone out over the side and let it go. (This wasn't a *very* big sacrifice; it had been days since he'd had service.) (He would have dropped it anyway.)

She wasn't there.

His phone was gone.

Once upon a time, in a land that was losing, a man sat at the edge of a river.

It's Adam. Adam is the man. He sat by the river, and he couldn't see the bridge. The bridge was gone. The road was gone.

The rain was still feeding the river, and the river was eating everything, and Adam was watching it go—that's when he finally saw her. She was still far away, but he saw her.

"Hello!" he shouted, falling onto his stomach in the mud and reaching into the water.

"Adam!" he heard her shout.

She was coming closer to him. Swimming toward him.

They caught each other's arms and held fast.

"You're alive!" she cried. "I've been looking for you, hoping."

"I was looking for *you*!" he said. "You left the bridge."

"I didn't leave. I just came unstuck. And then I was caught up, like everything else, in the river."

"We've found each other now," he said, grasping at her arms, trying to haul her up onto the bank.

"No," she said, pulling back. "Adam, what are you doing!"

Her arms slipped away from him. They caught each other by the wrists.

"I can save you!" he said.

She laughed at him. Her lips were red. Her teeth were pointed. Her skin was the color of a green tea Frappuccino.

"It's still a no," she said, squeezing his hands tight.

She was stronger than he was. Bigger than he was. She was trying to hold on to him without pulling him in.

"Are you here to save *me*?" he asked.

"Oh . . ." she said sadly. "No." She pulled herself carefully toward him. "But I'm glad you're alive. You've always been lucky."

"The road is gone—is this what you wanted?"

"No."

She was a dark shadow in the water. But he wasn't a fool—he knew she had a tail.

"It will be easier for you now," he said. He was crying again. "I'm glad."

She shook her head. "This isn't easy. This is just another kind of hard. That's all that's left now, for any of us."

Adam still didn't understand. She shook her head, like she didn't expect him to.

Then she pulled herself close, so carefully, and raised herself out of the water.

"My prince," she said, and kissed him.

And then she let go.

Mixed Messages

Beth

Are you there?

Text me when you're there.

I might not text you back right away—we're going out to dinner for our anniversary. (Not our wedding anniversary.)

Jennifer

Happy anniversary!

You're there!

Well, I'm here.

Are you at work?

Indeed. I'm the only copy editor working today. I wonder if everyone else was laid off. It wouldn't be the first time that's happened . . .

Can you talk?

Talk? No. Text? Yes.

Beth

I meant text.

Jennifer

Well, here I am. What anniversary is it, if not your wedding anniversary?

It's our together anniversary. Like, our kissing anniversary. I like it better than our wedding anniversary. The weather is better.

You're the one who wanted to be a June bride . . .

I just didn't want to wait for the weather to change to lock that down.

Got to lock it down.

Is that what you wanted to text me about? Your anniversary?

No.

Okay . . .

I'm nervous to tell you.

Is it about me?

No!

No. Sorry. It's about me.

Are you sick?

No. Sorry.

Stop asking me urgent questions, so I can finish typing it . . .

Sorry, sorry. I'll wait my turn.

I think I'm pregnant.

Really?

Yeah.

Why did that take you so long to type?

Oh my God, Jennifer. It started out longer, but you kept interrupting me.

You really think you're pregnant?

Maybe.

Is that . . . possible?

Are you asking whether Lincoln and I still have sex?

I am NEVER asking whether ANYONE is having sex.

Well, we do. We have sex. That's not a problem.

Okay, I'm glad.

We should talk about sex more.

You and Lincoln?

No, you and me.

You have chosen the wrong best friend.

Women are supposed to talk to each other about sex. It's supposed to be healthy. And empowering.

Jennifer

> Well, I've never been much of either.
> ¯_(ツ)_/¯

Beth

> > There is a shrug emoji, you know.

> I'm old-school. I like this guy: ¯_(ツ)_/¯

> He's like "Meep."

> > Do you type him out every time?

> I've got a shortcut on my phone.

> Meep. ¯_(ツ)_/¯

> > Jennifer. I really think I might be pregnant.

> So that's . . . possible? You still get your period?

> > I would have told you if I stopped having periods.

> Would you?

> > Yes!

> It's been so long since I had a period, I sort of
> forgot people our age get them. In my mind,
> periods are for teenagers.

> > Like snap bracelets? And jelly sandals?

> And cyber-bullying.

> > 1. I'm sorry to flaunt my uterus privilege.
> >
> > 2. I feel like you're not really responding to my
> > pregnancy concerns.

1. Hey. It's okay. I don't think either of us has much uterus privilege.

2. I'm not sure what to say.

3. Why aren't you at your anniversary dinner?

> I'm meeting Lincoln outside the restaurant. He's late.

You're eating inside a restaurant?

> It's Nia's—they have outdoor seating, but you have to go inside and wait for it. But you can't get in line until your whole party is here.

Wear a good mask.

> I always wear a good mask.
>
> You don't think I'm pregnant.
>
> Do you.

I don't think anything; talk me through your thinking.

> Oh my God, some young guy just winked at me.

Beth, I think we need to have a little talk about the birds and the bees. That's not exactly how it happens.

> I just peeked inside the restaurant to check on the line, and he winked at me!

What did you do?

> I got the hell out of there! I'm a married woman, and he's clearly a maniac.

He wouldn't have to be a maniac to flirt with you. People flirt with you all the time. I've seen it.

Beth

Are you talking about that time we were at the Chili's in the Fort Worth airport, and that waiter called me "mama"?

Jennifer

Yes.

It's because I was wearing an empire-waist sundress. He thought I was pregnant.

Well, he was clearly into it.

I haven't been flirted with in a century.

In *this* century?

That's correct.

Your husband flirts with you.

Mitch hasn't flirted with me since nineteen hundred and ninety-three.

That's a lie; I've seen him flirt with you; once, with a tuba. But I can't argue with you right now—Lincoln is going to be here any minute. Do I tell him I might be pregnant?

Have you taken a test?

No.

Talk me through your thinking . . .

My period is late.

How late?

A week.

And that's unusual? It's usually pretty regular?

Historically.

Like . . . ten years ago, historically?

No. Usually. Recently. Mostly.

Okay. Well. You could take a pregnancy test.

You think it's menopause, don't you?

No. I don't know what to think.

You think it's perimenopause.

I don't even know what perimenopause is.

No one knows what perimenopause is! It's just what you blame when you're old and you feel fucked up.

I don't think that. I don't make presumptions about other people's perimenopause.

Don't distract me with alliteration.

I'm sorry. (People with ovaries can be so touchy . . .)

How does it feel to think you might be pregnant?

I'm not pregnant.

You could take a test.

I told myself I'd never take another test.

I know.

Beth

> Oh my GOD. That cute guy is still staring at me.

Jennifer

Wait—is he young or is he cute?

> I think he might be BOTH. What the fuck.
> Should I tell him I'm infertile?

You could just tell him you're married.

> I'm not telling him anything. This is unnerving.

What are you wearing?

> Why—do you think I might be asking for it?

¯_(ツ)_/¯

> Look, it's my anniversary. I'm
> trying to lean into my assets.

I hear you, mama.

Oh God, sorry—I was trying to be funny.

> No, it's okay. It *was* funny.

> I was just moving so that guy can't watch me.
> Who goes to a tapas bar in the suburbs to flirt
> with middle-aged women?

Where is Lincoln?

> I don't know, he's supposed to be getting
> his hair cut.

He's cutting his Covid ponytail?

Yes. Finally.

Won't you miss it?

Maybe? I don't think so.

I thought you liked it.

I did at first. It was like being married to MacGyver.
And then it was like being married to late '90s Eddie
Vedder. But now it's kind of like being married to the
guy who opened Omaha's first health food store.
Like, he won't wear it down, and he won't wear it in a
bun, and he won't let me braid it. So it's this very low
ponytail every day. It's becoming A Look.

I can't believe he won't let you braid it. That's very selfish
of him. My girls won't let me braid their hair anymore,
either.

We are surrounded by selfish people.

(Your girls used to let me braid their hair when they
were little, I loved it.)

If Lincoln would wear his hair down, it would be very
early-'90s Eddie Vedder, and I might still be into it.

I wish Mitch would have grown a Covid ponytail.

At least he can go back to the barber now that he's triple
vaccinated.

He refuses to go back. He says he doesn't want to pay for a
haircut when I can give him a perfectly good one for free.
I guess I'll be cutting his hair until I die or develop a tremor.

So much to look forward to in this scenario.

INDEED.

Beth

I can't tell Lincoln that I think I'm pregnant.

Jennifer

Why not?

Because it makes me sound crazy. I'm *being* crazy.

You're not being crazy. It's possible.

If it were possible, it would have happened. It didn't happen. It isn't happening.

You could take a test.

I'm not taking a test.

Okay. You can just wait and see.

This is what happens, right? Everything stops working. This is the progression. Virgin, mother, crone. I just skipped the middle phase.

Is it virgin/mother/crone? Or virgin/whore?

You're thinking Madonna/whore.

I think it's madonna/whore.

Something/mother/crone.

Snap bracelets and jelly sandals/mother/crone.

I can't tell Lincoln that I'm a crone now.

You're not a crone. Your period is just late.

My period is checking out. It's moving on. My Aunt Ruby is getting too old to travel.

I don't miss my period, but I do miss the estrogen. My skin is so dry.

God, I'm sorry. I really shouldn't complain to you about any of this.

No, it's okay. Who else are you going to complain to? I don't compare your pain to mine when you're hurting.

That's very kind.

It's only middling kind.

No, it's good. It's like—"Love means never having to say you're sorry."

It's more like—friendship means never having to check your privilege.

Well, I appreciate it.

Besides, how many times have I complained to you about my kids . . .

Oh my God—I would never resent that.

I know.

For what it's worth, I don't think you have to tell Lincoln that your period is late or irregular. People don't talk to their husbands about their periods.

I do.

Why?

I don't know. Because it's happening. Because I need somebody to get me bananas in the middle of the night, so that I can take my Advil.

Jennifer
You still get cramps?

> **Beth**
> Yeah. Like clockwork.

I don't miss cramps.

> I never thought I would either—but now I think I'll miss the whole thing. The routine of it. The cycle. The *clockwork*. I could depend on it.
>
> What can I depend on now?

Time marching on?

> You're not very comforting.

I know; I never have been. But I'm very good at commiserating.

> You are a genius commiserator.
>
> You're commiserating with me now, and you don't even have ovaries.

Just because you talk to your husband about your period sometimes doesn't mean you have to talk to him about it this time. Do you think he'll notice that you're late?

> No . . . but I think he's already noticed that I'm anxious.

You could tell him why you're anxious?

> What if *he* thinks I might be pregnant? What if he *hopes*?

Would he hope?

> I think he always kind of hoped.

Well, you hoped, too.

> Yeah. But not anymore. I put that behind me.

Maybe he put it behind him, too.

> I don't want to remind him.

You don't want to remind him that you don't have kids?

> Honestly? Yeah.
>
> I try to keep him focused on everything we have. I lean into our assets.

Do you mean that you try to keep yourself focused on what you have?

> It's the same difference!
>
> And I hate to say this, but you were better at commiserating before you went to therapy.

Mitch says the same thing.

> Always with the insightful questions now.

I know. I apologize.

> I can't say, "Lincoln, it's our anniversary, and all I'm thinking about is that my period is late, and that that doesn't mean what it used to mean; it means that it's finally over."

Don't tell your husband, on your anniversary, that it's finally over.

> But it is! You know what I mean!
>
> That isn't going to happen for us now, and I already knew it wasn't going to happen, and I never fought that hard to make it happen. But now it's over. It's over. I'm diminishing. It's time for Galadriel to head into the west.

Jennifer

Is that the Lord of the Rings speech?

Beth

Yes! How did you know that?!!

I know some things. Occasionally.

I think it might be a little melodramatic to announce your perimenopause with a speech from Lord of the Rings.

You know . . .

Normally, you're the one telling me not to be melodramatic and negative.

That was old Beth, flush with estrogen and optimism.

This is new Beth. Crone Beth.

Crone Beth shoots straight. She tells it like it is.

You know what I noticed after my hysterectomy? When I went through overnight menopause?

I remember there were hot flashes . . .

I had so much less patience for people's shit. I think estrogen makes you an enabler. All those mothering hormones—you let people walk all over you. And you feel sorry for everyone. The other day, I was reading People Magazine, and it was some sob story—it's always some sob story—and I thought, "I don't have enough estrogen for this."

You were reading People Magazine?

On my phone. In the News app.

Remember magazines?

Remember newspapers?

I'm part of the old world. I'm a twentieth-century woman. I'm a relic of a forgotten age.

Is this more of your speech?

Lincoln told me that he never planned on having a family. Before we started dating.

Does that mean he didn't want kids?

No, I think it just means he never planned it.

Well, he's not much of a planner.

I am. I had a plan. Four kids, remember? Three years apart?

I remember.

That was so stupid of me.

It wasn't stupid.

I tempted fate.

I don't think you actually believe in fate.

No. I believe in entropy. Which is worse.

I'm going to float a few options here . . .

They're just ideas. You can take them or leave them—or you can keep spiraling. If I were in your position, I'd probably choose the spiral. (Who doesn't love a good spiral?)

Option 1: You could take a pregnancy test. Just to settle that part of your mind.

Option 2: You could set this all aside for a month. This might just be a blip. You might have years of bleeding and cramping left in you.

Beth

I'm not very good at setting things aside.

Jennifer

Me neither.

I'm good at centering them.

Same.

Focusing on them until they take up my entire field of vision.

Is it "naif"?

Is what naif?

Naif/mother/crone.

Definitely no.

Lassie?

Lassie/MILF/rapping granny

We could just google this.

You know I don't like to google. I think it's making our brains rot. Google-assisted dementia.

The other day I was thinking . . .

We think of ourselves—of everything—as having an ideal state. Like, we mature to an ideal state, and then we decay.

What if the middle isn't the ideal? What if every moment along the curve is ideal? Because it's all happening the way it's supposed to happen?

A seed isn't any better than a piece of fruit. Maybe a rotten piece of fruit isn't any worse. It's supposed to rot.

We're supposed to rot.

Maybe the middle part isn't any better than the end.

The middle feels better.

Right. Well. I was thinking all that . . . And then my period didn't start, but I had cramps anyway—and I thought, "A rotten piece of fruit is obviously worse than a seed."

You had cramps anyway?

Yeah. I'll probably have cramps 'til I die.

You know, Lincoln is getting older, too.

Yeah, but men don't radically change. They don't go off. Like a dairy product. They just weather.

That cute guy just walked outside. What is my life.

Is he being creepy?

I don't think so. I'm trying not to look at him.

Beth was sitting on the curb, texting someone. Probably one of her sisters or Jennifer.

She was wearing a sweater he liked. And jeans he liked. When she sat like that, her sweater inched up, and he could see the small of her back. If he got a little closer, there'd be freckles.

She stood up as he was walking toward her. (He'd have to go looking for the freckles later.)

He touched her arm, and she jumped.

"Sorry," he said. "I thought you saw me."

Beth looked startled, wary.

"Beth?"

Her eyes got wide. "Lincoln."

"Sweetie"—he touched her arm again—"are you okay?"

Beth still looked startled. She grabbed onto his new sweater and buried her face in his chest. "Lincoln."

"Hey." He put his arms around her. "What's going on?"

"I didn't . . ." Her words got lost in his chest.

"You didn't what?"

"I didn't recognize you."

"You didn't *recognize* me?" He tried to push her away, but she stayed buried.

"Your hair," she said. "And the mask."

"Hey . . ." Lincoln said. He pushed her shoulder away from him, then reached up and pulled down his mask. "Is that better?"

She looked up at him. Her face and neck were bright red. She nodded. "There you are."

He touched her chin. "Twenty years isn't long enough for me to make an impression, huh?"

She tried to hide her face. "I'm so embarrassed."

He laughed. "It's okay. Hey—" He caught her chin. "Don't hide—it's okay. I wondered why you didn't acknowledge me. I thought you were having some heated text argument."

She laughed, too—finally. "I thought you were some young, cute guy flirting with me!"

"Now you're just covering."

Beth was looking up at him. Her glasses were hanging from her neckline. She couldn't read with them on, and she wouldn't get bifocals. He kissed her forehead.

"I'm not covering," she said. "I did. Ask Jennifer."

"Jennifer will lie for you."

Beth laughed, more and more like herself. "I'll show you." She was still holding her phone. She woke it up and showed him the screen.

"That cute guy just walked outside," she'd texted. *"What is my life."*

Lincoln grinned. He barked out a laugh. It had felt bad for a minute, to think she hadn't known him—that she wouldn't know him anywhere—but now it felt a little better . . .

"Is he being creepy?" Jennifer had replied.

"I don't think so. I'm trying not to look at him."

A new text popped up. *"Beth, are you okay? Is he bothering you? Tell him you're pregnant, and he'll leave you alone."*

Lincoln stopped grinning.

"What?" Beth asked. She turned the phone toward herself, and her face fell. "Oh," she said. "No, that's a joke."

"Oh," he said.

"I'm not pregnant," she said.

He nodded.

"My period's just late."

"Your period's late?"

"Yeah, but not . . ."

"So that isn't why you wanted to go out tonight . . ."

"Oh God—*no*." Her phone buzzed. She pulled her other hand away from him to furiously text Jennifer back. Then she dropped the phone into her purse and looked at him. "No. I'm so sorry. I didn't mean to—I was just talking to Jennifer. About periods and stuff. Menopause. Virgin, mother, crone, et cetera. Not—I'm sorry. I didn't mean to get your hopes up like that."

He shook his head. "It's—" He touched her cheek. "Are you okay?"

She nodded. "Just . . . I really wish my period would start. So that I could stop worrying about it." She laughed. Tearful. "Or I wish it would stop altogether. So that I could stop worrying about it."

"It's 'maiden,'" he said.

"Maiden?"

"The three faces of the goddess. Maiden, mother, crone."

"The goddess?" Beth said.

He pushed his fingertips into her hair. "The goddess."

"Is that something you know from Dungeons & Dragons?"

"And religious history."

"I thought it was just a way to sort women . . ."

"You can't sort women like that. Women are all three."

Beth snorted softly and looked down. "Not me."

Lincoln pulled her closer to him, cradling the back of her neck. He rested his head against hers. She smelled like coconut. "It wasn't hope," he said.

"When?"

"Just now. It wasn't hope. It was surprise."

"I'm sorry about it anyway. The confusion."

He pressed his eyes closed. "I didn't think that was . . . a thing that could happen."

"I don't think it is," Beth said.

He kissed her hair. "Were *your* hopes up?"

She huffed softly. "Always, I guess. Against all odds."

Lincoln found a way to hold her even closer—one arm around her waist, one hand on her neck. "I like that about you," he whispered.

"What?"

"Hope. Against all odds."

"Yeah," she said, "but it's getting a little pathetic."

"Would you really want . . . *that*? Now?"

"I . . ." She took a big breath, and when she exhaled, she sank deeper into his chest. "I'm forty-nine," she said.

Lincoln nodded.

He was forty-nine, too. He liked being forty-nine together. He liked that they moved through the world at the same pace. That they'd gotten here at the same time. Like they were meant to do this together.

"It's more like I never stopped wanting it," Beth said. "Like I never took the time to stop. To close the open window on my desktop. You know?"

He nodded.

"And now my period is late—and I realize that I've got all this old hope sitting around, and I'm not really sure what to do with it."

He took a deep breath, and when he exhaled, he held her closer still.

"I like your haircut," she whispered.

"You won't miss my ponytail?" The stylist had cut off even more than Lincoln was expecting. He hadn't worn his hair this short since high school.

Beth shook her head against his chest. "I missed the back of your neck."

"If you want," he said, "I'll let you pretend I'm a young, close-cropped stranger."

She laughed. "I don't want that. Lincoln?"

"Hmm?"

"Would you want . . . *that*?"

"To pretend to be a stranger? I think it might make me jealous."

"No." She shoved at his belly. "For my period to be late. For the usual reasons."

"Oh . . ." *Would* he want that?

Lincoln had never really dreamt of becoming a father. He hadn't grown up with one—maybe fathers were off his radar.

But Beth wanted kids, Beth had a plan, and Lincoln . . .

Well, Lincoln had wanted Beth.

More than he knew it was possible to want another person.

He felt so lucky to have her, he would have gone along with any plan.

He didn't know how to be a good father, but he figured he'd cross that bridge when they came to it . . .

And then they just never came to it.

They tried a few things. Prescriptions. Injections. He'd wanted it *then*—because Beth wanted it so much.

It was her decision to stop trying.

And Lincoln mourned. But he couldn't have told you, even in the moment, whether he was mourning his own loss or mourning hers.

"I'd be happy," he said now, "if that happened . . . but I wouldn't wish for it."

She didn't respond.

"Is that okay?" he whispered.

Beth nodded. Her shoulders were shaking.

He pulled away from her, putting some air between them, worried that he'd find her sobbing—but it wasn't that bad. Just tears.

"I'm sorry," he said.

"It's okay," she said. "It is okay. That's not why I'm crying."

"Why are you crying?"

"I don't know . . ." Her freckles disappeared into her cheeks when her face got red. "Because I'm old. Because it isn't going to happen, and it's been so long since I actually thought it might. I'm old, you know? I'm a crone."

"There's nothing wrong with being a crone."

"Lincoln"—she thumped his chest—"you're supposed to lie and say I'm not a crone."

"Sweetheart, they're the three faces of the goddess. They're all holy."

"*Lincoln.*"

He brought his hand up to her jaw. "You're exactly where you're supposed to be, Beth."

"You mean, like, '*wherever you are, that's where you're supposed to be*'? Like mindfulness, and Zen Buddhism, and Buckaroo Banzai?"

"No." He shook his head. "I meant—you promised to get old with me, and here you are, keeping your promise."

Beth made a noise like a laugh. She was still crying. She fell back onto his chest, like she was giving up. "We should go put our names on the list."

He put his arms around her again. "I already did."

"I thought we both had to be here."

"We *were* both here."

"Oh. Right."

Lincoln laid his head against hers. "I was coming to tell you, it's going to be at least another twenty minutes."

"I can't believe I didn't know you . . ." she said.

"Hmm?"

"When I saw you tonight. With your mask on."

"You knew me. You just didn't see me right away."

"Did it hurt your feelings?"

"A little . . . I kind of liked being 'that cute guy' again."

"*Ha.*" She was leaning on him, her hands lazy on his sides, playing with his sweater. "I think I would be happy . . ." Beth said, "if it happened. But first I'd be scared. And I'd feel like I was losing something."

"Losing what?"

"What we have now. What the future looks like now."

"Yeah . . ."

"I don't think I'd wish for it," she said. "A baby. Now. Is that okay?"

"Of course it's okay."

"I'm not pregnant, Lincoln."

He nodded his head.

"I'm just getting old."

He wrapped his arms tight around the small of her back. "Keep getting old, Beth," he whispered.

You can read more about Beth and Jennifer in the novel *Attachments*.

Snow for Christmas

BAZ

MY STEPMOTHER SAID SHE DIDN'T WANT A CHRISTMAS gift this year. She just wanted me to meet her for tea when she came up to London to do her shopping.

Daphne grew up in a small town in the north. She gets a kick out of shopping at the big department stores and having tea at Fortnum's with all the tourists.

When I meet her in the lobby, she's laden with shopping bags.

"Basilton, dear," she says, standing on tiptoe to kiss my cheeks. "How will I get all this back to Oxford? Don't you wish there was a Mary Poppins spell? I'd kill for that carpetbag."

"I could ship them for you," I say, taking as many bags as I can. "Or send them; Penelope Bunce has a spell . . ."

"Oh, I'll be fine." Daphne pulls one of the bags away from me. "Don't peek—that one's for you."

I use magic to get us seated right away—the same spell my father always uses, "Ready, set, go"—and Daphne is as pleased as a little girl when the waiter brings us a three-tiered platter of scones, sandwiches, and cakes. It's a damned shame that Simon isn't here. He told me this morning that he's never had a "fancy tea-place tea."

"Your grandmother throws a fancy tea every time you show your face," I said.

"Yeah, but she doesn't have a cake trolley."

"Her entire *house* is a cake trolley."

Simon was standing at the end of his bed, swinging his sword like he was slicing someone in half in slow motion. "Gareth told me that Fortnum's has a cake trolley with Battenberg cake"—he sliced the sword the other way—"*and* Victoria sponge, and a chocolate one . . . and some sort of apple cake. And you can have as much as you want, on top of all the little third-tier things—the éclairs and the what-do-you-call-them, the little cakes wrapped in icing . . ."

I was standing in front of him, tying my necktie, trying very hard not to look impressed with his sword-show. (It's a *constant* effort.) "Petit fours," I said.

Simon swung the sword again, tapping the flat side against my hip. "That's right."

"When did Gareth tell you all that?"

"First year. His mum took him to tea for his birthday."

"I think that's the sum total of what you learned at Watford first year."

"Not true." Simon spun the sword between us and tapped my other hip. "Learned you were a git."

"You're the git." I shoved his chest, and he fell back on the bed, laughing. "I'll bring you back some petit fours in my pocket," I said.

"You better—and cast 'Safe as houses' so they don't get smashed."

I rolled my eyes and pretended I was going to leave without kissing him. It's a good game. He sprang off the bed and pushed me against the wall. (Simon must never get more furniture for this flat; he needs an unusual amount of clear wall space.)

He kissed me soundly. "Hurry back. With cake in both pockets."

"*Mordelia* wanted to come," my stepmother says, jolting me back to the present. "But I told her that I never get you to myself, and that I needed to talk to you about Christmas Eve."

Daphne is spreading a huge glob of strawberry jam onto a scone. She told me she hadn't eaten a single carb all week—not even a carrot—because she was saving them for today.

"What about Christmas Eve?" I ask.

"Well, your father and I hope that you'll be there . . ."

"Of course I'll be there. I always come home for Christmas."

I don't even have to worry about leaving Simon alone this year because Lady Salisbury is going to throw him twenty years' worth of Christmases. He's probably going to get a train set and a rocking horse.

Daphne has paused in her strawberry spreading. She's beaming up at me. "And we hope you'll bring a guest."

"A guest," I say.

She leans forward. "*A guest.*"

My stepmother is a very pretty, dark-haired woman with a toothy smile and toned arms. She's less substantial than my mother in every way. Thinner. Smaller. Less opinionated. Less powerful.

"*It's like,*" my aunt once said, "*your father decided after a lifetime of drinking gin that he wanted a glass of water.*"

Aunt Fiona meant that as an insult. She always makes it sound like my father *left* my mother for Daphne—instead of mourning my mother for years and then washing up, a shell of his former self, on Daphne's shore.

"Like . . ." I say, taking a scone from the basket, ". . . a friend?"

"Like . . . whomever you might like to spend Christmas with," my stepmother says. "I was thinking Simon Snow might appreciate having a place to celebrate."

My mouth drops open. My tongue actually clicks. "Simon Snow."

Daphne is still beaming. "Yes. Your friend."

"My friend Simon Snow . . ." Talking to my family is like playing tennis. You just keep lobbing euphemisms back and forth to avoid saying what you actually mean.

"I've spoken to your father, Basil—"

"You *have*?"

"And we both agreed that it might be very nice for you to have company at Christmas, someone your own age."

I drop the scone on my plate and commence rubbing my eyes with both hands. "Mum. You sound like you're suggesting I bring a friend along on a *ski holiday* . . ."

"Basil, I thought you'd be happy about this."

"Happy?" I look up at her. "You *know* I can't bring Simon home for Christmas. Firstly, because he drained every last bit of magic out of the Pitch family estate—"

"We're prepared to let bygones be bygones. Your father was very impressed with Snow's role in the whole . . . *mess* this summer."

(The mess. When my stepmother joined a magickal cult. And my boyfriend saved the day.) (My boyfriend. Simon Snow.)

"And," she continues, "we agreed to set the past behind us."

"So . . ." I spread my napkin in my lap with a flounce. "Nobody's going to mention the Mage or the Mage's Men or that time Simon arrested Uncle Cyril . . ."

"Why would we? Your father can't stand your uncle Cyril."

"All is forgiven?" I say. "All of it?"

"Basil, none of it will even come up."

"And no one will mention . . ." Am *I* going to mention it? Can I just say it? The thing we're really talking about here? That I'm gay. That I'm practically living with another man. That the reason I'd bring Simon home for Christmas is because I'm in love with him?

Daphne reaches over the table to touch my arm. "No one will mention *anything* that troubles you, Baz. And I know that *you* won't mention anything that troubles your father. We'll have a lovely meal.

And we'll open gifts. We've cleared out the attic and made it into a guest-room—it's all ready. We'll put Mr. Snow up there and you on the sofa. It'll be marvellous, you'll see. It will be a start."

I frown down at my scone, picking at a sultana. Simon in the guest-room. Me on the sofa. No one saying anything to upset each other.

"It's awfully nice of you to invite him, Mum. But Simon Snow is having Christmas with the Salisburys this year."

"Oh," Daphne says. She sounds surprised. And disappointed. "Of course. How very nice for him."

Simon isn't home when I get there. I did bring back petit fours for him and a piece of Battenberg. (I didn't have to use my pockets; they gave me a box.)

I try to study. I have a research paper I'm working on, and I should be happy to have the flat to myself. Simon's out with Penny. Eventually he texts to say he's on his way back. Then an hour later, he texts to say he's *actually* on his way back. I give up on coursework and try to watch a football match, but I can't focus.

When Simon finally gets home, I'm slumped on his pink sofa with my feet on the coffee table.

He walks in and takes off his coat. He's wearing a blue woollen jumper underneath. Simon's a great one for jumpers now that he's figured out how to fold his wings up tight and then hide them under one.

"How long have you been home?" he asks, looking down at the table. "You're still wearing your shoes."

"Oh," I say. "Sorry." I kick off my Oxfords, surely scuffing the backs. They fall in two thumps onto the table. I push them off.

"For fuck's sake," Simon says. "What's got into you?"

"Nothing . . . Long day. Couldn't concentrate."

Simon pulls his jumper over his head and shakes his red dragon wings out behind him. He's wearing one of his new shirts, with flaps that wrap around his wings and cleverly button where he can reach them. "Are you cross with me for getting home late?"

I frown at him. "What? No. Weren't you with Penelope?"

"Yeah."

"Why would I be cross about that?"

"I don't know." He flops down on the sofa next to me, dropping his jumper onto the floor. "Why *are* you cross?"

"I'm not," I say. Crossly.

Simon frowns at me. "You're still wearing your suit." He reaches up and carefully starts to loosen my tie. He's become very skilled at this over the last few months.

"I'm not cross with you," I say.

"Good." He gives the tie a sharp tug and slides it out from around my collar. Then he unbuttons my top button.

"I had tea with my stepmother."

"I know. Did she piss in your Darjeeling?"

"Don't be crass."

"Don't be coy. Tell me what happened."

"She wants me to bring a date home for Christmas."

Simon sits back a little. "A date? Where are you supposed to find a date?"

"Not *a* date," I say. "You. She wants me to bring *you* home for Christmas."

He looks as stunned as I was seven hours ago. "But your stepmother doesn't like me."

"I know."

"And your father *hates* me—I ruined your house."

"I *know*. Daphne says they're letting bygones be bygones."

"Do you believe that?"

"I believe they won't *mention* any of it."

"But . . ." Snow still looks confused. I can see where he's headed next. "I thought your dad didn't know that you're . . ."

"He knows," I say grimly. "He just doesn't approve."

"So why do they want you to bring home your boyfriend?" *(My boyfriend.)*

"I don't know," I say. "To appease me, I think. My stepmother says it'll be 'a good start.'"

Simon sits there with his face all screwed up like he's thinking. His very handsome, freckled face. He's scratching the curls over his forehead with one hand. "Yeah," he says. "All right. I'll go."

I sit up. "Simon, you can't. I already told Daphne you're having Christmas with Lady Salisbury."

"I'll do one day with Lady Ruth and one with you. She'll understand."

"No," I say emphatically. "You're not giving up a loving Christmas with people who accept you to spend the day with people who don't even *like* you."

"They don't even *know* me," Simon says.

"They blame you for the Mage and the Humdrum—"

"You said they won't mention any of that."

"They won't, but—"

"Good." He shrugs. "I won't mention it either. I hate talking about all that shit."

"Simon. My father still refers to you as 'the Mageling.'"

"Your aunt calls me worse than that, and you make me have lunch with her all the fucking time."

"I don't *make* you—and besides, that's different. My aunt at least . . . Well, my aunt doesn't pretend we're just good pals."

"I thought you said your dad knows you're gay."

"He does! But he won't acknowledge it."

"Do you want him to?"

"Simon, they're going to put me on the sofa and you in the guest-room."

"Do you want to *sleep together* in your parents' house—are you mental?"

"I . . ." I feel agitated. I feel thirsty. I should have hunted while Simon was out. I stand up and take off my suit jacket. "I want . . . I don't want to be *closeted* in *my own home* on *Christmas.*"

"*Baz.*" Simon waves his arm and makes a face like I'm an idiot. "They already know you're gay—everyone knows you're gay! Are you upset that you didn't get to give a speech? They invited you to bring your boyfriend home to meet them properly. I've watched enough telly to know that's a good fucking sign. How will you be *less closeted* going alone—than with me right there, sitting next to you?"

"You don't understand," I say.

"I really don't."

I lean over to put on my shoes. "I'm going hunting."

"All right." Simon stands up, reaching for his discarded jumper.

"No, I'm going alone. I need to think."

"All right." He lets his arms hang, still holding the blue jumper.

I finish tying my shoes and grab my coat. I stop in the doorway. I don't turn around.

"I'm coming back," I say.

"I know," Simon says behind me.

When I get back to the flat, Simon is in bed. I don't say anything to him on my way to the shower. All my things are here now. All of my toiletries. My razor. Simon uses whatever soap I leave in the shower. At first I didn't like it. I wanted him to smell like himself, not me. But he still smells like himself.

I climb into the bed. He has a real bed now. I brought my down duvet from my aunt's flat, and my pillows. Simon hogs them. He has all three pillows when I climb into bed. I reach out and pull one, and he rolls towards me, letting me have it.

I feel his arm come round my waist. "I'm sorry," he says.

I don't answer him. But I find his bare stomach. His warm skin.

"I'll go wherever you want me to go," he says. "I'll spend Christmas with Lady Ruth and Jamie. Like I planned."

I bring my hand up to his chest and push. He goes where I want him—on his back, so I can lie with my head on his shoulder. He hooks an arm around me.

"You don't understand," I say.

"You're right," Simon whispers.

"They won't acknowledge me."

"I know."

"We could be married with children—"

"*Could* we?"

"—and my family still wouldn't acknowledge what we are to each other."

Simon is quiet. He's playing with my hair.

"What," I say.

"Nothing."

"I can *hear* you thinking, Snow. It's a grinding noise. Like an engine stuck in gear."

Simon gives my hair a yank. "I still feel like the invitation *is* the acknowledgment. But I hear you, Baz—I do. I understand what you're saying. That you feel . . ."

"Gaslit," I say.

"Right."

"And shamed."

"Right." He kisses the top of my head.

"Like, everything I am is something no one can mention."

"They know you're a vampire, right?"

I lift up my head to frown at him. "*Yes.* They know *everything.* I don't have any secrets from anyone—apparently!"

He's carding his hand in the back of my hair. "Babe. That's not true. Lady Ruth doesn't know you're a vampire. And nobody at school believed me when I told them."

I let my forehead drop on his shoulder and groan.

"Hey." He kisses the top of my head again. "Why don't you come to Lady Ruth's for Christmas with me? We can be as gay as we want there. We can be extra gay, as a treat."

"You're not even gay, Snow."

"I am. For all intents and purposes."

That makes me laugh. He always gets me in the end. I move closer to him, settling onto him. "I'm sorry," I say.

"For what?"

"For leaving without kissing you good-bye."

"Make it up to me."

I lift my chin, and he finds my mouth in the dark. (It isn't hard; I'm always in the same place.)

We kiss. In Snow's bed. (It's our bed. For all intents and purposes.)

I pull away. "I want to go home for Christmas."

"All right," Simon says.

"And . . ." I close my eyes for a second. "I want you to go with me."

"All right," he whispers. He kisses my cheek. "Whatever you want, Baz. Always. Always whatever you want."

Later, as I'm falling asleep, Simon nudges me. "Did you remember to bring me cake?"

"Yes."

"What kind?"

"Battenberg and petit fours."

"Wicked."

"But I ate it."

"You ate my cake? Crowley, you *must* have been a wreck."

SIMON

The plan is, I'm going to ride down to Oxford with Baz today for Christmas Eve, then drive back to London in the morning to have Christmas with my grandmother. Baz borrowed his aunt's car—I'm not sure whether she knows I'll be driving it.

I'm glad Fiona won't be there today. She's spiteful and rude, and her husband gives me the full-body creeps.

Baz's aunt married an *actual* vampire. They all say he doesn't murder people anymore, but "anymore" isn't a very reassuring word. Fiona can't bring Nico home for Christmas because Baz's dad would stake him. I think I'd help.

We have to leave soon, but Baz keeps changing his mind about what I should wear.

He's got me in a tartan suit now. Grey and blue and green, with a little bit of red. Spelled so snug, I can hardly sit down.

"It's a little much," I say, "isn't it?"

"My father will think so."

Baz is wearing tartan, too. Purple and gold trousers, with a dark red, polo-neck jumper.

"Why aren't *you* wearing a suit?" I ask.

He's fussing with my necktie. "Because my father expects me to."

"Yeah, but you *like* wearing suits."

"I can wear a suit every other day." He frowns at the tie and yanks it off. It catches on my collar and pulls my head forward.

"You're really going out of your way to get under your dad's skin," I say. "I'd think bringing me home would be aggravating enough."

Baz opens up my collar and murmurs, "That's better."

Even this little bit of undressing gets to me—I try to catch his mouth. He won't let me, he's all business at the moment. Smoothing down my shirt. Straightening my lapels.

"You don't have to hide your wings," he says, brushing off the back of my jacket, where my wings are folded flat. "My parents know about them."

"I don't want to scare the kids."

I'm nervous about being around his sisters and his baby brother. I never know what to say to kids. I bought them Christmas gifts. Baz told me not to, he says they're spoiled rotten, but I did it anyway.

I hope they're too little to remember the last time I came for Christmas—when they had to flee their house in the middle of the night.

That's the same Christmas I killed the Mage.

And lost my magic.

That's the Christmas when I first kissed Baz . . .

I look up. He's stopped patting and picking at me. He's just standing there, watching me, like he's thinking deep thoughts, too.

"You're the most handsome man I've ever laid eyes on, Simon Snow."

I grin. I get my arms around him. "I thought you said vampires could see themselves in the mirror."

~~~

After I made their castle unlivable, Baz's family moved to a hunting lodge in Oxford. I don't know what I was expecting a hunting lodge to look like, but it's not this—another giant, rich-person house. This one looks right out of a fairy tale. Timber-framed with a thatched roof. A huge wreath on the door.

Baz is getting out his key—it's the size of my hand, an actual metal key—when the door opens. His stepmother is standing there, wearing a floor-length red dress. Baz's stepmum looks like if Billie Piper and Kate Beckinsale had a daughter. She's much younger than his dad. And much nicer, as far as I can tell.

"Basilton," she says, pulling him into a hug.

"Mum," he says, hugging her.

"And . . ." She smiles at me, and it's only a bit strained. I'll chalk that up to embarrassment; the last time I saw Daphne Grimm, she was getting catfished by a magickal cult leader. "Mr. Snow," she says.

"Call me Simon," I say.

"Simon, of course. Welcome. We're so glad you've come."

I'm holding a box of gifts, so she and I are both saved from a hug. She just waves us in and takes our coats away.

Two little girls are already climbing up Baz's legs. That'll be Sophie and Petra. He says I shouldn't bother trying to tell them apart. They're dressed like little dolls—in red velvet dresses, with shimmering gold bows tied at their waist.

"You're too heavy to pick up," Baz groans, lifting them each for a hug. "This is my friend Simon. You've met him before, but you don't remember."

"Hullo," I say.

They narrow their eyes at me. (Maybe disliking me is in their genes.)

One of them pulls on Baz's jumper. "Basil, are you staying the night?"

The other pulls on the other side. "Mum says you're staying the night."

"Mum says we're to be nice to your friend even if he's stupid."

"No—even if he *does* something stupid."

"I'm glad you've been warned," Baz says. "Now get off me. You're ruining my jumper."

Another girl in a matching red dress walks by. She has head-phones on, and she's watching something on her phone. Mordelia.

Daphne's back, and she's holding a toddler (Swithin) wearing a little grey suit with a red waistcoat. Merlin, the whole family is dressed like a royal Christmas card.

"Let me show you the guest-room," Daphne says to me, handing the baby off to Baz. "It's in the attic, I'm afraid."

"I don't mind," I say.

I'm following her out of the room when Baz's dad walks in from the other side.

Everyone changes.

Mordelia pulls off her headphones. Daphne and Baz stand a little taller. The twins stop jumping on Baz and hold their hands behind their backs, as if they're used to being naughty and having something to hide.

I brush my hand against my hip like I've got a sword hidden there. (I don't.) (Baz wouldn't let me bring it.)

Malcolm Grimm is looking right at me. He's as tall as Baz, with a dark suit and snow-white hair. He's handsome, in a cruel and elderly way. Baz and his dad don't really look alike, but they sort of move alike. Stand alike. Frown alike.

Mr. Grimm steels himself at the sight of me. He clears his throat. "Mr. Snow," he says. "Welcome to our home."

"Thank you," I say, deciding not to tell him to call me Simon.

He turns to Baz, and his eyes immediately drop to the purple trousers. His frown deepens. (Has he not seen Baz's flowered suit? It's *much* worse than this.)

"Basilton."

"Father."

"You're looking well."

"Thank you, sir. As are you."

"Yes, well . . ." His dad clears his throat again.

"I was just taking Simon up to show him his room." Daphne links her arm in mine and pulls me towards the stairs.

Baz catches my eye as I go. He looks worried. I wink. We'll both survive this. We've survived everything else so far.

Dinner can't start soon enough.

We spend what feels like hours in the sitting room—just sitting. There isn't a television in here. The twins are fighting over a stuffed toy, and Swithin is climbing over an enormous dog. (A Tibetan mastiff. It's so massive, I thought it must be magickal, but Baz says it's just expensive.) Mordelia is sitting very prettily on a chair, with a blank, bored look on her face.

I've been given a tumbler of scotch, but I'm trying not to drink it. I don't think alcohol is a good idea for me, generally speaking—I've got too much in my life I could fuck up—and it's *definitely* not a good idea tonight. I need to keep what wits I have about me.

I'm sitting on the sofa with Daphne, and Baz is across the room in a chair. We didn't make any effort to sit next to each other—we might not have, in any case—but it feels strange, knowing that I couldn't touch him right now, even if I wanted to.

I never used to like touching Agatha in front of her parents. I didn't want to *remind* them that we were doing stuff together. I wanted the Wellbeloves to trust me and let me be at their house all the time.

Baz's parents will never trust me. And even though we're sitting as far apart as possible, I can tell my being here is making his parents miserable. Daphne won't stop smiling at me, like she's constantly reminding herself to do it, and his dad won't look at me at all.

I tried to get Baz to explain to me in the car why they're so homophobic.

"They're not homophobic," he said. *"They're hetero . . . philic. They're obsessed with making the right choices and being the best at everything."*

"You are *the best at everything."*

"I'm the worst at marrying a powerful girl and having powerful babies, and inheriting my family estate."

"You have to have babies to inherit the House of Pitch?"

"I have to continue the line."

"Fuck that, I'm glad I ruined the place."

"My father looks at me, and he sees a wrong turn. I'm all that's left of my mother, and I'm a dud."

"Can I freshen your drink?" Daphne asks.

"Ah, no," I say. "I'm good." I'd like to ask for water instead. I'm thirsty and hungry, and I can hardly breathe in these trousers.

I suck on a piece of ice and try not to stare at Baz.

He's wearing a dark grey jacket over his red polo neck. He must have magicked it up, because I know he didn't bring one.

I can tell he's on edge. Nervous.

The first time I saw Baz around his family, he was just a boy. But he was cool, calm, aloof. One of them.

Now . . .

Now he's his own man. He stands out. His hair is longer and looser. His clothes are louder. (I know for a fact now that Baz isn't untouchable.)

He looks like he can't quite settle or slide into place. He's on his second drink, and he keeps plucking at his trousers, like he's covered in invisible lint. He isn't looking at me. But he can't seem to focus on anyone else either. His dad keeps having to repeat his questions.

We're all relieved when Daphne says it's time for dinner.

We follow her into the next room. The only time I've seen a production like this was the last time I had Christmas with the Grimm-Pitches. The dinner table is covered in red and gold cloth, and there's a showy red bow tied around each chair. The whole table is filled with silver platters and flowered dishes and coils of decorative ribbon.

"You sit here by me, Simon," Daphne says.

Baz takes a chair at the opposite end, at his father's right hand. There's a gigantic flower arrangement in the centre of the table, and I can hardly see him once I sit down.

"Sorry about the tight squeeze," Daphne says when I accidentally scoot my chair back into the wall. "This table fit perfectly in our old dining room."

The old dining room, in the house I ruined. I wince.

Petra and Sophie are fighting over who gets to sit to the right of Baz.

"Stop this arguing at once," their father says.

"I'll just sit in the middle." Baz starts to get up.

His dad stops him. "No. We don't cave in to their tantrums. Mordelia, come sit next to Basilton."

I stand up so quickly, my chair slams into the wall again. "I'll move."

Baz's dad is looking at me for the first time since he said hello. He doesn't look pleased. "Thank you, Mr. Snow."

"It's Simon," I mumble, trying to get to Baz without knocking into anyone. This room really is much too small for this table.

Baz is gripping my leg before I've even settled down next to him. He's pinching so hard, I think he might be narked at me. But his face is placid and bored.

One of his little sisters flops into the chair next to mine, whimpering.

"Stop making my sisters cry, Snow," Baz says in a droll voice.

He's still clamping down on my thigh. I lay my hand over his, and give it a squeeze. He grabs my hand and holds it tight—and I feel a little giddy with relief. It feels like years since I've touched him. (I might also be giddy from hunger—it feels like years since breakfast.)

The food is already on the table. It's probably been ready for hours and kept fresh with magic. Nobody's been in the kitchen since we got here.

Baz's dad picks up a platter of roasted potatoes and passes it to Baz. "So, Mr. Snow—"

"Honestly, sir," I interrupt. Baz squeezes my hand, but it's too late for me to stop now. "*Please* call me Simon."

"Simon . . ." his dad says. His whole face is pinched up, like that was painful. "What are you studying in university?"

Baz lets go of my hand to give me the platter.

"I'm—"

"He's taking a break," Baz says.

His dad ignores him and looks at me. "A break?"

I'm fumbling with the potatoes. One falls in my lap. "I was study-ing social policy, but it was a bad fit. So I'm . . . taking a break. I've got a job."

"What sort of job?"

Baz hands me a basket of Yorkshire puddings without taking one.

"I work for a builder," I say.

His dad leans towards me. "You're a builder?"

"No." I've taken too many puddings, but I don't think I should put one back. "I'm sort of a messenger for a builder. I am getting my forklift licence though."

"Your forklift licence . . ." Mr. Grimm says. He looks more shocked than disapproving—though I'm sure he *is* disapproving.

Everyone expects me to be doing something great, because I was the Chosen One. But none of my skills are worth anything in the Normal world. Honestly, I'm thinking about joining the RAF—but every time I mention it, Baz throws a fit, and Penny says I'll never pass the physical. I went to a recruiting event for the London police, and neither of them would speak to me for days afterwards.

"What can you do with a forklift licence, Simon?" Daphne asks.

"Um. Lift things, I suppose."

"Can't you use your wand?" one of the twins asks.

"He hasn't got a wand," Mordelia says.

Baz hands me another platter. "Simon is considering the Air Force," he says. "He wants to be a pilot."

I look at him, confused. He very much does *not* want me to be a pilot.

"The *Normal* Air Force?" his dad asks.

I turn to him. "Is there a *magickal* Air Force?"

"Why would you want to be a pilot," Mordelia asks, "when you have wings?"

"*Mordelia,*" her mother says.

"It's not a secret that he has wings!"

"It's impolite to speak about any body part that isn't visible."

"A pilot?" Baz's father says.

"It's just something I've thought about," I mumble.

"He'd be very good at it," Baz asserts.

I spin my head back to Baz, and I hope my face says, *What the actual fuck?*

He hands me the platter of turkey without looking at me.

I take it. I give myself some turkey. "First, forklifts," I say. "Then maybe aeroplanes."

Baz is sitting very stiff and tall, and staring down at his plate rather than making eye contact with anyone.

That's when I notice that he hasn't given himself any food—or hardly any. He's taken the smallest possible serving of everything that's gone by. He didn't take any turkey.

I frown at him and put two slices on his plate.

His father was about to hand Baz the gravy boat. He freezes. They've all gone still. Baz might not even be breathing.

"I'll take that," I say, reaching over Baz. I pour gravy over his turkey, then mine. Then I help Sophie (or maybe Petra) with hers, then hand it on to Daphne.

I put one of my extra Yorkshire puddings on Baz's plate. Then I lay my hand on his thigh.

He can do this. I know he can do this.

⌒

BAZ

I take a deep breath.

The turkey smells heavenly. Vera must have helped Daphne with dinner; that's Vera's onion gravy.

I'm not thirsty. We left London early so I could stop in the woods at the edge of my family's land. I drank an entire deer. I let Simon watch.

I'm still so full of blood that the people around me just barely tug at my fangs. My throat doesn't ache. My sinuses don't burn.

But my fangs don't differentiate between my hungers. They want to drop now. They want to help.

I glance over at Simon—I should throttle him.

He looks in my eyes. He nods.

Then he looks down at his own plate and takes a bite. "This turkey is delicious, Mrs. Grimm."

He squeezes my leg.

He's the only one not watching me.

I take a deep breath.

I breathe.

I pick up my fork. Sophie has leaned over her plate to stare at me. Her hair is dragging in her gravy.

I pick up my knife.

"Really delicious," Simon says.

I cut a piece of turkey.

I breathe.

I feel my fangs twitch.

I remember when they came in—I was eleven. I was at home, in our old house, alone in the kitchen, eating a beef pie that Vera had made for me. My dad had just got remarried. Mordelia was a newborn.

My fangs broke through my gums in the middle of a bite. They sliced into my lips. I ran and hid in the bathroom—I didn't know what was happening. There was blood on my face and hands. I licked away all that I could, then I went looking for more.

Daphne was in the sitting room.

Mordelia was in the nursery.

We had a dog . . .

This is an animal response, I think now, *and you are not an animal.*

I think about contracting. Withdrawing.

I think about how Fiona was the one to find me that night. I was hiding in the barn.

It was late, by then. I was covered in blood. More blood. I burrowed into the straw when I heard her coming.

I thought they were probably all hunting me.

I was glad that it would be Fiona to find me, and not my father.

She saw the dog before she saw me.

"Good on you, Basil."

I sat very still. I didn't breathe.

"I mean it," she said. "What a fucking relief. Come on, come out."

I didn't move.

"Don't make me cast on you," she said.

She was right; that would be ignominious. I stood up, brushing away the straw.

Fiona pointed her wand at me anyway. *"Clean as a whistle!"*

The blood disappeared from my new Watford jumper.

Fiona walked over to me and took me by the chin. She turned my head this way and that. The fangs had long retracted. The cuts on my lips were already healing.

She put her hands on my shoulders.

"You did well," she said. "I'm proud of you."

"Fiona," I whispered.

"Shhhh. You mustn't say it, Basil, ever."

"But Fiona—" I cried.

"Hush now. Look at me. You did well, darling." She shook my shoulders. "I'm so proud of you."

"But—I—Father's dog."

"That was very resourceful of you, Basil. Strong. Smart. I expect no less from Natasha Pitch's son."

I sobbed. Fiona shook me again.

"It was just a *dog*," she said. "And that over there is just a horse. Those are just sheep out in the fields. And deer in the woods. Do you understand?"

I nodded.

"I know you can handle this, Baz. You're a Pitch first and foremost. Everything else is a footnote."

I nodded again.

She wiped my cheeks with her thumbs. "You tell me if you need help, all right? If you get yourself into a scrape. You come to me, not your father—and not Daphne Grimm, all right?"

"Yes."

"I couldn't be prouder of you, Basil. I just couldn't."

I am a man, I think now, sitting at my father's table. *I am a Pitch.*

Simon has his hand on my thigh. Squeezing. Grounding.

I take a bite of turkey. *(Contract, contract, pull back.)*

I swallow.

My fangs stay hidden. I don't have to cover my mouth.

I cut another bite.

"Could you pass me the salt?" Simon asks.

I'm chewing.

Simon lifts his hand to my arm. "Babe? The salt?"

"Of course," I say, reaching for it. I swallow. It's fine.

I glance up at my father. His food is untouched, and he's openly staring at me. His eyes are shining.

At the other end of the table, Daphne is weeping.

"This is excellent," I say. "You've outdone yourself, Mum."

Mordelia is gawking at me. The twins are watching their mother cry. Only Swithin and Simon are eating. (They have very similar table manners.)

"Basilton," Daphne says, through tears. "You didn't get any potatoes." She holds out the platter. Simon takes another serving before he passes them to me.

"Here's the stuffing, Baz," Mordelia says, sending down the dish.

All the plates are coming at me from every direction.

Simon starts laughing. I laugh with him. I have food in my mouth. It's uncouth.

Then my father stands up.

He walks out of the room.

I turn to my stepmother. She's confused, too.

But then he's back—he's got a bottle of champagne. He pops it open with one hand and pours it into my empty water glass. He pours for Simon next. Then for Daphne and a little for Mordelia. And for himself.

"Merry Christmas!" my father says, holding his glass in the air. His eyes are still shining. There's champagne drenching his cuff.

We all hold our glasses up. "Merry Christmas!"

SIMON

I think I got drunk with Baz's dad at dinner.

Not too drunk—because I ate half a turkey and three servings of Christmas pudding.

But his dad kept popping open champagne bottles. And his step-mum kept offering us more food. I thought she was going to feed Baz his pudding herself with an aeroplane spoon.

I've never seen him eat so much.

At one point, when his dad was fetching more champagne, I leaned over and whispered, "They know you're still a vampire, right?"

Baz pushed me back. I was sliding off my chair. "Darling," he said, "you're drunk."

"I can't help it. I can't say no to your dad. He scares me."

"He scares everyone," Mordelia said.

I suppose they were all just happy to see Baz eating. They haven't shared a meal with him since he was twelve or thirteen or whenever it was that his fangs came in.

I can't blame them. It makes *me* happy to see Baz eating, too. If they think this is good, they should see him eat with his giant fangs. They should see him drain a red deer! He's gorgeous. I love him like this. Full. Fed. Easy.

I'm a little drunk.

I don't know how I was supposed to avoid it.

⟋⟍

BAZ

No one asks what's changed. Or what it means. Where my fangs have gone.

For them, the variable factor is Simon.

My father nearly embraced him after dinner. He did embrace me. "Basilton," he said. And, "Good show." And, "We're all very glad, aren't we?"

Simon suggested that my family might think I'm cured. If they do, I'll let them go on thinking it. Cured by homosexuality. Cured by Simon Snow's tender ministrations.

(I won't ever tell them about the Vampire King who taught me to eat with my mouth closed.)

My stepmother hugged me, too. And hugged Simon. The children were all riveted by Father's behaviour. I've never seen him in his cups, so I can't imagine they have.

"Time for this bunch to get to bed," Daphne finally says, when we've run out of champagne and trifle, herding my father and the girls away from the table. Swithin has already fallen asleep in his pudding. "Come along," she says, when the twins protest. "You have to fall asleep, so Father Christmas will come."

"I think Simon and I will stay up and watch a film," I say.

"I want to watch a film," Mordelia whines.

"You can watch a film with us," Simon says. "It's Christmas. Do you like *Die Hard*?"

Daphne frowns. "Come along, Mordelia."

"It's all right," I say. "She can stay up with us."

"If you're sure, Basilton . . ."

"It's fine."

"Yes!" Mordelia says.

Daphne leans close to my ear. "Do you know a sobering spell?"

"I do," I say, smiling at Simon. "I'm giving him a minute to enjoy himself. He never drinks."

She kisses my cheek. "Good night, Basil. Merry Christmas."

"Merry Christmas, Mrs. Grimm!" Simon says loudly.

"Merry Christmas, Simon."

I give Mordelia a shove. "Go and change into pyjamas."

"I'd like to change into pyjamas," Snow mutters as they all go. "I hate this suit."

I grab his shoulder and spin him around, then lift my arm and shoot my wand from my cuff.

"That's dead sexy," he says.

I point it at him. ***"Stone cold sober!"***

He grins. "Are you drunk, Baz?"

I frown. "Clearly not."

He giggles and pushes my shoulder. "I'm immune to magic, you big plonker."

"Eight snakes," I swear. "I forgot."

He wraps his arms around my waist and rests his head on my shoulder. "Change me into pyjamas, would you? I hate this suit so much. I can't even breathe."

The suit isn't immune to magic. I turn it into pyjamas. I let his wings fly free, and Mordelia is properly awed when she sees them— "Wicked!"

We sit on the sofa in the family room and watch *Die Hard* together. Even half-bladdered, Snow knows this movie well enough to skip through all the worst violence and nudity.

He sobers up a bit along the way.

"This was all right, wasn't it?" he asks, when I walk him up to the attic.

"Yes, Snow."

"It's a start, then, isn't it?"

"Knock on wood," I say, knocking on his forehead.

"I wish I could have met your mum. Like, not the ghost version. The real one."

"That was the real one," I say softly. "It wasn't a ghost. It was her."

"I would have liked to meet her like this."

I assume he doesn't mean tipsy and wearing magic pyjamas.

"She was even more traditional than my father," I say. "When she was headmistress, you could get expelled from Watford for—"

"Hey," he says, touching my cheek. "You don't know how she would have reacted."

"I can *imagine*."

"Well, imagine that she would have kept growing, you know? If she'd lived. Her mind would have changed about all sorts of things."

I look in his blue eyes. "Perhaps," I whisper.

"Perhaps," Simon whispers back, smiling. His eyes lose focus for a second, then his brows drop. "She asked me to give you something . . ."

"What?"

Simon holds on to my shoulders and stands on his toes to kiss my forehead.

Then he settles back on his heels and smiles at me. "That."

SIMON

Baz's twin sisters wake me up, both of them banging on the door. "Wake up! Father Christmas was here!!"

The door opens, and Baz peeks in. "They can't open their presents until everyone is awake."

I groan.

One of the girls pushes the door open. "Wake up, lazybones, you're ruining Christmas!"

Baz is grinning at me. He's showered and dressed in fresh clothes. He's drinking tea.

My pyjamas smell like champagne and gravy.

"Wake *up*," the other twin says. "You're being *shocking*."

I manage a quick shower and put on the green jumper and dark jeans that Baz packed for me. I'm only staying to open gifts; I need to get back to London. I wish someone could cast a spell on my aching head—magicians never have aspirin.

When I get downstairs, all the Grimms and Pitches are deeply unimpressed with me. (I suppose there's only one Pitch here. My one.)

Baz hands me a cup of tea, and Daphne gives me crumb cake. And the girls tear into their gifts.

Baz was right, I shouldn't have bothered bringing them books and crayons. The little girls got an enormous dollhouse from Father Christmas, and Mordelia got an actual pony. Baz gave all the girls and women hair barrettes—which pleased them far more than I expected. He gave his father honey made by magickal bees.

(Baz and I are exchanging gifts later. I'm giving him his own side of the room—plus a leather bracelet thing I bought from the spider-woman who makes my shirts.)

His dad isn't being as jolly as he was last night, but he's in a much better mood than he was when I showed up yesterday. He's stopped looking my way and sighing. And he seems genuinely pleased with Baz, who's been nibbling on cake this whole time. His parents are going to stuff Baz like Hansel every chance they get.

One of the twins brings me a gift to unwrap. "It's from everyone," she says. "It's an ugly jumper."

"It's a *lovely* jumper," Daphne says, mortified.

"Thanks," I say, ripping off the paper.

The little girl is leaning against the sofa, squinting up at me. "Delia says you have wings."

"Delia's lying!" the other twin says.

"She isn't lying," I say. "I do have wings."

"Show us!" they both shout.

I glance over at Baz. "You have to ask your brother to cast the spell."

Baz rolls his eyes, as if I'm constantly showing off my wings, everywhere we go.

"Do it, Basilton!" one twin says.

"Give him wings!" says the other.

"I'm not *giving* him wings," Baz grumbles, pointing his wand at me. "I'm setting them free. ***Like a glove!***"

My jumper reshapes itself around my wings, and I carefully unfold them. The twins gasp, and Swithin squeals. "Bird!" he says.

I spread my wings wide.

Baz's father looks dismayed again.

But Baz is smiling at me.

⌒

I get out while the getting is relatively good. Everyone's in a decent mood, and I haven't done anything to destroy their home.

Baz's parents thank me for coming—and they even walk me to the door (possibly to make sure I leave). It makes it awkward saying good-bye to Baz. He hands me Fiona's car keys and my overnight bag.

"I'll see you back in London," I say, "yeah?"

"Yeah," he agrees. "Wish Lady Ruth and Jamie a happy Christmas for me."

"I will."

"Drive safely, Simon," Daphne says.

"Don't worry," I say. "Baz has spelled that car into a tank."

I step outside. And down the steps.

"Simon!" Baz calls. "Your wings!"

I turn back, and he's coming down the steps with his wand out. I pull my wings in tight and wait for him to cast the spell.

"Cover your back!" he casts.

Then he touches my chest and leans in to kiss me. Quickly. On the mouth.

BAZ

I couldn't let him leave without a kiss good-bye. I'd only regret it later.

 You can read more about Simon and Baz in the Simon Snow Trilogy

In Waiting

In Waiting

ANNA DIDN'T SEE HIM APPEAR. HE WAS JUST THERE all of a sudden, walking around, looking disoriented.

"Hey," she said. "You're new."

"Yeah." He ran his fingers through his hair. "I guess so." He laughed. Nervously. Like he wasn't sure he was supposed to. He'd probably never laughed before.

"Hey," she said, more gently. "It's okay. Sit down." She scooted over on her bench. "Get your bearings."

He sat down next to her. He was older than usual. Solidly built. With broad shoulders and a wide face. His hair fell soft and strawberry blond over his forehead.

Everything about him was carefully rendered. Even his sweater had a pattern—a Fair Isle knit.

He pushed his hair off his face again and swallowed. "Am I . . . Is this . . . the story?"

"No. Not yet. This is like . . . the waiting room. You haven't been written yet."

"Okay . . ." He nodded. Then winced, shaking his head. "But I *feel* written."

"I know. It's weird. You'll get used to it—or maybe you won't. You might get drafted right away. That happens all the time."

"It does?"

"Oh, yeah. Usually, even."

"How long have you been here?"

She smiled at him and shrugged. "A while."

The man—he really was a full-grown man—kept looking at her. He was looking at her clothes. Her shoes. Her hair. He was trying to figure her out. He was frightened.

"We haven't had a redhead for a while," she said.

"Yeah?" He breathed out another nervous laugh. "I think I look like someone on a TV show she likes . . ." He shook his head. "But less handsome. Why would she make me *less* handsome?"

"Ah, don't worry." Anna nudged her shoulder into his. "You look very nice. I think if you were any handsomer, you'd be *too* handsome."

"You're being kind."

"No, I'm serious. 'Too handsome' isn't any good at all. If anything, it's creepy."

The man laughed. More naturally.

She went on—"When I see the aggressively handsome ones coming, I know they aren't meant for anything interesting. They can barely hold a conversation."

He was smiling at her. "You've really got the lay of the land here, huh?"

Anna smiled back at him and decided to be honest. She could tell this one was built for conversation—for banter, probably. His eyes were thoughtful, and he had a little smile constantly tucked in the corner of his mouth. It was disarming. Inviting. She should enjoy it while she could. "I've been here years. Since high school, if you can believe it."

"Since you were in high school?"

"Since *she* was in high school."

"That long . . ." He gave her a sad look. He'd been alive for three minutes, and he already pitied her.

"There've been a few close calls," Anna said. "She's gotten me ready a few times. Like, all wrapped up and ready to go. I've got incredible substructure—I even have parents."

"You have *parents*?"

She nodded. "They're kicking around here somewhere. I'll introduce you."

"But you've never . . ." He waved his hand out and vaguely down. ". . . gone *in*? Not all the way?"

"No," she said, and because she knew what the next question would be, she added, "I'm not sure why." She looked away from him. At the park they were sitting in. It was a lovely spring day. The trees were in bloom. The irises were up. There were people everywhere, if you looked for them. "It's been all teenagers and magicians around here for the last few years. She's hardly thought of me."

"Ah," he said softly. "I'm sorry."

Anna looked back at him, smiling broadly. She had small, even teeth and shallow dimples. Her eyes were a specific shade of blue, and her hair parted on the right. "Don't be. It's not a bad life. I mean—it could be worse. It's not like she writes horror stories. She doesn't even write villains, really."

"No villains?"

"Nope. Every once in a while we get what my dad calls a 'complicated character' . . ."

The man's eyebrows pulled up a bit in the middle. It was an advanced expression. Disbelief plus compassion. "I still can't believe you have parents."

"I have a best friend, too! And a career—I even have a cat!"

He grinned. "You're like Barbie."

"Ha!" She elbowed him. "That's something you'll like about this place. We all get each other's jokes."

He looked away from her. At the park. The pathways. The figures moving in the trees. "It never even occurred to me that I'd be here long—certainly not for years."

"Well. Not much has occurred to you, right?"

He turned back to her and settled against the bench, folding his ankle over his knee. "I guess you're right. Still . . . I sort of took shape feeling like I was about to go straight in." He held his hand flat and pushed forward.

"Right into battle."

"Yeah . . ."

"Well, maybe you are!" Anna didn't want to drag him down into the weeds with her. "She's always on deadline. There could be something brewing. You don't seem to be a teenager . . ."

"I'm thirty-two," he said.

"Oh yeah?" She turned toward him, sitting sideways on the bench. "I'm thirty-four. Do you have a birthday?"

"Sometime in February."

She leaned forward. "That's a *really* good sign! I mean, if you're hoping to be a main character."

He cocked a reddish-blond eyebrow. "Don't most people want that?"

"God, no." Anna laughed. "Not even the ones who get chosen. Lots of nervous types around here."

He frowned. "I don't feel very nervous . . . I mean, not constitutionally."

"Really? Hmm. You might not be a main character, then. You could be a romantic lead. Would you like that?"

He seemed to think about it. His chin got all rumply. "Maybe. I mean . . . I'm not against it. Everyone needs a little romance, don't they?"

"I wouldn't know."

His eyes jumped back up to her. "Oh God, sorry."

"Ha." She poked his arm. "I'm just teasing."

"Oh." He looked relieved. "Good. I mean. You know . . . you don't seem very nervous either."

"It's funny you say that." Anna folded her legs, crisscross applesauce. "I was once. I was *really* high-strung. But I've been here so long that there isn't much to be nervous about anymore. Plus I think I've sort of drifted . . ."

He lowered his eyebrows. "From what?"

"From who I was meant to be."

"Out of character?" He sounded shocked.

"I suppose. My mom says I've kind of taken on a life of my own."

"Is that even *possible*?"

"I mean—" She shrugged. "—who's going to stop me?" She held out her hand. "I'm Anna, by the way."

He took her hand. His had heft. It was warm. "I'm James."

"You've got a name!" she exclaimed, shaking his hand. "I didn't want to ask. That's an *extremely* good sign."

"Are there people here without names?"

"Loads! Some of us don't even have faces. There's a guy walking around who's barely a haircut."

James frowned again. "That sounds gruesome."

"Oh no—it isn't. It's a really great haircut. But, still . . . *a name*. That's the last thing she gets to. You're ready to go, buddy. You're the complete package."

"I wonder where I'm headed . . ." He looked around him, then down at his open hands. "It's strange, not knowing."

"Hmm." Anna narrowed her eyes at him. She wanted to help. "Let's think about this. You're thirty-two . . . Can you do magic?"

"No, I don't think so."

"Are you a vampire?"

"No," James said, affronted. "I'm a sociologist."

"You could be both."

He laughed. "I appreciate the encouragement. But I'm just a red-haired man with an overbearing mother and a Scion xB."

"James! You have a mother? You have a *car*?"

"I guess I do . . ." he said, surprised.

"You are not long for our world, friend—I shouldn't even bother getting to know you!"

His face fell. Compassionate again. "Anna, I'm sorry."

"Stop *apologizing*," she groaned. "I'm still just teasing. I'm *happy* to get to know you. I mean, I don't mind teenagers—or vampires, for that matter. But it's nice to talk to someone my own age."

She smiled at him. He smiled back.

His eyes were a *very* specific blue. Pale. Almost icy.

"Are you feeling any better?" she asked. "We could take a walk."

"Don't I need to stick around? In case she . . ."

"She won't call your number or anything. She'll just take you."

He was concerned, careful. "And she'll be able to find me? Even if I walk around?"

"Oh yeah, this is all the same place. You can't really hide from her."

"Okay, then, yeah. Let's walk."

Anna hopped off the bench, and James followed her. She led him along one of the paths, through oak trees. There was water flowing somewhere, but Anna had never been able to find it. It must belong to someone else.

James was quite a bit taller than her. He walked with his hands in his pockets. He was wearing faded green cotton pants and sensible leather shoes. He could be in any sort of story. He was stolid and reassuring. His face was freckled, and there were laugh lines around his eyes and his mouth.

"Do you usually stay around here?" he asked. "On the bench?"

"Oh no, I get around. I have a house."

"You have a house? I don't think I have a house . . ."

"At first, I just had a room," Anna said, "but there's a whole house now. Do you want to see it?"

"Yeah," he said. "Do you mind?"

"No, not at all. Come on."

She led him along the path. She could get to the house by deciding to get there, and it only took as long as she wanted it to.

She decided to give it a few minutes. She liked walking with James. She wasn't in any hurry. There was only so much she could show him anyway. There was only so much here.

The farmhouse appeared in the distance. They turned down the gravel driveway.

"You live on a farm," he said.

"Yeah, I think it's one of the places she lived when she was a little girl. I was a little girl when I first got here."

He stopped to look at her. "Wait, you grew up here?"

"Sorrrt of . . ." she said, cocking her head. "It's more like she *grew* me up. Revised me up. Over the years."

James smiled gently. His eyebrows were raised in the middle again. "Anna, that's so weird."

She goggled her eyes. "I *know*."

"How long have you been thirty-four?"

"A decade at least." She reached out and tugged on his forearm. "Come on."

She pulled him through the yard. There were chickens out pecking in front of the coop. There were goats, too, in the back. There'd been a horse for a while, but not anymore.

The front door wasn't locked. Anna took James through the old kitchen. There was a pump by the sink and a big table instead of counters.

She showed him the living room with the antique sofa and the television . . .

She never told anyone else about the television—they'd be so jealous. The house always made people jealous at first. Then, over time (it usually took longer than three minutes), they saw it as something pitiful. And then, over more time, it scared them. The older ones wouldn't come anywhere near it. They acted like it was haunted. Like Anna was the ghost.

But James wouldn't be around long enough for that. She showed him her bedroom, with the homemade quilt and stuffed animals. "I don't know why those are still here. Everything's a bit haphazard."

She showed him the bathroom with the pedestal sink and the cast-iron tub. "Do you have to go to the bathroom?" she asked.

"No."

"No," she agreed. "No one ever does."

They ended up on the front porch, on the old wooden swing.

"This is really lovely," James said. He was looking out over the wheat fields and unconsciously rocking the swing with one foot on the floor.

Anna crisscrossed her legs. "Thanks."

A fat orange cat ambled up the front walk. Anna held out a hand, snapping and clicking her tongue. "Here, Peaches."

The cat came to her, jumping up into her lap. Anna laughed, petting him.

"Even your cat has a name," James said.

"Well . . ." she said. "Sort of." She was blushing. "I mean—I named him."

"Can you *do* that?"

Anna glanced up at him. "Who's going to stop me? I'm sure she'll rename Peaches if she ever uses us. But she might *not* use us. She might make Peaches a dog in the end. He may as well have a name while he's here, right?"

James was watching Anna, smiling just with his eyes and one side of his mouth. "Yeah."

"You can pet him if you want."

James reached out and scratched Peaches between the ears.

"That is your first cat petting," Anna said.

"No," he said. "I've petted plenty of cats."

"In your backstory," Anna said. "But not here. It's different—can't you feel it?"

He kept scratching. Peaches closed his eyes, purring. "No," James said. "I don't think that I can."

"You will," she said, "if you try. If you have enough experiences here. You'll feel the difference."

"I feel like I'm being *pulled*," James said. He seemed agitated. He stopped touching Peaches and looked out over the fields. "Do you feel it, too? It's like I'm meant to get into my book. Like I can't be delayed."

"I'm not delaying you." Anna tried not to sound defensive. "I'm not a *trap*."

"No." James looked back at her. "I didn't think you were. But do you feel it?"

"Yeah," she said. "Everyone feels it. But you can't really act on it. All you can do is wait. You're here until she needs you."

"But why would she make me and then leave me here? Why would she leave *you* here, with all of this? It doesn't make sense."

"Well, she can't use all of us," Anna said. She tried to be practical. "Some of us are just extra."

"And you're at peace with that? You're not frustrated?"

"I was frustrated for a *while* . . . I used to get up every morning and get ready. But . . . I couldn't sustain that, you know?"

"How do you feel now?"

"I feel . . ." Anna sighed. She looked down at Peaches. She never really talked about this. Who would she tell? Her parents? Her best friend? That seemed unkind. They were only sketches compared to her. They might never get filled in.

Anna almost never met someone like James. Someone with clearly drawn outsides and clearly drawn insides. Someone with carefully developed emotional maturity. James didn't even realize how special he was. How lucky he was. He wouldn't be here long— she was surprised he'd lingered at all.

"I feel forgotten," Anna said. "Mostly. Like . . . I must have been fascinating once. For her to build all this for me." She looked around the yard. "I must have had promise. But then she just . . . set me aside. It's a bit like knowing someone has fallen out of love with you."

James listened. Even after she'd stopped talking.

Anna kept looking at Peaches. "I mean, not that I know how that feels . . ."

"You've never had a love interest?" he asked.

"No." She looked up at him. "Which is strange. Most people around here come in pairs."

"Maybe it isn't that you were forgotten," James said carefully. "Maybe she's saving you for something really good."

Anna smiled. "That's very optimistic of you, James."

"I think I might *be* optimistic," he said.

"Likable," she said. "Sympathetic. Almost creepily handsome. I have a good feeling about you."

He laughed and seemed to relax. He was still rocking the swing with his ankle. It was nice. Comforting.

Anna felt for him. She could still feel the pull, too, underneath everything. But she was so used to it. It was like gravity for her.

"Can you make friends here?" James asked.

"Yeah. Of course."

"Even if you're not meant for the same story?"

"I mean, *yeah*," Anna said. "Relationships don't have to be eternal. People come and go from your life."

"I suppose that's true."

"I've had a few friends here for years."

He rested an elbow on the back of the swing and rested his head in his hand. "Has anyone been here longer than you?"

"No one who's stayed."

"You mean no one who hasn't ended up in a story?"

"Not everyone ends up in stories."

He looked concerned. "What do you mean?"

"Well, some people fade," she said matter-of-factly.

"They *fade?*"

"Usually the ones who fade start out blurry. They just never take shape, and then they—" She waved her hand. "—fade away."

James looked concerned. "Has anyone with a name faded?"

"Yeah. Sometimes."

"That's awful."

"Oh." Anna should be more thoughtful. None of this was matter-of-fact for him. And he was *full* of feelings. His personality must be a mile deep. "James, that's not going to happen to you. You burst into life fully formed. That's *such* a good sign."

"You're sure?"

"Oh yeah. You're like a tool built for a very specific job. I really think you'll go in as soon as she has a chance to sit down."

He tipped his head into his hand and scratched his head. "I shouldn't let you comfort me like this. It's very selfish."

"I don't mind," she said. "I'm just being honest."

"Honest," he said. "Likable. Sympathetic."

"Stop," she said, smiling. "Are you hungry?"

"Is there food here?"

"So much food," she said, "everywhere you turn. There's always a cake on my kitchen counter."

"What kind?"

"Lemon with coconut frosting. Sometimes pineapple upside-down cake."

"And we can eat it?"

"*Yes.*" Anna stood up, scooping Peaches out of her lap and onto the porch.

The cake was delicious. The plates and silverware were antiques.

Anna's parents came home after a while. They were blurry; she could tell it made James nervous. She took him back out to the porch swing.

"Why do you think you still live at home?" he asked her.

"I don't think she's gotten around to figuring that out. This house is full of narrative inconsistencies. Ideas dropped on top of older ideas. It's a mess."

"I kind of like it," James said. The sun was setting over the fields. "Why does the sun set?"

"I don't know," Anna said. "To keep us sane?"

He laughed. "I feel tired. Is that crazy?"

"No. I think it's another good sign. Not all of us sleep."

"Do you sleep?"

"Yes. Sometimes I even dream."

James giggled. Like that was too much.

"You could stay here," Anna said, too quickly. Too hopeful.

He glanced at her. "Do you have room?"

Theoretically, she thought. "Yeah," she said.

They watched the sun set. James wanted to know more about main characters. Anna described every one that she could remember.

"They seem like a troubled bunch," he said. "Damaged."

"I guess so," she agreed. "But not irreparably."

"I'll take your word on it—but I don't think I'm a main character. I feel mostly fine."

"The main thing about main characters," Anna said, "is their definition. The light hits them differently. Like . . . they have blue veins in their arms and dry skin on their knees. They have a distinct way of holding their shoulders. They have nervous tics and a hundred smiles. They stand out from a mile away."

James was listening, watching.

"You're wearing brushed twill trousers, James. And even your freckles are in focus. Someone took a lot of care with you."

"I shouldn't let you comfort me," he whispered.

"I'm just being honest. Come on, I'll show you your room."

There'd always been a door between Anna's bedroom and the bathroom. It never opened. Tonight she tried it anyway.

It opened.

Into a hazy void.

Anna quickly pulled the door shut. "Let me try that again."

She closed her eyes and pictured a room. What kind of room would James like? Something simple. Reassuring. She pictured a bed like hers, but with a green wool blanket. With clean white sheets and three feather pillows. With lace curtains. And a window cracked to let in the breeze. She added a pitcher of water and a basin. Even though that seemed antiquated. She imagined it all. Then she opened her eyes and smiled up at him. She opened the door into the room.

"Anna . . ." James whispered. "Did you do this?"

She didn't answer.

"Can everyone do this?"

"No," she said softly.

"How . . ."

"I've been here so long," she said, "I think I might be merging with the equipment."

James huffed out a laugh. Like he was overwhelmed and also a little spooked. "Is it safe?"

"I can't hurt or hide you," she said. "And I wouldn't. It's safe. It's all the same place. I promise."

"Okay." He looked down at her. "I believe you. Thank you."

"You're welcome . . . There'll be breakfast in the morning. Homemade biscuits."

"I'll see you then. Good night, Anna."

"Good night, James."

Anna lay in her bed, listening to the wind and feeling . . . light. Feeling exhilarated. She'd never had anyone stay the night before. She hadn't met many people like James. People who were her age. People who could talk the way he could talk. Who could sleep. And eat cake. And got scared in a way they could articulate.

She thought about his strawberry-blond hair and his pale blue eyes.

She was waiting for him when he came downstairs the next morning wearing the same green pants and cream sweater.

Anna had changed. She had a closet full of dresses—and matching shoes if she wanted. Even some hats. She really was like Barbie.

"Looks like the house didn't eat you," she said.

"Good morning," he said.

"Good morning. Did you sleep?"

"Like a baby—and you were right."

"About what?"

"It *was* different. From my memory of sleeping."

She gripped her coffee cup in both hands. "*Yeah?*"

"*Yeah.*" He seemed excited, too. "Like, the texture was different. If I thought about it too hard, the feeling slipped through my fingers. But it was still there."

Anna nodded her head. "That's it exactly. It's everywhere," she said. "That feeling. Everything is a little different here. This experience is different."

James shook his head. Shaking it off. "It was wild. Can I have some coffee?"

"Your first cup of coffee," she said.

He laughed. "I guess so."

They ate breakfast, and she asked if he wanted to meet some of the other people who lived here. That seemed to make him uncomfortable.

"Maybe if I end up staying," he said. "But if I'm only going to be here for another day or so . . ."

"That makes sense," Anna said. "Besides, you'll just make them all jealous."

She was glad he'd said no. She wanted him to herself. After breakfast, they took a walk in the wheat fields. James had grown up in a city. This was all new to him. He asked her more questions. About how the world worked. She couldn't answer all of them, but she could answer better than anyone else here.

They came back for lunch. Grilled cheese sandwiches. "Does your mom make these?" he asked.

"No, they're just part of the house. Vestigial narrative."

That amused him. Anna amused him. He was always smiling at her. It was incentive to keep talking.

After lunch, they sat on the porch again. James told her what he knew about himself. He was a sociologist. He worked at a university. He got excited when he realized they were both from Nebraska.

"That's nothing," she said. "We're all from Nebraska. It's like how Stephen King's characters are all from Maine."

"Oh." He hunched back into the swing, disappointed. "Well. I'm a professor, but I do research, too. I was married once, in my twenties, but it didn't last. I'm not very good at dating."

"You are *such* a love interest," she said.

"Wouldn't not-being-good-with-girls make me a *bad* love interest?"

"Uh. No. Sweet that you think so."

James was blushing. "Well. I . . . mostly deal with my mom and the guy in the office next to mine—I wonder if they're here?"

"Can you picture them?"

"Not really."

"Probably not, then. But you might have an office."

"My office . . ." he said. "The whole campus. How would we find it?"

"You just have to set your mind to it," Anna said. "If it's here, we'll get there."

James stood up. He walked off the porch. Anna followed him up the driveway and down a path, onto a university campus. She'd never seen anything so expansive—it took her breath away.

"James . . . this is magnificent."

"I think she went to school here," he said. "That makes it easy to conjure, right?"

The buildings got fuzzy when you got close to them, and they kept changing places. But the building where James worked was solid. The staircase smelled like wood polish. The door to his office was open. He was delighted. "This is it," he said. "This is mine."

"It's gorgeous," Anna said. There were papers on his desk with actual writing. There were framed photos with real people in them.

James sat in his desk chair and spun around. Anna leaned against his desk. "You're happy here," she said.

"Because it's mine."

"No—you're happy here. Canonically. You like your job."

"Oh." He looked thoughtful. "I think you're right. That's nice, isn't it?"

"It is."

"I want to show you the vending machines," he said. "The break room has the best vending machines."

She followed him to the break room—the only other door that would open—and he bought her an ice cream bar.

"Are you happy in your house?" he asked, biting into one of those pre-wrapped cones.

"I am," she said, "but I don't think I'm meant to be."

"Explain."

"I think I'm meant to feel comfort there, but also fear."

"Fear of what?"

"I don't know," Anna said, "and that's why it's sort of faded. I don't think she's ever thought that part through. The threat."

"So you've just decided not to be afraid of it?"

"I guess so."

"That's extraordinary, Anna. I can't even imagine not feeling what I'm meant to feel."

"That's because you're new," she said. "You're still infused with purpose. And you don't have contradictory experiences."

"I must seem like a baby to you."

"You seem mint in box," she said. "Internally consistent."

That made him smile.

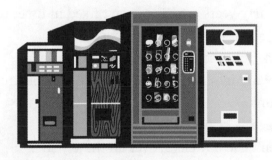

They wandered around campus for a while, but the farther they got from James's office, the more faded everything was.

Eventually he asked if they could go back to her porch swing.

"You don't want to look for your house?" she asked.

"I don't think I'm meant to feel happy in my house," he said.

"What do you remember feeling there?"

He thought for a moment. "Lonely."

"Fuck that," she said. "You can wait at my house."

They spent another evening on the porch swing. Anna kept expecting him to disappear. She didn't know what was taking so long—he was so *ready*.

She'd met people over the years who started to disappear as soon as you said hello. People who flashed before your eyes. That's one reason Anna liked to sit in the park. To see who showed up. To see how long they stayed.

It used to make her bitter. She used to sit there hating them. Hating *her*.

But now . . . Anna was just curious.

They found beer in the refrigerator, in her kitchen. Miller beer in clear bottles. Anna had never tried it. There wasn't a bottle opener, so James knocked the caps off on the porch railing. "These beers are thirty years old," he said. "Look at the labels."

Anna looked. She didn't know what beer labels looked like these days. She wasn't sure if she was supposed to be thirty-four years old *now*. Or thirty years ago. She wasn't fixed in time, really. It was another thing about her that was undecided.

"I hope I'm going somewhere with a porch swing," James said, kicking the swing into motion. "What sort of book are you meant for, do you think?"

She shrugged.

"You haven't had any clues, over all these years?"

"I don't think she knows," Anna said. "I think that's one of the problems. I think she built me before she knew how to build a story. So I'm more of a daydream than anything else."

James nudged her with his elbow. "Don't say that." He took a sip of his beer. "You're too well developed for that."

"Well, thank you," she said. "But . . . it's a cheat, I think." She took a second. She might as well tell him, he'd be gone soon. It would be nice to tell someone. "I'm pretty sure *all* of this is autobiographical."

He shrugged. "Everything is autobiographical, right? Like my campus?"

Anna pursed her lips. "Mmm. It's different. There's borrowing details and settings and traits. And then there's . . . Well. Then there's . . ." She looked down at her beer. She didn't really like the taste. She was going to offer it to James when he finished his.

"There's you," he said, watching her.

She nodded. And then she sighed. And nodded some more.

"That's got to be an advantage," James said softly. "For getting in."

"I think it was, at first," Anna said, earnestly looking up at him. "You know how you shove yourself forward when you're young? But then, over time, maybe you don't want to show people all that. Maybe there are things that are more valuable if you keep them to yourself."

"You can't be sure of this," he said. "You're just theorizing."

"I guess I've had plenty of time to tell myself stories."

James smiled at her. He looked down at her lap. "You don't like beer?"

"This," she said, holding up the bottle, "is my first beer."

He clinked his bottle against hers.

"And my last," she said. "You can have it."

He smiled and took it. "At least I won't be leaving you here alone with a drinking problem."

"You won't be leaving me here alone," she said.

The next day, they took another walk through the fields, and Anna showed James the tree she'd used as a playhouse when she was a little girl. It was more real than his office. You could even see the patterns in the bark.

The next day, James woke up with a last name. MacIsaac. He was giddy about it. So Anna was giddy, too. She called him "Mr. Mac-Isaac." They celebrated with lemon cake.

In the middle of his second slice, he said, "I'm not a sociologist anymore. I do something for the government."

"She's working on you," Anna said. "Right now."

They both sat still at Anna's table, waiting for James to change before their eyes. His sweater was replaced with a white button-down shirt. The top button was undone. She could see the freckles on his chest.

But he didn't disappear.

~~~~

The next day, crazy old Renee got called up. (Or down. *In.*) Renee had been here for years. She wasn't even a *character*. She was just a tank top with an obnoxious laugh. She sounded like a donkey.

James had never met Renee, but he was devastated by the news.

"Don't be jealous," Anna said. "She'll probably get sent back."

"People get sent *back*?"

James went inside and got a himself a beer, then he took a long walk in the fields. He didn't want Anna to go with him.

Anna waited for him on the porch swing. She wasn't sure James would make it back without her.

He did. Long after dark.

He walked in slow strides up to the porch. "Hey," he said.

"Hey," Anna said. "I didn't know if you'd be able to find your way."

"The fields disappeared as soon as I couldn't see the house. But . . . it was all here again when I came back for it."

"I'm glad," she said.

"Can I sit with you?"

"Of course."

He dropped down onto the swing, and it rocked for a few seconds.

"There's dinner inside if you want it," she said. "My parents are in there watching TV."

"I should be nicer to your parents."

"I know they make you nervous."

"Still . . ." He sighed and rubbed his face. "I just want to go *so bad.*"

"I know."

"It feels so *urgent.*"

She nodded.

"And I don't even know why! I just feel like I'm supposed to be somewhere else. Like I'm a piece in a larger puzzle, and all I want is to click into place."

Anna didn't say anything. It didn't seem like she should. She didn't feel anything urgently. (Except maybe urgently wanting James to stay.)

It hardly bothered her anymore when other characters were called in. She was so used to it—sometimes she was relieved. They got some unbearable smart-asses around here. Good riddance to them.

It was a little insulting to think that *Crazy Old Renee* got the call before *Anna,* but Anna still wasn't upset about it.

"I feel like I have a job," James said, "and she won't let me do it. It's *infuriating.*"

"I'm sorry," Anna said.

"I don't work for the government anymore, by the way—I'm writing a book."

"What about?"

"I don't know." He sounded glum. "It feels like she's losing the thread."

Anna put her hand on his knee and gave it a reassuring squeeze. "She's just working on you."

James covered her hand with his own and squeezed back. "I realized tonight . . . she doesn't have to use me. She could come up with someone entirely new. And then I'll just fade out."

"That won't happen," Anna said. "You're too lovely."

James breathed out a laugh. He rolled his eyes. "I'm lucky you found me in the park. I'd still be wandering around like a lunatic."

"Someone else would have helped you. Everyone here is pretty helpful. Even the ones who don't have faces."

⟋⟋

The next day, they were walking in the fields, and the snake was there. How had Anna forgotten the snake?

She froze. Just like she always did. Every time, no matter how old she was.

"What the fuck," James whispered.

The snake rattled its tail. It wound its way closer.

"Don't move," Anna said through her teeth. "It won't hurt us."

"Then why are you afraid?"

The snake slid closer. It wouldn't hurt them. It would brush over her foot and against her ankle. She just had to stand still.

It got closer. Anna was just as afraid as she'd ever been. She'd never acclimate.

The snake was close to her shoe.

James lifted up his boot—he had boots now—and stomped on it.

"Mother *fucker*," James said, rubbing both hands through his hair.

Anna took a shuddering breath. "You killed it . . . You killed it! How did you do that?"

"*Fuck*," James said. "Was that a rattlesnake?"

"Yeah. You killed it. I didn't know—"

"Anna, that wasn't a setting—that was a scene. Do you have *scenes*?"

"A few."

"Jesus." He put his hands on her shoulders. "Are you okay?"

"I'm fine."

"Does it usually bite you?"

"No, it just touches me."

"Fuck." He pulled her into a hug. "I'm still glad that I killed it."

Anna leaned against his chest. He had a distinct smell. Like soap and antiperspirant and beer. (Why did James have a *smell*? Was he a character or a fantasy?)

He squeezed her. "I hope it never comes back."

"Me, too," she said.

"Christ."

She laughed. She pulled away. "Let's get out of here."

They went back to her house and ate Banquet TV dinners out on the porch.

"I haven't had one of these since I was a kid," James said.

She was fascinated by his backstory. Anna didn't have much of a backstory. Even though she had an elaborate setup. She was like a doll sitting in a dollhouse, surrounded by furniture.

James had *memories*.

Anna had memories, too, but they were mostly of this place. Her backstory was only a few scenes long. A few disjointed flashbacks.

James's character kept shifting. It was driving him crazy.

"Oh God," he said, when they were done eating.

"What?"

"Nothing." He looked upset.

"James—what?"

"I'm not James anymore. I'm Isaac."

"But your last name—"

"Not anymore."

"She's working on you," Anna said. "It's a good sign."

He sighed.

"She's kept all the important parts," she said. "You've still got red hair and nice shoulders."

That made James laugh. He rolled his eyes, he tried to relax. "So, your character has shifted a lot over the years?"

"I mean, I was eight when I started, so yeah."

"Have you always been 'Anna'?"

"Yeah, but . . ."

"What."

"Well . . ." She looked at him for a second, deciding whether to say more. "For a while, I could open portals into other dimensions."

James—Isaac—guffawed.

"It's not funny," Anna said, laughing.

"How did that even work?"

"I don't know." Her shoulders were shaking. "She never hammered it out. My eyes glowed."

James—she was just going to keep calling him James—was still laughing. "You really were a Stephen King character."

"I had siblings for a while."

"And then they faded? That sounds traumatic."

"It wasn't so bad. I'd already been here for years, and they were so sketchy. Like, sometimes there were three of them, and sometimes there were four . . ."

James leaned back in the porch swing. He was looking up at the stars. "Do you think people remember this place? After they leave?"

"No. Why would they?"

"Maybe some of it sticks," he said. "In our subtext."

"Maybe," Anna said, crossing her legs, letting him rock the swing. "But I don't think so." She looked at his face. In profile. He had strong cheekbones and a strong nose. A dramatic jaw. Everything about him was solid. "Why do you think we want to be in stories?" she asked.

He turned back to her. "Because that's what we are?"

"Yeah," she said, "but as long as we're here, we get to keep going. The story is the *end*."

"It's not the end, it's the destination."

"But everything stops then, right? Everything gets locked down. As long as we're here, we're doing new things. We're changing. But once we're in a book . . . that's it."

James had one eyebrow cocked down. Thoughtfully. "Once we're in a book," he said, "we've landed exactly where we belong, and we get to stay there forever."

She smiled at him. At his stolid face and his blue eyes. The red hair falling over his forehead. "You're very optimistic, James."

He smiled a little at the name. "I am," he said. "Unwaveringly."

He made an effort to talk to her parents on the way up to bed. He couldn't quite look in their eyes.

Anna said good night to him at his door, and then went to her room and changed into her nightgown. (She had multiple nightgowns. She had a winter coat. She had a hint of backstory about ice-skating.)

There was a knock at her door. She went to open it. James was standing there, grinning.

"Anna," he whispered. "I'm James again."

She grinned up at him. "Good night, James."

She went to bed, knowing that he was still changing. That he might disappear. She wished that she had a camera. Or a way of keeping part of him.

"Don't you get bored?" James asked. They were sitting on the swing, watching the chickens.

"Not really," she said. "If you weren't here, I'd be at the park, meeting the new people and chatting with friends. Everything's always in flux."

"Why haven't you taken me back to the park?"

She looked at him. He'd wanted to wear something different today, so she'd lent him an oversized blue cardigan. "I thought it might discourage you," she said. "To see people come and go."

He didn't argue. They were drinking lemonade. "What kind of book *wouldn't* you want to live in?" he asked.

"A horror novel," she said. She didn't have to think about it. "Or a war story. What about you?"

He cocked an eyebrow, thinking. "I really hate space."

That made Anna laugh. "Why do you hate *space*?"

"There's nothing there but death."

"And aliens," she said. "And Han Solo."

"No, thank you."

"What kind of book are *you* hoping for?" she asked, leaning her shoulder into his.

"I think, when I first got here, that I wanted to end up in something like . . . a dramatization of historical events."

Anna snorted.

"But now," he said, "I think that's the kind of book I'd like to read, not live in."

"So what *do* you want?"

"I just want to grow," he said. "I want to feel more comfortable in my life. I want more supporting characters."

"You might *be* a supporting character," she teased.

"You told me I had leading man written all over me."

"I told you you looked like a love interest—there's a difference." She was trying not to smile, but she was still smiling. Her lips were twitching.

James was smiling, too. His eyes were twinkling. "I'll take it," he said. Then, "What about you? What kind of book are you hoping for?"

"As long as it's a book," Anna said, "I don't really care. She better not waste me on a short story."

That made James laugh. "Are you kidding? It would take half the story to describe your weird house."

～

A week passed, and James didn't change very much. Anna could tell he was disappointed, that he felt abandoned. But he didn't storm off again. He told her he wanted to meet more of the people here.

She walked around with him, dutifully making introductions. "What is *he* doing here?" a rare unused vampire asked Anna behind James's back. "He's practically in 3D."

"I know," Anna whispered. "He'll probably be gone soon."

The vampire shook her head. She had a very distinct sense of humor but only a blur of a face. "The only one around here with that much precise detail is you, Anna."

Anna shrugged. She hoped that James hadn't heard. He wouldn't like being compared to her.

When they got back to the farmhouse, James was tired. He didn't want to sit on the porch, so they watched TV with her parents.

"What are we watching?" he asked, twenty minutes into the show.

"*Gunsmoke,*" her dad said.

"I don't think your parents are much older than you," James said, so that only Anna could hear him.

"They've never been revised," she explained.

After her parents went to bed, Anna and James stayed up, sitting on the couch. He seemed lost in thought.

"What's wrong?" she asked.

"I was just thinking—now that I'm not a sociology professor, I can't go back to my office and buy ice cream bars."

"I'll bet the vending machines show up somewhere else," Anna said. "She liked those."

"I really wanted to be in a book with those ice cream bars," James said sadly.

Anna laughed.

They were sitting right next to each other on the couch. Her mother had turned off the TV but left on a lamp.

"I don't want to be in a book with any of this stuff," Anna said quietly.

James lifted his head away from the couch to look at her. "What do you mean? You've got great stuff here. It's all so vivid."

"I don't know what sort of story she has in mind for me . . ." Anna said. "But it's not a romantic comedy."

He was just watching, listening.

"This is a story with a little girl who's supposed to feel scared all the time. I may not feel it anymore—I may not be a girl anymore—but it's in the bones of this house. It's why she built it. She put a snake in the field that I can't run from . . ." There were tears running down Anna's cheeks. She wiped them with the back of her hand.

James helped her, wiping her cheeks with his big thumbs. He looked concerned. And worried. "Anna . . . Are you hiding here? From your story?"

She shook her head no. Her voice was very low: "But maybe *she's* hiding me here. For a reason."

James was frowning. Probably because he couldn't think of anything optimistic to say. He put his arm around her instead, and hugged her into his side. He was still wearing her sweater. He was big and warm. And temporary.

James woke Anna up the next morning. Knocking on her bedroom door.

Anna sat up in bed. "Come in?"

He ducked in. He was already dressed—in a new cardigan of his own. "Up, up," he said, "we have plans today."

"Plans?" Anna never had plans.

He pulled her quilt down. She folded her bare legs under her nightgown.

"We're going to have a picnic," he said, "by the lake."

"James, there isn't a lake."

He grinned. "Oh, there's a lake."

"Do you have *a lake* now?"

He nodded, still grinning.

"Do you also have a picnic?"

He knelt one knee onto her bed. "No. You're going to make the picnic."

"How?"

He covered her eyes gently with one hand. "You can do this, Anna. I know you can."

James's hand was warm and real. Anna imagined a picnic. A basket with a red-checked lining. Sandwiches with olives on toothpicks. A green-plaid thermos with iced tea. A cherry pie.

When she opened her eyes, the basket was sitting on her bed, and James was beaming down at her.

Anna put on a yellow sundress with white tennis shoes—they were clothes she'd had since she was a girl, but they still fit.

James waited for her out on the porch.

Please, she thought, *don't take him. Not until after our picnic. I've never had a picnic.*

"Why do you have a lake?" she asked him as they walked through the yard.

James had taken her hand. He was leading her. "I don't know yet. Let's hope it doesn't disappear before we get there."

His lake seemed to be connected to her farm. Anna squealed

when she saw it. And James laughed. The lake was small and clear, with a little pier at one end. They sat on the pier and took off their shoes, letting their feet dangle in the water. There were fish swimming farther below.

"You have your own fishing hole," Anna said.

He grinned at her some more.

"Are you still someone writing a book?" she asked.

"I'm not sure. That feels fuzzier. But I have an apartment now. I can see it clear as day."

"An apartment with a fishing hole?"

"I think they're disconnected."

"Ooh," she said. "You have multiple settings."

He turned to Anna and looked earnestly into her eyes. "I really think she's *working* on me."

"I do, too. You get better every day."

He was still looking in her eyes. His freckles were stark in the sunlight. There was a breeze playing with his peachy hair. He had scruff on his cheeks—that was new. He was smiling at her. He was always smiling at her.

James brushed his thumb along her cheek. "You have an eyelash," he said, "just . . . there."

"Thanks," she murmured.

"Anna, I . . ." His hand stayed on her face. It wrapped around her jaw. She could feel his palm. She could feel every finger. She tipped her chin up, hopefully.

James leaned down to kiss her.

She'd imagined this a lot. Kissing. Boys and girls. Men and women. Never their faces—they didn't have faces. Or names.

James's lips were soft. His mouth was wet. Someone had given him teeth and a tongue and a soft way of sighing.

Anna let herself touch his bristly cheek.

When he pulled away, she looked at her lap—afraid of his reaction, that he might regret it. But he was laughing breathily. He lifted her face up by the chin. He was smiling.

"That was my first kiss," Anna said.

"Mine, too."

～

James was made for kissing.

They kissed on the porch swing.

In the wheat fields.

Lying on top of her bed, on her homemade quilt.

He was soft and gentle, and he never stopped touching her—his hands on her face, in her hair, on her back.

He smiled while he kissed. He laughed.

"I shouldn't," she said one afternoon between kisses.

James was holding her face with his thumb on her chin. "Shouldn't what?"

"Kiss you," she said. "You're meant for someone else."

He lowered his eyebrows, thinking. He was leaning on one elbow. His shirt had come unbuttoned an extra button. "You said that we won't remember what happens here."

"We won't, I don't think. That doesn't seem practical."

He rubbed her chin with his thumb. "I don't know what's right," he said. "But I know that I'm acting in character."

Anna smiled. She felt it all the way up to her hairline.

James kissed her cheek. "If she didn't want me to kiss you, she shouldn't have made you so kissable."

Anna laughed. He was kissing her ear, her neck . . . He was laughing, too.

"And likable?" she said.

"So likable. So sympathetic."

Anna wrapped her arms around him. "She shouldn't have left a dream like you sitting around unattended."

"I haven't been unattended," he said. "Not for a minute."

∾

James had an English accent for three hours one morning. They both found it unnerving.

∾

James taught her to play double solitaire. It took her ages to imagine up a full deck of cards.

∾

They took walks. They went fishing. They lay on their backs in her front yard, looking up at the stars.

They sat in her bed, with James leaning back against the head-board and Anna straddling his lap. He took her hair down, and Anna imagined that it had never looked so clean and shiny.

∾

"There's a new girl in the park," Anna's mother said.

Anna and James were playing cards on the porch. She was wearing her yellow sundress, and she'd kicked off her shoes. His button-down shirt was untucked, and he was holding Peaches.

"Does she need help?" Anna asked.

"She seems fine, but I thought you might want to say hello. She's about your age and clear as a summer day. Hair down to her waist and wearing corduroy slacks. Corduroy! You can see the ribs. A main character if I've ever seen one."

Her mother went on into the house.

Anna looked at James. "Do you want to go say hello?" she asked.

James shook his head. He didn't look up from the cards.

∾

James wanted to change his clothes. "I want jeans," he said.

Anna really focused on him, and she could manage it for a few minutes, but the jeans kept reverting back to his green chinos.

She hadn't seen James this frustrated since the day Renee was called in.

～

"Is your backstory still changing?" she asked. "You haven't mentioned it lately."

"Not really," he said.

They were lying in her bed. His head was on her chest, below her throat.

"Maybe she's refining you in ways you don't notice," she said.

James didn't comment.

Anna ran her fingers through his thick red hair. "I'm sure she's still working on you."

～

The woman—the main character—was still here. James still didn't want to meet her.

One day, the woman walked right up to the farmhouse; Anna's parents must have shown her the way. She stood in the yard and looked up at the house. She had long brown hair. The same color as Anna's. She was wearing glasses and a very cute cardigan.

Anna and James watched from behind her bedroom curtains.

"We should go talk to her," Anna said.

"No," James said. His voice was hard.

Peaches walked up to the woman and rubbed against her ankle. She leaned down to pet him.

After a few minutes, she walked away.

～

That night, after her parents went to bed, Anna sat on the couch with James. He kissed her urgently. With fewer smiles.

"Anna . . ." he said. "Can I come to bed with you tonight?"

Her heart leapt in her chest.

She thought of James's green trousers and the woman wandering around the park. "We shouldn't."

"Don't tell me we shouldn't," he said. "Tell me you don't want to or that you're not ready. But don't tell me we shouldn't."

He was holding her close. His face was flushed, and his breath was hot. Anna wondered if her own desire was anywhere near that well expressed.

"I *do* want to," she said. "I want you."

James groaned and buried his head in her neck.

She climbed off the couch and led him upstairs to her room. They knocked the stuffed animals off her bed. (They'd all be back again the next day.)

For a moment, Anna worried that James wouldn't be able to un-dress. But his clothes fell easily onto her floor and stayed there. He must be made for this, too.

She climbed under the covers, still wearing her sundress.

James took it off and cast it aside.

He kissed her. He was smiling again, but his eyes were a little wild and worried; he was capable of nearly infinite mixed emotions.

Anna had never done this before. She'd barely imagined it. She didn't worry about getting pregnant—she couldn't even use the bathroom.

James hunched over her. He lay between her legs. He kissed her face while he was inside of her. "Anna," he said. "Anna."

~~~

Neither of them were tired. After. The window was open. There was a breeze. James lay with his head on her chest, below her throat.

"I love you," he said.

She stroked his hair.

"I don't want to love anyone but you, Anna."

She didn't say anything at first. She didn't reassure him. What could she say? She couldn't revise him. And she couldn't hide him. She couldn't control anything that mattered.

"I love you, James," she said eventually. Because she *did* love him. And it might not change anything, but it was still true.

～

James had grown mulish. Stubborn. Maybe he'd always been that way. He frowned more. At the fields. At the stars.

"This is a life," he told Anna, with his eyebrows furrowed. "Whatever comes next, this is real."

She didn't argue.

She held his face in her hands and let him kiss her as urgently as he wanted.

～

She wondered if James still felt it pulling at him. His story. He must—he seemed so restless sometimes.

Anna imagined taking the scissors out of the kitchen drawer— there were scissors in the kitchen drawer—and cutting the ties that bound him to his book.

But that might be worse. If she decided not to use him in a story, he might fade away. Anna couldn't bear to watch James fade away.

～

People didn't fade when they got called in.

It was more like they unraveled. Like they were slowly being taken apart and put back together somewhere else. It was a joyful moment usually. Ecstatic. Anna had watched it happen before. She'd hugged someone as they came apart in her arms.

The day that James unraveled, Anna was standing with him on the porch. They'd just come back from a walk.

"Anna," James said in a strange voice.

She turned to him—his face was shocked, he was staring at her.

"James," she said, looking down at his shimmering feet.

"Anna." He rushed toward her. He grabbed her arms. "You're . . ." He was staring at her hands. At her fingertips. They were shimmering, too.

"Oh my God," Anna said. She backed away from him. "No . . ."

Peaches was at her feet. She picked him up. "*No*," she said. She ran to the pillar by the front steps and wrapped an arm around it. "*No!*"

"Anna . . ." James was trying to pull her away from the pillar, but his hands were collapsing. "Sweetheart, we're going together."

"James—it won't be like this!"

"I know." He got his arms around her waist. They slipped through. He put them around her again.

"We might not even know each other, there."

"Come with me, Anna."

It wouldn't be the same, wherever they were going. And they weren't going anywhere good—Anna knew this was true, because this was *her* story, and her story was never going to be good. Poor James. His arms slipped through her waist again.

"Anna," he said, "I love you. Come with me."

"No!" she screamed, and Peaches fell through her disappearing arms. "It won't be us!"

James was reaching for her. He didn't have hands. He didn't have legs. The sun was still shining in his hair. "I was meant to be with you," he said, his voice thready. "Wherever it is we're going."

Anna imagined him staying, but imagining it didn't make it so.

So she imagined herself staying. Her feet immediately felt more firmly grounded.

"Anna!" James looked horrified. There wasn't much left of him, but he could see what she was doing.

She reached out a solid hand, imagining he'd catch it and become more solid.

But he shook his head. He was almost gone. "Come with me."

He disintegrated.

James was gone, and the story was whipping around Anna, pulling at her ankles.

She imagined herself solid.

She imagined herself staying.

Who was to say what she was meant for? She'd been born too long ago. She'd waited too long with no direction. She'd given most of her memories to herself.

Who was to say where she belonged?

This was life. *This* was real.

She imagined herself eating lemon cake.

She imagined herself walking along the paths, making her own way.

She imagined herself in her bedroom with James, listening to the rain pitter-patter on the roof.

James.

The story pulled at her.

James was in it. James was there. He'd never come back, and no one else would ever replace him here. No one who'd come before was anything like James.

Anna wondered if the lake was gone . . .

Was it in the story already?

She wondered if there was another first kiss there waiting for her.

What would Anna end up as? After sitting here unused for so long. Maybe she just wanted to get rid of Anna, throw Anna into a crowd scene. Maybe she just wanted to clear her head.

The chicken coop was gone. The wheat fields were flashing. Peaches . . . Where was Peaches?

Everything was leaving Anna—but the pull on her skin was fading. She felt almost as solid as ever.

This is a life, she told herself.

But James was a life. And James was gone. And what had he said? *"We'll land where we belong, and we'll stay there forever."*

"You owe me something good!" she shouted into the circling emptiness.

James was something good.

Was James waiting for her?

There was barely a tug on Anna's center of gravity.

"I've been waiting for so long," she whispered. "You owe me something good."

Anna closed her eyes.

She imagined herself letting go. She imagined herself arriving someplace better than the place where she'd always belonged.